THE COPPER HEART

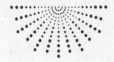

SARAH PAINTER

Text Copyright © 2020 by Sarah Painter

Published by Siskin Press Limited

Cover Design by Stuart Bache

For my wonderful readers,
thank you for taking Lydia Crow under your wing

CHAPTER ONE

It was a typical spring day in central London. A dense grey sky crouched over the city and the air was damp with threatening rain. Lydia was clinging to the cold metal of a steel cylinder, her feet braced against more steel, and she was trying, very hard, not to think about the thirty floors below her. One hundred metres of empty air ending with solid tarmac.

The Shard, London's tallest building, was a tapering pyramid of glass panels held together by a steel cage and, according to the website Lydia had looked at, a concrete core. The metal struts were accessible on the four corners of the pyramid and the evenly spaced horizontal pieces looked invitingly like a narrow ladder. From the ground, at least. Close up, the rungs were too far apart, and the upright beam too wide to comfortably grasp. Lydia had a pouch of chalk and was wearing grippy climber's shoes, but she still felt she could slip at any moment.

Ignoring the trembling in her muscles, she hauled

herself up another rung. The spring breeze was stronger at this height and a gust blew bits of hair into her face. She hugged the pole for a while, taking a mini-rest and spitting the strands from her mouth. Lydia had scraped her hair back into a ponytail but it evidently wasn't enough. She should have worn a swimming cap.

Lydia focused on the smooth metal inches from her face. She didn't want to look up, to see how much more towering skyscraper she still had to climb. And she definitely didn't want to look down. Just imagining the tiny people on that hard, hard ground, was enough to make her stomach flip. She was a Crow, she reminded herself. She wasn't afraid of heights.

Being a Crow, of course, was exactly the problem. It was the reason she was clinging to one of the most iconic buildings in London, breaking the injunction against trespassing the owners had been forced to institute to stop people from doing, well, exactly what she was attempting.

The sun broke through the cloud at that moment, early light reflecting on the glass and shining steel and almost blinding Lydia. Clinging where she was, muscles burning and shaking, was not a tenable position. She knew this so she forced herself to start moving again. One foot up onto the next rung, then sliding her hands up the pole, wrapping them around for a better grip and then, with increasing effort, the second foot up. The fear was circling. Every time she moved upward there was a moment when her body was too far away from the building for comfort, when she had to trust muscle and grip and momentum. The test was to get as far up as possible, which required careful calculation as well as guts. If she climbed until her energy was completely gone, she wouldn't be able to descend safely. There was no rope, no harness, no giant bouncy pillow. Nothing to stop her from breaking every bone on the unyielding ground far below.

That was it. She was going back down. For a second, just the thought of descending made her body go liquid with relief. Lydia began reversing her movements, at first finding them even worse than climbing up. Each time she moved a foot down, it was reaching blindly for the rung below. The urge to just stop and cling to her position, both feet firmly on a metal strut, both hands gripping, was almost overwhelming, but she knew that if she gave into the urge, she would die. Her muscles, already exhausted, would quickly tire and she would fall. There was nobody coming to help, so she had to keep moving. She moved her hands, bent her legs and sent another foot downward.

The sounds of the city began to flood back as she descended. Traffic, car horns, a pneumatic drill, and intermittent sirens. It gave her a jolt of adrenaline. The ordeal was almost over. Lydia took a deep breath and forced herself to keep moving steadily and safely. This was no time to rush. She was still twenty floors up when a voice by her ear made her jump in surprise. She adjusted her grip, making sure it was firm while looking around. The voice had said her name. Just once, but very clearly. There was nobody there. Only glass and steel and a glimpse of grey sky and other buildings, an unwelcome reminder that she was way too far off the ground. Of course there was nobody there. She was experiencing an auditory hallucination because she was exhausted. It would be something to do with the build-up of lactic acid in her muscles. Something like that. 'Sod off,' she said, anyway. Just in case. Living with a ghost had taught her that there were all sorts of people in the world and some of them were non-corporeal.

'Lydia,' the voice said, again. It sounded human, if that human had an extremely sore throat. And had smoked approximately three thousand cigarettes.

Lydia wanted to close her eyes. She touched her forehead to the metal pole, increasing her grip as best she could. Her fingers were numb and she was frightened the strength in her hands was ebbing away. What would happen then? She saw, in horrible technicolour, her fingers uncurling and slipping, her body leaning away from the metal scaffolding, her arms pinwheeling uselessly in the empty air as she fell backwards and down, down, down.

There was a crow perched on the metal frame of one of the sheets of glass, its head cocked. Lydia blinked, expecting to dispel the image, but no. It remained. Chunky body, powerful black beak, black feathers and a single, shiny black eye fixed upon her, as if waiting.

'What?' Lydia knew she sounded rude, but it was hard to modulate her tone. She was, in all likelihood, about to slip and fall to her death. 'I could do without an audience,' she said. 'I'm not having the best day.'

The crow shifted its feet and a small shiver ran along its body, ruffling its feathers.

'Yes, you're very beautiful,' Lydia said. 'And you can fly, you smug bastard.'

There was something about seeing the crow which had cheered her up a little. She wasn't alone. And she was a Crow. A rush of energy ran through her body and she continued climbing down, her pace steadier.

ONCE SHE GOT to the last few feet, Lydia was dismayed to see that there were plenty of people on the pavement. She had started before dawn and the area around The Shard had been almost deserted. She hadn't been that long, but already commuters and street cleaners had filled the thoroughfare. Hell Hawk. That was London for you.

Aiden was waiting where she had left him. He had his phone in his hand and was still filming. 'You can stop, now,' Lydia said, holding her hand up.

'Not bad,' Aiden said.

'Feel free to head on up there yourself,' Lydia said, drily. Her limbs were like jelly and her heart was thudding. She was managing to resist the urge to drop down and kiss the ground, but only just.

Aiden flashed a smile. He looked better these days, a bit of colour in his cheeks and a body that was young-skinny, rather than malnourished. When Lydia had taken over the Family from her uncle Charlie, she had inherited Aiden as a right-hand man. He was one of her many cousins, and only twenty years old, but he had worn the haunted expression of a much-older man. 'Nah, you're all right,' he said, easily.

'You get it all?' Lydia said, falling into step with Aiden as they joined the crowds milling around the London Bridge station. 'Because I'm not doing that again.'

'Unless someone challenges you,' Aiden said.

'What?' Lydia had thought that climbing the highest building in the city was an induction thing. Like a hazing. 'I thought it was one and done.'

Aiden shrugged. 'Only if you'd reached the top. You've left it that someone can challenge you by climbing higher.'

'You're kidding?'

'No one's going to do that,' Aiden said. 'It would be... Disrespectful to challenge the head of the Family.'

'Damn right,' Lydia said, smiling to show she wasn't offended, while inside she swore. Feathers. Another tradition to worry about.

BACK AT THE FORK, Lydia sat at her favourite table and waited for Angel to bring her breakfast. There were perks to usurping Charlie Crow and one of them involved a full English, gratis, and brought to her with the bare minimum of scowling. 'What's happening with Charlie's house?' Angel surprised her by asking.

'What do you mean?'

'If you're not moving in there, is it being sold? Seems like a waste.'

Lydia knew that it seemed odd, ignoring a massive house in favour of her little flat above the cafe, but she had no intention of leaving Jason. He could leave the building if he hitched a ride inside her body, which was exactly as weird and uncomfortable as it sounded, but otherwise was confined to quarters. 'What's it to you?'

Angel's expression closed down and Lydia mentally kicked herself. She hadn't meant to be so blunt, but every day since stepping into her role as the head of the Crow Family had been a barrage of questions. People looking to her for decisions and her having to pretend she knew what she was doing. Not easy when every day brought fresh horror as the full extent of Charlie's business practices came to light. Lydia was dismantling the criminal side to the Crow Family business while, simultaneously, trying to keep the members of the family happy. Or happy enough that they didn't mount a rebellion. It was exhausting.

Her phone buzzed with a text from Aiden.

Everyone is very impressed. Good job, boss.

Lydia wondered if he learned this style of handling from dealing with Charlie. Lydia found it risible, but there was a part of her that liked it. A part that she would have to watch.

Upstairs in her office-slash-living room, the landline rang. 'Hi Mum, everything okay?'

'Everything is perfect. Your dad sends his love.'

In the few weeks after Mr Smith had used his healing mojo to restore her father's mental capacities and stop the series of small strokes which were eroding him further, Lydia had spoken to him on the phone regularly. It had seemed, in the past, that her presence made Henry Crow worse and she didn't know whether Mr Smith's cure would extend to keeping him well or

7

whether she still needed to stay away. There was only one way to test it, and she didn't want to risk making him ill again. Her parents agreed, without them ever needing to have a frank discussion on the subject. They had been on a six-week cruise, returning the week before and Lydia guessed things would return to normal with Lydia mainly speaking to her mum and visiting rarely.

'He's sorry to miss you, now,' her mum was saying. 'He's just catching up after our trip.'

'Snooker?'

'Table tennis,' her mum replied and Lydia could hear the smile in her voice. 'He played on the ship and now he's talking about joining the local league. He used to play with Charlie, back when they were kids, I think. But, yes, the telly's been on twelve hours a day while he catches up on everything he missed.'

Lydia winced at the mention of her Uncle Charlie. She tried to imagine him wielding a ping pong bat and failed. Lydia hadn't told her parents that she had traded Charlie's freedom for a mystical cure of her dad's illness. She told them, instead, that he was out of control and had tried to kill her. Both true, but she still hadn't done it lightly and she felt sick when she thought of Charlie incarcerated in a secret government facility. Then she remembered that he was the man who had murdered Jason and she stopped feeling bad.

LYDIA LET herself into Charlie's house. He had been very careful and there hadn't been much in the way of incriminating evidence to clear from his study, but in visiting the house to look it over, Lydia had started a habit that she wasn't ready to break. She checked in on the place every few days and viewed the video from the security cameras, which were set to record only when triggered by movement. This meant scrolling through carrier bags blown in the wind and post deliveries. Luckily, the local canvassers were well-trained to avoid the house and Lydia didn't have to watch random charity-collectors ringing the doorbell. She also got confirmation that her Crow power was stronger than it used to be. She ought to be caught on the video approaching and leaving the front door, but the footage went fuzzy with white snow. She had known that Charlie had that effect on video recording, whether consciously or as a side effect of being a powerful pure blood Crow, and now it seemed Lydia did, too. Occasionally, Lydia's surveillance would be rewarded in other ways. An old contact of Charlie's would appear, a baseball cap pulled down low in automatic-camera-avoidance. Sometimes they shoved cryptic notes through the letterbox. 'Call K'. 'H sends regards.' Stuff like that, usually scrawled on the outside of a piece of junk mail. Today, there was a neatly-folded note on the polished wooden floor. Lydia pulled on a pair of nitrile gloves and picked it up.

It's later than you think.

With the note safely sealed in a plastic bag, labelled with the time, date, and location, Lydia moved through the rest of the house. She checked the doors and windows for signs of forced entry, just in case the cameras had glitched, then, when she was satisfied that nothing was out of place, she went up to the training room.

It ought to be a place of bad memories. She had hated being forced to train by Charlie and had spent the entire time trying to keep her power in check, to moderate how much of it she allowed Charlie to see. She knew that he had pushed her cousin, Maddie, beyond breaking point, causing the mental instability and psychotic rage Lydia had experienced first-hand. Lydia had tried to keep herself safe, holding the warnings she had grown up with firmly in her mind. She had no wish to be used as a tool or weapon by Charlie Crow. Not to mention the time he had attacked her, trying to provoke a bigger, stronger reaction. Well, he'd got what he'd wanted. Lydia had discovered that she wasn't the weak link she had always believed. And she also wasn't just a battery, powering up those around her. In that moment of terror, maybe as a result of all the training that Charlie had forced, she had discovered a new facility. She had accessed a well of power that seemed both within and without herself. She had reached out and found a thousand wings beating, a thousand hearts beating, every single one giving her strength.

It had been almost three months since Charlie had been taken by Mr Smith and his government department. Spring sunshine poured through the tall windows, reflecting off the wall of mirrors and turning the sprung wooden flooring yellow-gold. Lydia stood in the middle of the room and closed her eyes. Her coin was in her hand and she extended her arm, placing the coin in mid-air. In her mind's eye she saw it suspended there and then made it spin, first clockwise and then counter clockwise, before adding coins, one by one, and holding them in different points around the room. Making them spin in unison, or randomly. It was a warm-up or a meditation, this routine, and Lydia found it calming. The sun was welcoming on her upturned face and she felt her power humming both within her and in that liminal space beyond. The place where wings spread in the high blue sky.

Her phone was ringing. Lydia opened her eyes, wondering how long it had been before she had noticed. For one second the room was still full of gently turning coins, and in the next second, they were gone.

Her phone was on top of her hoodie and she felt something as she bent to pick it up. A wash of dark feeling. A premonition.

'Sorry,' Fleet's voice sounded strained. 'I know you're training.'

'What's wrong?'

'Alejandro Silver is dead.'

CHAPTER TWO

Lydia walked to St Thomas' Hospital by Westminster Bridge. The day had developed from the unpromising grey start to a pleasant late afternoon, with a blue sky and fluffy white clouds. The iconic sights of Big Ben, the London Eye and the Houses of Parliament looked like a tourist postcard in the sunshine, but Lydia's mind was distracted. How could Alejandro Silver be dead?

St Thomas' sat on the opposite bank to parliament and Lydia imagined the ambulance that would have rushed across the bridge, siren blaring, hours earlier, carrying the stricken head of the Silver Family. That was how she still thought of him. Alejandro might have told Charlie that his daughter, Maria, was the new head of the family now that he was heading into politics, but nobody had believed it. Least of all Lydia.

Fleet was waiting for Lydia at the main entrance of the hospital. He led the way to the north wing and down to the lower ground floor, filling her in on the details as they walked. 'He collapsed in the street, that's all we've got so far. It seems as if he was en-route to the house for a vote on a new clause on a finance bill. Didn't sound especially significant, but we're looking into it.'

'Was he attacked?'

'Not that I have heard,' Fleet didn't look at her, was scanning the list of departments on the wall.

'Where did it happen, exactly?'

'Victoria Embankment, not far from that floating pub.'

'The decommissioned ferry?' Lydia was momentarily distracted. She had always thought it was odd that people would choose to go to eat and drink on the water without going anywhere. It seemed like all the downsides of being on a boat with none of the benefits. It was something different, though, something novel. For tourists and corporate events, presumably.

'Yeah, that's the one. Concerned passer-by called an ambulance then stayed with him until paramedics arrived. It took six minutes, which is good going, but by the time they got him to the hospital, he was gone.'

They took a right out of the lift and, finally, saw the discreet sign for the mortuary. Hospitals never shouted about this department and Lydia couldn't blame them. It was evidence of their failure. The limits of their power. Nobody liked to be reminded of that.

'Did he speak to the good Samaritan?' If Alejandro had been conscious, perhaps he would have handily explained exactly what had happened before he expired.

'I'll find out,' Fleet said.

'Is Maria here?' Lydia wasn't looking forward to a

reunion with Alejandro's daughter. They had history and none of it was good.

'I don't think so. I'm not even sure if she knows, yet. She's in court.' He looked at his watch. 'They'll finish soon, though. Judges don't work late.'

'Don't they need to wait for her to see him before the post-mortem? Isn't this a bit fast?'

'I don't know.' Fleet looked uncomfortable. 'These things usually take a little longer, but I'm assuming it suits the CPS to fast track it through. I mean, it's high profile and there is a good chance it wasn't natural.'

Something was definitely off about Fleet's manner. 'What's wrong?'

He still didn't meet her gaze. 'I'm not on this. Officially. A friend told me because they know I'm connected to you.'

'Right...'

'I've asked to be assigned, but they haven't returned my call.'

There was clearly something else going on there, something that was bothering Fleet, but there wasn't time to get into it.

Inside the first door to the mortuary was a small waiting area and another door, this one with a keypad and an intercom. Fleet pressed the button and identified himself. There was a buzz and they were inside a short corridor with several closed doors leading off and double doors at the end with another keypad lock. Lydia steeled herself for the mortuary itself, remembering the clinical whiteness and horrifying steel tables from her last visit to one. She could smell bleach, formaldehyde and other things that she didn't want to think about too closely.

A man wearing a surgical cap and gown and carrying a mask, pushed through the double doors. 'What can I do for you DCI?'

'We're here to observe the Silver post-mortem.'

'I don't think so,' he said shortly. 'I'm the lead pathologist and this is the first I'm hearing about it.'

Fleet had already got his credentials out and he flashed them at the doctor who looked unimpressed. 'I've not had notice that you were coming,' he repeated.

'Why is it an issue? I just want to get your initial impressions ahead of the formal report. I won't quote you anywhere, but I'm sure you know this is a high-priority case.'

'He's high profile, I am aware. We've had to shuffle the schedule to accommodate the requested turnaround time.' He looked at his watch in a meaningful manner. 'I really need to get started.'

'I'm not going to hold you up,' Fleet said. He paused. 'But I'm not going anywhere. I can wait while you phone my gaffer. It's up to you.'

Lydia watched the doctor wrestle with his desire to pull rank over Fleet and the equally pressing desire to get moving and get home in time for dinner. The second urge seemed to win out.

'I'm about to start,' he said. 'You can go into the viewing room, but nowhere else. I may be able to spare a few minutes after, depending on how long it takes. And I will put this interruption into my notes, too. This isn't a bloody circus.'

'I appreciate your cooperation, sir,' Fleet said smoothly.

The doctor opened a single door, revealing a square room with what passed for comfortable seating in an NHS hospital and a large window in one wall with sliding shutters which were currently open. There was a table in one corner holding a vase of plastic flowers and someone had gone to town with a lemon-scented air freshener.

'I wonder if they have done the formal identification yet.'

Lydia made a non-committal sound in reply. Truthfully, she wasn't paying close attention to Fleet. The pathologist had appeared through the double doors which she now saw led into the examination room she was looking at through the glass viewing window. He looped his mask around his ears and approached the table in the middle of the room.

'You okay?' Fleet touched her arm, but she couldn't look away from the viewing window. The body of Alejandro Silver was lying on the metal table. His dark hair was swept back from a lightly lined forehead, his short beard was neatly clipped and there were a few silver-grey hairs at his temples. In life, he had looked young and vigorous for his age. In death, he looked... dead. That was the nature of it. There was something unmistakable and alien about a person once their spark had gone out. What did they used to call it? Soul case? Alejandro's soul case was unmarked, at least from where Lydia was standing. And he had a white sheet covering his lower half.

Lydia reached out her senses, but they felt choked by the artificial lemon scent. She thought she could taste a little hint of Silver magic, but it was an after-image. Nothing like the raw power she had felt from Alejandro in life. In fact, it was so faint it could almost be her imagination, something she expected to feel. She closed her eyes and produced her Crow Family coin, gripping it to help her focus. The sense of Silver remained elusive, seeming to disappear the harder she tried to grasp it. Lydia wondered if it was because there was a solid wall and double-glazed glass between them. Or, perhaps, Alejandro's 'Silver' essence had dissipated now that he was dead. She had sensed 'Fox' from the deceased Marty, but his ghost had been in attendance. She had a good look around the room, just in case Alejandro's spirit was hanging about, watching the proceedings, but didn't really expect to see anything. If Alejandro's spirit had been present, Lydia was pretty sure she would be tasting Silver at the back of her throat.

A door on the far wall opened and a small figure, also gowned, walked in. His mask was pulled down around his neck and he looked surprised to see visitors through the window.

The pathologist walked to the wall and a speaker set in the corner crackled into life. 'This is my technician,' the pathologist said, through the speaker system. 'And he's late.'

'Sorry,' the technician muttered. 'There was a queue at Pret.'

Lydia's stomach turned over at the thought of food.

The pathologist turned away from the window and

got to work. He switched on a recording device and began to examine the skin surface from the head down, making his observations out loud. There was no bruising or broken skin, no signs of trauma. Lydia was conducting her own examination, reaching out her senses for Alejandro's ghost, trying to see if there was any kind of supernatural signature. Once she was sure there wasn't anything she could detect, she touched Fleet's sleeve and shook her head. 'I'm going to wait outside.'

AN HOUR LATER, Fleet met Lydia on Westminster Bridge, next to one of the ornate Gothic triple-lanterned lampposts. 'When you said "outside" you really meant it.'

'Hospitals,' Lydia shrugged. Given the choice, who in their right mind would sit inside a linoleum palace of pain, when they could be outside, looking at the slow water of the river, instead? The sky was tinged with lavender and a few lights had flickered into life, but Lydia couldn't see the sinking sun. It was hidden behind clouds and pollution. 'What's the verdict?'

'Inconclusive,' Fleet replied. 'Pathologist didn't find any evidence of trauma and preliminary exam shows cause of death as heart failure. Which is usually a coroner's way of saying "I don't know, yet. Go away officer and let me finish my job in peace." He'll finish up tomorrow, but we'll be waiting a bit longer for lab results.'

Lydia was leaning on the green-painted iron balustrade, keeping her gaze on the wide expanse of the Thames. She had been mulling over the ramifications of

Alejandro's death ever since she heard the news, and was no closer to working out what she needed to do. Two Crows had been killed in Wandsworth prison and now this, the head of the Silver Family. She had suspected that representatives from a mysterious company, JRB, were intent on causing rifts between the four magical Families of London, which would put them – whoever they were – at the top of the list of suspects for this latest outrage. If that was the case, Lydia needed to know their endgame. 'Who would benefit from a war between the Families?'

'It's not necessarily murder,' Fleet said. 'No signs of trauma, no defensive wounds. It could be natural causes. He wasn't *old* old, and was in good shape, but it's not unheard of.'

'Please,' Lydia said, impatiently. 'Alejandro Silver was hale and hearty. Alarmingly so.'

'You were frightened of him?'

'I had a healthy respect for his power,' Lydia said witheringly.

'Well, I'm glad. I sometimes wonder if you have a realistic view of the danger you keep courting.'

'I don't court danger,' Lydia said. 'All I want is a quiet life.'

Fleet pulled a 'yeah, right' face and Lydia went up on tiptoes to kiss him. Cool air on her skin, the sounds of the city all around, and Fleet's warm lips on hers. For a few seconds she could forget that she was supposed to be in charge of the Crow Family business or that Maria Silver was probably, at this very moment, sharpening a sword ready to plunge it directly into

Lydia's soft parts at the next available opportunity. Probably one of her Family heirlooms. The Silvers were the kind of people who had antique weaponry on their office walls.

Lydia blinked and realised that Fleet was no longer kissing her. His face was still close, though, and his gaze was searching. 'I lost you, there. Do I need to brush up on my technique?'

Lydia smiled. 'Sorry. No. Your technique is on point, as always.'

'Glad to hear it.'

'Maria Silver is going to blame me for Alejandro's death.'

'I know.'

'I need to find out who did this, and fast. I need to be able to prove to Maria that it wasn't the Crows.'

'Any point in me telling you that you don't need to get involved, that the police will investigate?'

'None at all.'

Fleet nodded. 'Thought as much.'

BACK AT THE FORK, Lydia found Jason sitting on the sofa with his laptop. She ignored the whisky bottle and got a beer from the fridge, instead.

Jason raised an eyebrow. 'Still on that health kick?'

'My body is a temple,' Lydia said, popping the cap and taking a long swig.

He was still looking at her and his expression was unnervingly sympathetic. 'What?'

'You might want something stronger.'

'I know about Alejandro, I've just come from the mortuary.'

'Wait. What?' Jason frowned. 'What about Alejandro?'

'He's dead.' Too late, Lydia remembered that Jason's wife (of one day) had been a member of the Silver Family. Back in the 1980s, but still. 'Sorry for your loss,' she said. 'He collapsed by the Thames this morning. I assumed you'd seen it on the news or...' Lydia trailed off, realising that he clearly hadn't. Couldn't have, in fact, as it hadn't been reported, yet. 'Never mind. What's your thing?'

'It's nothing,' Jason shook his head. 'The broadband is down. Alejandro Silver died?'

'Yeah,' Lydia sat next to him on the sofa. 'It's a problem.'

Jason's eyes were wide and he was vibrating slightly. 'Maria is going to blame you. She's going to flip... I mean, she's going to –'

Go on a Crow-killing spree. Lydia straightened her spine. 'We'll find out who did it. Deliver their head on a plate. Easy.'

'Or prove it was natural causes. Could it have been natural?'

Lydia shrugged. 'Anything's possible, I suppose.' Alejandro had looked peaceful in death, something she didn't associate with the man. She had expected him to go down swinging and coldly furious, even while suffering a heart attack. His cool, measured voice rang in her mind as she imagined him telling a myocardial infarction that it didn't have an appointment. 'There wasn't anything obvious in the post-mortem. Nothing obvious the pathologist shared, anyway, and I'm no expert. I just had to stop myself from throwing up. Now we have to wait for the blood and tissue tests.'

'You saw him?'

Lydia grimaced. 'He looked fine. I mean, he looked dead, but wasn't cut up or covered in bruises.'

'Poisoning, then, maybe. Like those Russians in Salisbury.'

'I hope not,' Lydia said. If it was a nerve agent like Novichok she had just been exposed to it. 'Although you're right. They do love their poisonings.' Had he pissed off the Russians? Or maybe he had been an agent or a double agent all along. Lydia shook her head gently. The business with her overly friendly spook, Mr Smith, had put spy nonsense into her mind. This was more likely to be a political move. Or something to do with his role as head of the Silvers. A bit of good old English corruption.

'He's only just left the law firm. Could it be a disgruntled ex-prisoner? Someone he helped to put away?'

'That's a good shout,' Lydia said. 'He was a criminal barrister, I think. Before he stepped into corporate law. It was a while ago, but that would give time for somebody dangerous to have served their time.'

'And if they've been nursing a grudge...' Jason turned his palm upwards.

Lydia was quiet, thinking it over.

'Do you need me to ask him?'

She grasped his offer immediately. 'I didn't see his

spirit at the hospital, but I could go to where he collapsed. See if there's anything hanging around. Although,' a thought occurred. 'I think he died in the ambulance. Could his spirit have got caught in that?'

Jason shrugged. 'Well, if you get a whiff of Silver, I'm happy to hitch a ride and play twenty questions. I mean, it could be the quickest way to solve his murder.

CHAPTER THREE

F leet had arrived at The Fork later that night and was gone at dawn. He kissed her before he left. 'Sorry. Don't wake up.'

'Too late.' Lydia had kissed him back, half-hoping to delay him for a more thorough awakening and half-wanting him to head out the door so that she could get on with her own day. She needed to hunt for Alejandro's spirit and should really have got started the previous evening, but had been exhausted; her muscles complaining about their early-morning free-climb. Even the prospect of Maria Silver hadn't been enough to make her get the tube to the embankment.

'Stay safe today, okay?' Fleet said, one hand on her bedroom door.

'You, too,' Lydia said.

He hesitated. 'I'll let you know as soon as the coroner's full report comes in.'

'Great. Thanks.'

Fleet was clearly working up to saying something else. 'What?' Lydia prompted.

'It's not just Maria you need to worry about,' Fleet said. 'Until we know who hit Alejandro, we can't be sure they aren't going after all the major players. That includes you, now.'

Well that was a cheery thought.

THE EMBANKMENT WAS LINED with tour coaches and people thronged the pavement. It was a sunny spring day and the great white wheel of the London Eye was just across the Thames, turning slowly. Like the floating restaurant, Lydia didn't see why anybody would voluntarily sign up for an hour inside the Eye. Heights were bad enough, even without being locked up inside a glass bubble with a group of farting, sweating, *talking* tourists.

Lydia wasn't sure of the exact spot where Alejandro had collapsed and there was no handy crime-scene tape marking out the area, so she just walked slowly up and down the stretch. At one point she ended up at Cleopatra's Needle and realised she had gone too far, walking back she could see Big Ben in the distance and the Whitehall Gardens on her right. On her left, the river flowed slowly, unchanged and unconcerned. It had seen more death and destruction than Lydia could even imagine, and held the secrets of countless unlucky Londoners in its murky depths. A couple were standing next to one of the orange lifebuoys for a picture.

As she approached the staid green arches of Westminster Bridge, Lydia stopped. She sat on a bench so as not to look too conspicuous and closed her eyes, reaching out with her senses. There was exhaust fumes from the traffic, a waft of spicy fried food which made her stomach rumble, and the scent of perfume. Something very strong with jasmine and patchouli. And then, just when Lydia had decided that she was wasting her time, she got a hit of Family magic. Unfortunately, it wasn't the clean bright tang of Silver, but a woody musk. Fox.

'Enjoying the sun, Little Bird?'

Lydia opened her eyes. Her head was already tilted, giving her a full and uncluttered view of Paul Fox. He was wearing his standard uniform of black jeans and a fitted black T-shirt, emphasising his narrow waist and wide shoulders. They had worked together off and on for long enough now, that she had become inured to the animal magnetism which was bundled into the Fox signature. She was still human, though, and the view was pretty magnetic all on its own. 'Working.'

'I heard.'

'And you decided to just hang out here on the off chance I would show up?'

Paul smiled. 'Close enough.'

They might have an active truce and a decent working relationship, but Paul Fox still couldn't answer a straight question with a straight answer.

He sat next to Lydia on the bench. 'Should you be out and about?'

'It's fine,' Lydia said, waving at the crowded street. 'Maria isn't going to kill me with this many witnesses.'

Paul gave her a long look. 'Somebody took Alejandro out with exactly this audience.'

The man had a point. Not that Lydia was going to concede it. Although how he knew the details so quickly was an interesting question. She was going to ask Paul if the story had hit the news sites, already, but she decided to save her breath.

When it became apparent that Lydia wasn't going to elaborate, Paul shook his head. 'Please tell me you're not staying at The Fork, at least.'

'Crows don't run,' Lydia said. 'And I'm the head of the Family, now. I can't bail.'

'You need a new HQ. Somewhere with better security. Or with more privacy. Too many people know about your current location.'

'Because it's my place of business,' Lydia said. 'I'm not closing Crow Investigations.'

'But why not? You've got enough to do. I've been watching and you haven't drawn breath since Charlie disappeared. You can't do it all. Not forever. And it's not like you need the work, now.'

Lydia decided to ignore the 'I've been watching' part, to assume he meant it figuratively. 'Since when did you start doling out life advice? I'm fine. And I like my work.'

Paul held up his hands. 'Just saying.'

It didn't matter how much trust had built between her and Paul Fox, she wasn't about to start sharing and caring. This wasn't a sleepover and Paul didn't have enough hair to braid. A memory of running her hand over his buzz cut, the way it felt on her skin, jumped into the front of her mind and she felt colour in her cheeks. *Hell Hawk.*

'So, what's the plan, Little Bird? And please don't tell me you're going to visit Maria with your condolences. You're too soft-hearted for your own good.'

Lydia glared at him. 'Classified.'

'I'm asking around,' Paul said. 'Seeing if anybody knows who might have the balls to take on Alejandro. I can share the whispers with you,' he paused. 'If you want.'

Lydia forced herself to stop glaring. 'That would be helpful.' She needed to give him something back. She might not want to start sharing and caring, but she had to do a bit of the former, at least. It was the price of doing business, she told herself. Just business. 'You know I told you about how Marty died? That he had been frightened to death by something he thought was the ghost of his ex-girlfriend?'

Paul nodded. 'I remember.'

'I found out by speaking to Marty's spirit.' Lydia decided to leave out the part involving Jason. Or the fact that she could sense Family magic. One revelation at a time. 'I came here on the off-chance that Alejandro's would be hanging around.'

Paul looked at her for a beat. Then he said, 'That's a very useful party trick for a detective.'

Lydia shrugged. 'I have my skills.'

'Yes, you do.'

Lydia broke eye contact and ignored the way her stomach was flipping. She scanned the view, instead, without any real hope. 'He's not here, though.'

Paul stood up. 'I'll go and speak to my live and kicking contacts, then. See what I can dig up.'

'Thank you,' Lydia said.

'And if you change your mind about moving out, you know where to find me.'

'You're offering me a place to stay? Don't think your family would be too pleased if I turned up with my toothbrush.'

Paul's stance shifted and he became something feral, dangerous. 'I've told you before,' he said, voice low. 'I'm the leader, now. It's my den, my rules.'

The frequency of his voice set off a fluttering in her stomach. Lydia took a steadying breath and told herself that it was just a primal fight or flight reaction, nothing more. She forced a nod and then watched him walk away. Within a few steps he seemed to melt into the crowd, disappearing from view. The after-image of something red, moving through dark green undergrowth, flashed across her mind. Being this close to the most powerful Fox in London was possibly not the best idea she had ever had. Still, better the devil you know. And with the Silvers probably amassing contract killers as she sat, it was better to keep her alliance with the Fox Family. However confusing she found it.

BEFORE HEADING HOME, Lydia spoke to the people running the booths next to the Westminster Pier. There was one selling tickets for tourist boat trips and another offering dodgy-looking burgers and ice cream cones. It was busy enough that they didn't want to get into a long conversation, but Lydia thought they were telling the truth when they each denied seeing anything. Lydia was walking away when a skinny young guy with bleached blond hair and a neat black beard, caught up. 'I saw the ambulance,' he said. 'Just up there,' he indicated back along the wide pavement, away from the bridge.

Lydia confirmed that the time matched Alejandro's collapse. 'Were there a lot of people around?' Lydia gestured around. 'Was it this busy or quieter?'

'About the same,' he said.

'Do you know if he was on his own? Did you see him speaking to anyone before he collapsed?'

He shook his head. 'I didn't really see him. Just the ambo.'

'You work here often?'

'Every day,' he said.

Lydia gave him her card and a twenty-pound note, and told him to call if he remembered anything else. He might not have seen anything useful this time, but another pair of eyes was always handy.

AIDEN WAS WAITING BACK at The Fork, a cup of coffee on the table. Lydia slid into the seat opposite him and tried to keep the irritation out of her voice. 'What now?'

He looked offended. 'Charlie liked to be kept up-to-date on everything. I had to keep him informed. We all did.'

'I told you, just keep everything going. I gave you my rules, but everything else you can use your own initiative.'

Aiden opened his mouth to argue and then seemed to think better of it. He nodded, tight lipped.

Lydia sighed. 'What?'

'It's not that simple. People know Charlie isn't around. If you let people get away with stuff, word is going to spread.'

Lydia resisted the urge to rub her forehead. 'What stuff?'

Aiden went quiet. After a moment he reached for his coffee and Lydia stopped him with a look. 'Don't make me ask again.'

'People want to speak to you. They need to see you around, too. Not all the time and not everyone. But there's a hierarchy. Those at the top need to feel they've got special access, special consideration, or they start to wonder if they really are.'

'Are what?'

'At the top.'

Lydia hadn't banked on spending her time massaging egos. She had a new understanding of why Fleet was so stressed and unhappy at his work these days. He had mentioned that managing teams of people sounded important and powerful, and that he would be able to delegate all the dull grunt work and be left with the pick of the tasks, but the reality was that he spent his time at his desk or in interminable meetings, putting out fires. 'I wish that wasn't metaphorical,' he had said. 'At least I'd be more active.' Looking at Aiden and considering the prospect of meeting and greeting the crème of Camberwell in order to keep the peace, Lydia felt closer to Fleet than ever. She too would prefer a nice old-fashioned burning building right about now.

UPSTAIRS, Lydia let herself into her flat and headed out onto the roof terrace. She sat on one of the metal bistro chairs and got her phone out ready to make a list. There was nothing like a nice neat 'to-do' list to make her feel more in control. And to put off actually doing any of the tasks. Jason materialised in the middle of the terrace, almost making her drop the phone. 'Feathers!'

'Sorry,' Jason said.

'That's okay.' Lydia felt bad for swearing. Jason couldn't always control where and when he appeared.

'I didn't know you were out here.'

'Don't suppose you'd agree to wear a bell?'

Understandably, Jason ignored that. 'Any luck at the embankment?'

Lydia shook her head. 'Nothing. Not even a hint of Silver.'

'It was a long shot,' Jason said. 'You're in one piece, though, so that's a result.'

'I don't know why everyone is so worried about me. I'm the head of the Crow Family. I'm basically untouchable.' Lydia didn't like everyone being so nervous. It was making her jumpy. 'Besides, Maria must know I wouldn't make a move on Alejandro. She might front up for the look of it, but she won't think I'd be that stupid. Maybe I should just go and see her, clear the air.'

'What? You're just going to stroll into her office and explain that you didn't kill her father. Yeah, that's a wonderful idea.'

'There's no need for sarcasm.' Everyone's a critic, Lydia thought. First Fleet, then Paul, and now Jason.

'I'm just saying,' Jason said. 'Maybe Fleet should do it. She's not going to kill a cop.'

'I'm not sending Fleet to do my job. I can't look weak.'

'Better than looking dead.'

CHAPTER FOUR

Since he had banished his father, Tristan, Paul Fox was the head of the Fox Family, Maria had stepped into Alejandro's place as the head of the Silvers and, now, Lydia was the head of the Crows. The Family had adjusted pretty quickly, all things considered. Lydia had expected more resistance, but it seemed that her status as Henry Crow's daughter had gone a long way. Of course, the tricky matter of where, exactly, Charlie had gone, and why he hadn't said goodbye still had to be resolved. Most, though, seemed to decide that it wasn't their business. If Charlie had left Lydia in charge and gone into retirement, as per Lydia's story, then all was well. And if Lydia had killed Charlie in order to take his position, it was probably better not to ask questions.

John, Maddie's father, had been one of the few exceptions to put up a bit of a fight. He had cornered Lydia at a pot luck dinner, and asked a few searching questions. 'What did Charlie say? Why didn't he talk to anybody else? Why doesn't he want anybody to get in touch?'

Lydia had shrugged and done the whole 'you-know-Charlie-law-unto-himself' act, but John hadn't been derailed. He had taken Lydia's arm and moved them to quiet corner. 'Are you in trouble?'

'Not at all.'

'Where is he? I know you know.'

Eyes wide. 'I know as much as you, Uncle John.'

Then, John losing his temper, and forgetting his tone. 'Stop it. We need to know. If there are going to be repercussions. Will the police be involved? Is he dead? I need – we need – to know.'

Lydia had snapped into her new role. 'Pull yourself together, John. Charlie has retired. It's lovely news after his long years of faithful service to the Family.'

'But...' John had begun to argue, but Lydia hadn't let him continue.

She fixed the old man with a firm stare, pushing a bit of Crow behind it. John had sagged back against the wall, defiance draining from him in an instant.

'He's got what he deserves,' Lydia had said. 'And I don't want to hear any more about it.'

Now, looking at her coffee and thinking about Alejandro's body in the mortuary and Maria Silver somewhere in the city, no doubt plotting her revenge on the world, Lydia experienced a confusing mix of sympathy and anger. She also knew she couldn't afford to make a mistake. She was the head of the Crow Family and if she didn't act like it, someone would challenge her for the position. And those kinds of challenges often were the 'last woman standing' variety. Apart from the possible-death aspect, passing on the reins to a willing successor wasn't so bad in theory, but only if that successor was up to the job and not batshit crazy. Lydia might not have dreamed of being the head of the Crows as a little girl, but she was damned if she was going to lead her Family into madness and ruin.

She needed to act like a leader. And, whatever Paul, Jason or Fleet might think, that meant showing no fear. Lydia called the Silver and Silver office and asked for Maria.

'Ms Silver is in court today, can I take a message?'

'Are you expecting her in the office later today?'

'It's possible,' the assistant replied. 'But there are no available appointments.'

'That's all right,' Lydia said. 'It's not urgent. What's the case?'

Having obtained the name, Lydia opened the case list on the Old Bailey website. The name belonged to a Bulgarian HGV driver accused of manslaughter when twelve female immigrants were found suffocated in the back of his lorry, due to a lack of oxygen and space. It was being held in court five and this was the third day of the trial. Lydia guessed that the law didn't allow for grief and that Maria would have to postpone her feelings until it was completed. Unless she was allowed to sub in a different barrister and it was just her own professional pride that was keeping her working. Maria was a Silverhearted murderous witch, but on this point Lydia could relate. The show must go on.

Lydia decided to catch Maria on her way out of court. Outside the Old Bailey had to be one of the safer places for a chat. It wasn't private enough, but Lydia didn't have a death wish. No matter what the men in her life seemed to think. Court five was in the new building so Lydia waited outside the Warwick Passage entrance, hoping that the barristers didn't have a secret exit that wasn't listed on the visitor guide.

It was easy to see when the court let out, with a sudden stream of people coming from the public gallery. Once this had petered out, Lydia adjusted her stance against the soot-stained façade of the building and waited thirty minutes until staff members began leaving. There weren't any in the distinctive barrister's robes which either meant they were changing inside before leaving for the night, or she was waiting at the wrong place. Not for the first time, Lydia realised the limitations of being a one-woman-band. She added 'take on an assistant' to her mental to-do list. There ought to be a line of young Crows looking to be helpful, and money was no longer the pressing concern it had once been. Aiden had made it clear that her new role came with a generous stipend. She had yet to access it, but there would come a time when her hand would be forced. She wasn't taking on as many paying clients as her time had been swallowed by her new duties.

Giving up for the evening, Lydia walked to Black-friars station and caught an over ground train to Denmark Hill to head home. Minutes into the journey and she felt a compulsion for a different destination, so she got off at London Bridge and changed trains to one heading to Honor Oak Park.

WHEN LYDIA HAD BEEN a child and had yet to realise the extent to which her family was not the same as the other families in their street in Beckenham, her father had taken her to visit her ancestors. As always, he spoke to her as if she was an adult, which meant that she felt valued and respected, if occasionally confused. 'Not all of them, unfortunately, burial grounds get squeezed around here. Remains are moved. Still. It's good to pay our respects.'

Henry Crow had explained that the Camberwell Old Cemetery which was, in fact a couple of miles away from Camberwell proper and closer to East Dulwich, had only been built when St Giles church ran out of room in its graveyard. 'Too many bodies. The curse of modern life.'

'They moved Grandma?'

'No, lovey. This was years and years ago. And, luckily enough, it didn't really matter to us. Crows aren't buried in churches, anyway.'

'We're atheists?' Lydia had asked, having just learned the meaning of the word and utterly thrilled to get the chance to use it so quickly.

'I wouldn't say that, no. Just not very Christian.'

'But we're here?' Lydia remembered the ironwork gates of the cemetery seeming extremely tall, and the word 'Camberwell' picked out in black against a white sky. It was winter in her memory and the metal was freezing to touch.

They walked past fallen gravestones and up a hill, which felt to Lydia very steep and very long. At the top there was a copse of trees and, on the other side and covered with dark green ivy, a structure which looked, more than anything, like a stone Wendy house. It was only when Lydia got closer, that she realised that the peaked roof of the house was formed from carved grave-stones with ancient, crumbling inscriptions, and what she had thought were little windows were recesses for more engraving. The lettering in these was better preserved, as it was protected a little from the elements. She began sounding out the chiselled letters, trying to find words she could read, but when she turned to ask her father a question, she found him standing between two trees, looking in the opposite direction. 'Over here,' he said. Lydia held his hand, her finger bones like a tiny bird in his giant palm. Down the slope, beyond granite grave markers and green hedges, the distinctive London skyline hung pale grey, like a ghost of itself, or a mirage in a black-and-white world. 'Crows' final roosting, some-where up high, where we can see the city.'

Walking up the hill now, it seemed like a gentle slope. The trees around the tomb were still wild and overgrown, but there were far fewer than Lydia remem-bered, and when she approached the edge of the rise to look out at the view, the suburban sprawl seemed closer and larger than in her memory. The view of the city was still there, though, and she fixed her sights on it, ignoring everything else. This was a good thinking place. And, with her increased knowledge of her own powers, or perhaps her relationship with a deceased person, she felt the presence of the Crows who had gone before. It was faint, though. She didn't think the spirits of the Crow Family stayed anchored here in the earth, however pleasant the view. We're up there, she thought, tilting her neck to look at the blue expanse of sky. She heard beating wings and felt air running over her feathers, like a caress. Comforting and exhilarating all at once. Home.

She patted the stonework as she passed, looking for the sundial that she liked as a child. It was blue-weathered bronze and on the southern side of the tomb. The old-fashioned lettering which had confounded her as a small person, now leapt out. 'Life is but a passing shadow, the shadow of a bird on the wing.'

LYDIA WALKED BACK to The Fork from the cemetery. It took almost an hour, but pounding the pavement had always been good for her thought processes. Besides, it put off the moment when she had to walk back into the building which no longer felt like her refuge and home.

It was late in the evening and the cafe was shut. Angel should have been long-gone but the lights were on downstairs. Lydia recognised Aiden's outline through the window and steeled herself for another unwelcome surprise, or another piece of Crow business she would instantly wish she didn't know.

'Hang on,' she said to Aiden, crossing to the counter to make a strong coffee. The ritual was soothing, but it was really a delaying tactic. It didn't put off the inevitable for long, though. Sipping the bitter liquid, Lydia was trying not to think about how much she was relying on Aiden to act as the conduit between herself and the rest of the Crows. He had worked closely with Charlie and everybody seemed to like and trust him, so it made sense. But the fact that he had worked closely with Charlie meant that Lydia didn't know how loyal he still was to his old boss. Aiden was running through various issues, most of which he had already sorted out, and he seemed in his element. But how much could she trust him?

He had been one of the most pragmatic in the Family after Charlie's disappearance, but Lydia wasn't stupid enough to take people at face value. Especially not Crows. She loved her family, of course, but they were known to consider every angle. To work every possible advantage and to think several steps ahead. Lydia realised that Aiden had stopped speaking and was looking at her expectantly. If the niggles and petty rivalries and minor theft had been sorted out, why was he telling her about them? Oh yes, Lydia realised, so that she would know he had sorted them out. Aiden was looking for a pat on the head. Management didn't come easily, but Lydia forced a smile. 'Good work.'

Aiden looked momentarily confused, then his cheeks pinked a little. 'Everyone is satisfied with your climb.'

'Good,' Lydia said. She sensed there was more, though. 'What? Is it Alejandro? Has the news got out?' She made a mental note to check online. If it was out, there would be questions and concern. A lot of concern.

'It's not that.'

'Really. I'm monitoring the situation and will update everyone as soon as I have solid information.'

'People are still whispering. About Charlie.' Aiden hesitated. 'Some people have wondered why you aren't looking for him.'

'He doesn't want to be found,' Lydia said smoothly. 'And if people want to talk to me about it, they can do so. Anytime. It's not like they don't know where to find me.' She gestured around the cafe.

Aiden stood up. 'Right. Right, I'll tell them.'

'You do that,' Lydia fixed him with her best Charlie-stare. Dead-eyed. 'Let them know I'm not a fan of whispers.'

LYDIA WAS CLIMBING THE SHARD, but this time the wind was whipping at her face and hands like it wanted to rip her from the building. Her muscles were trembling and her fingers were numb from the cold. She flexed them tighter, willing herself to hold on. Eyes watering, she forced herself to reach for the next rung. The sound of giant wings beating, dangerously close, made her heart hammer faster. She was sweating with fear and exertion and she wanted to close her eyes, to pretend it wasn't happening. This is a dream, she realised. She was reliving her climb. If she looked over, she would see the crow. The dream state continued with that immersive, cold dread. The premonition that if she looked, she would see something terrible and unforgettable. Lydia wasn't going to give into fear, not even when asleep, so

43

she turned her face and looked. It was her cousin, Maddie. She was bruised and broken and had blood running down her face. Her eyes were beseeching. When she opened her mouth to speak, her mouth was a graveyard of broken teeth. 'Why don't you fly?' With that, Lydia felt her hands slip and, with an awful weight-lessness, she was falling backwards and down, the air suddenly rushing past her ears.

Lydia woke up in a tangle of duvet, her face and neck clammy with cold sweat. She thought she had been woken up by the nightmare but then realised that her mobile was ringing. It was an unknown number and Lydia's befuddled brain just had time to process that it might be the burger van guy she had given her card, before the theory was smashed by Simon's voice.

'It's Ash,' he said.

Lydia sat up, her brain firing, now. Simon had been taken by the Pearls at the age of sixteen and had spent three years partying with them against his will. They had rechristened him 'Ash', although that was likely to be the least worst of the liberties they had taken. Time had run faster outside of the Pearls underground home and twenty years had passed by the time he was released.

'I can't get used to Simon,' Ash said. 'I'm just going with Ash. I know it's probably Stockholm Syndrome or something, and I should stick with the therapy, but I feel like Ash, now, so...'

'Lots of people change their name,' Lydia said. 'It's your choice.'

'Yeah,' Ash said, sounding a little brighter.

'I don't want to be unsympathetic,' Lydia began, squinting at her phone screen. 'But it's three-thirty.'

'Shit. Sorry. I lost track.'

'What's up?'

'I think I found it.' Ash's voice went up in excitement.

'Found what?'

'Their lair. The entrance to it.'

'Please tell me you're at home.' The audio quality sounded like he was outside, but perhaps he was standing in his parents' back garden, enjoying the air.

'Highgate,' he said.

Lydia focused on the grey shapes in her room, letting her eyes adjust to the gloom. 'Go home. Please. I told you I would find them for you.'

'But you haven't,' Ash said. 'I'm not complaining, I know you're busy, but I need closure.'

That was the therapy talking, Lydia supposed. Was closure a real thing? Something human beings actually got? It sounded like things had to stop changing, to Lydia. And that meant death. 'Closure is overrated,' she said. 'Breathing free air is pretty great. Why don't you focus on enjoying that instead?'

'I can't.' Ash's voice had faded, like he had moved his mouth away from his phone. Then he said: 'Gotta go. I think I see something.'

'I'll come to meet you,' Lydia said. 'Don't do anything until I get there.'

A pause. Lydia heard a siren in the background, then Ash's voice. Frightened, now. 'Back up would be good.'

CHAPTER FIVE

I t didn't take Lydia long to dress and head across the river to Highgate. She took her car, counting on reasonable traffic given the unreasonable hour, and arrived at Queenswood Road half an hour later. The road cut through the middle of Queen's Wood, which was Highgate Woods' lesser-known neighbour. There were spaces marked along the side of the road and, praise be, plenty free for parking. The trees reached their limbs across the thoroughfare, forming a tunnel of branches and foliage. It was eerily quiet, traffic noise from the main roads curiously muffled. The last time Lydia had set foot in some London woodland, she had felt like she'd taken an acid trip. Or, at least, how she assumed one would feel. Lydia had bypassed the drugs-as-rebellion stage, figuring 'forbidden relations with Paul Fox' was bad enough.

She checked her phone for updates and, not seeing any, used the flashlight to head into the wood at the next proper path. It looked like people had cut into the woods at different points, wearing unofficial paths up the sloped bank and into the woodland, but Lydia wasn't straying today. It was dark enough to conceal all kinds of threats, even if the Pearls weren't up to their old tricks.

She heard Ash before she saw him. A dull thump followed by an exhalation, surprisingly soft. The first sound had been a punch, Lydia realised, as she turned the corner. Ash was doubled-over, his arms wrapped protectively around his stomach. There were five figures surrounding him at a distance with one, likely the puncher, closer. He was wearing a baseball cap and baggy jogging trousers which looked cheap but had a logo on the back, so might have been expensive. One of the others saw Lydia first and shouted at her to 'just fuck off'.

Lydia stopped and sized up the situation. They were very outnumbered and that was even assuming Ash was fit and able to hold his own. But the faces turned to her looked young, barely in their teens. 'Police' she slipped her ID from her jacket pocket and flipped it open, holding it up briefly. 'Unless you want a trip to the station, you lot can do one.'

The group didn't move and Lydia jerked her chin up in the international signal of 'get on with it'.

After another moment of bravado, with nobody moving a centimetre, the leader gave Lydia a long look up and down and shrugged. 'Boring here, innit.' And they moved off, a pack of kids who ought to have been safely tucked up at home, killing things on their Play-Stations.

Lydia watched them move up the path until they

disappeared into the trees, taking one of the unofficial paths off the main route. There was a chance they would double-back for a re-run and, kids or not, things could get tricky. Especially if they were carrying blades. Lydia grabbed Ash's arm. 'Come on,' she marched him back the way she had come.

'I've got to show-' Ash began.

'Shut up,' Lydia said.

He didn't try to speak again until they were out of the woods and at the road. 'You can let go of my arm, now.'

'Can I?' Lydia said, but she dropped her grip and stood in front of him, arms folded.

'You're angry,' Ash said.

'You're an idiot.'

'I didn't ask you to rescue me,' Ash said. 'I would have been fine.'

'You called me,' Lydia said.

'Oh, yeah,' Ash passed a hand over his face. He looked tired. His face was washed yellow by the street-lamp, dark shadows under his eyes and cheekbones. 'I wanted to show you what I found. A doorway. I think it's them.'

Lydia was pretty sure the Pearl court had a way to enter their underground home in Highgate Woods, but she was also certain that it wouldn't be findable unless they wanted it found. Fleet and his team hadn't seen anything when combing the area for Lucy Bunyan earlier in the year and the sense that Lydia had got was of very old, very strong magic. That sounded ridiculous and it wasn't something she was in a hurry to say out loud, but there was no other word for it. The Pearl Family had appeared to be diluted and weak, their family members scattered throughout London, running shops and stalls and working as hotel receptionists or accountants, their Pearl ability a shadow of what it had once been, but Lydia had recently learned that there was a core section of the Pearl Family which was extremely powerful. They looked young and beautiful but Lydia had glimpsed their true faces, and seen that they were very old indeed. Possibly even the original Pearls. At once, the fairy stories of how the Pearls had come into existence had seemed entirely plausible. Once upon a time, a fae and a mortal had a baby girl... 'Look,' Lydia forced herself to speak gently. 'You can't keep looking for them like this,' she indicated the deserted street and the woods beyond. 'It's the middle of the night and you're alone. And what was your plan if they popped up in a clearing for a chat, anyway?'

Ash pulled a knife from inside his black bomber jacket. It was very shiny and had an intricately-decorated handle. 'It's iron,' he said. 'I've been reading up on the lore and they don't like iron.'

Looking at the blade, Lydia decided she wasn't a huge fan, either. Several possible responses ran through her mind, but she settled on the mildest of them. 'Put that away before you hurt yourself.'

Ash's expression hardened, but he obeyed. 'I'm not playing,' he said. 'They stole my life. They might have done it again. They could have a new hostage down there. I can't just get on with my life and forget it happened.'

50

'Let's go for breakfast,' Lydia said. 'My treat.'

AS THEY CROSSED THE RIVER, Ash yawned so wide his jaw cracked. 'You want me to drop you home, instead?'

'It doesn't feel like home.'

Lydia took that as a no.

'Don't you want to know what I found?' Ash said, his face turned to the window.

'I can guess,' Lydia said. 'A place in the woods which felt odd. It went really quiet and the air felt funny, electric like there was about to be a storm. Maybe you saw the trees moving like they were growing.' She didn't take her eyes off the road, but could feel Ash staring at her.

'How did you know that?'

'Finding the entrance isn't the problem,' Lydia said. 'It's getting in without an invitation.' And getting out alive, she added silently.

It was almost five when they arrived at The Fork and the sky was lightening. Lydia left Ash prowling around the cafe, looking at the framed pictures on the walls, and went into the kitchen to forage breakfast. Angel wouldn't be thrilled, but she wouldn't say anything. Not now. Lydia cracked eggs into hot oil, and put bread into the toaster. The cooking gave her a little more time to think. It was true that she had dropped the ball on Ash's investigation. She could argue that she had been very busy and that would be accurate, but it still wasn't a satisfactory excuse. Lydia had offered to help Ash because she felt guilty about letting him down before, not investigating his case quickly enough when she thought his concerns were down to poor mental health. She seemed to be repeating her past mistake, rather than atoning for it.

She piled everything onto a tray and carried it out to the cafe. Ash was sitting at one of the central tables, lining up the little packets of sugar. He swept them into his hand when he saw Lydia.

'Eat,' she said, putting the tray down on an adjacent table and unloading it. She put a plate with fried eggs and bacon and buttered toast and a mug of tea in front of him. It wasn't up to Angel's standards, but Lydia wolfed her portion down, realising as she ate that she had forgotten to have dinner the night before. She was going to have to watch that. She had cut down on her whisky, after realising that her powers were much stronger when she wasn't drinking a bottle or so a day, but the unstable hours of a private eye weren't conducive to a healthy lifestyle.

'Why did you say you were police?' Ash said, after a few minutes of picking at his food. 'You could have told them your name and they would have run away.'

Lydia was pleased he thought so. 'That would be like using a machete to give a hair cut.' And she didn't want to advertise her presence in the Pearls' manor. They seemed to have a penchant for using kids as scouts and there was a small chance word would have been passed on. Lydia thought about her own network of informants around the city. It was still pretty small, but growing steadily. One day, she would be like her old boss and be able to find out anything at all with a well-placed phone call or a couple of site visits with some crisp twenties in her pocket. 'You can't put yourself in danger like that,' Lydia said. 'I'm sorry progress has been slow-'

Ash opened his mouth to speak and Lydia held up her hand. 'You're right to be impatient. I've been distracted. I haven't given it my full attention and I'm sorry. But I will from now on, okay? But you've got to promise me that you'll stop hunting them on your own. I can't do my job if I'm worrying about baby-sitting you at the same time.'

'I want to be involved. I can't stop thinking about them and I need to be a part of it. I can't just...'

'And you will be. But we go together. With a plan.'

Eventually, Ash nodded.

Lydia mopped up the last of her egg with a crust of toast and smiled at him. 'Trust me.'

CHAPTER SIX

'**B**rain aneurysm,' Fleet said.

'Good morning,' Lydia managed. She wiped drool off the side of her face and sat back in her chair, the bones of her spine cracking. It was almost ten and the sun was pouring through the window. She had driven Ash home just after six and had intended to forgo sleep, sitting her arse in her desk chair and beginning to work through the notes from Aiden. Instead she must have fallen instantly asleep. At least it had been dreamless.

'Lydia?'

'Yep. I'm here. Just processing.'

'It's being marked as natural causes. No criminal investigation necessary.'

Hell Hawk. That wasn't good.

Fleet sounded relieved. 'It's not murder, that means there's nobody to blame.'

Lydia heard the subtext. *Natural causes means*

Maria can't blame you. Shame he was wrong. 'Has Maria been informed?'

'Officers are on their way to her now. They thought it would be better in person. Top brass want it handled with the utmost sensitivity. He was an MP, after all. And the rest.'

Yes, the rest. Alejandro Silver, until recently, had run the most successful law firm in the city. Plus, there were still people in London who believed the old stories about the magical Families and had a little dose of extra respect for the head of the Silvers. 'It doesn't make sense, though,' Lydia said. 'He was very fit.'

'Hidden killer, apparently. Unlucky bastard.' Fleet paused. 'At least it was quick.'

'I thought he died in the ambulance?'

'Fairly quick,' Fleet amended. 'Doc said that he wouldn't have known, wouldn't have been conscious.'

'She's not going to believe it was bad luck. And she's definitely not going to be satisfied with no investigation.' Lydia felt a spurt of empathy for Maria. She would feel the same in the circumstances. Brain aneurysm or not, a lack of police investigation would feel like a smack in the face. Disrespect to her father and her whole family.

A pause. Then Fleet's voice, trying to be reassuring. 'You don't know that.'

Something was bothering Lydia, but she wasn't sure how to identify it from all the things that were troublesome. 'You watched the autopsy, right?'

'Some of it,' Fleet said. 'Why?'

'I don't know. Probably nothing.'

'Am I seeing you later?'

'I hope so,' Lydia said. 'Will you let me know if you hear anything else?'

'Of course. Will you stay away from Maria Silver?'

Lydia couldn't promise that, so she didn't answer. 'Have a good day. See you later.'

AIDEN HAD TOLD Lydia that she had to make herself available to the community and her solution had been to set a kind of open house in The Fork on a Tuesday. She had thought that by providing set hours, she could contain the business-side of being the new Charlie, and keep the rest of her time free. Of course, investigation work didn't sit well with a regular schedule of any kind and it was, invariably, awkward timing. Sadly, today was the day and she had missed the last two, so she had a quick shower and dragged herself downstairs. She poked her head into Jason's bedroom on her way to say 'hello and goodbye'.

He looked up from the large pad of paper he had propped on his knees. 'Going to dispense your wisdom? People lining up to kiss your ring?'

'What?'

'The Godfather, you know. Marlon Brando.'

'Never seen it,' Lydia said. She was about to say 'before my time' but didn't. She was trying to be a better person and that included not reminding Jason that he was a ghost living out of his natural timeline, having died in the mid-eighties.

'It's a classic. We should have a film night.'

. . .

Downstairs in the cafe, Angel was behind the counter. She nodded at Lydia and turned to pour her a coffee without being asked.

There were a few punters at tables, tucking into fried breakfasts, but Lydia spotted a man sitting on his own, nursing a mug of tea and looking worried. She took her favourite seat at the back of the room and waited. Once Angel had delivered her coffee, the man got up and walked nervously to her table.

'Ms Crow?'

'Lydia,' Lydia said. 'Have a seat.' She indicated the chair opposite and the man sat down. He was in his fifties with a grey beard and a mostly bald head. 'What can I do for you?'

'I have a problem,' he began and Lydia dug her fingernails into her palm to stop herself from snapping 'obviously'. People didn't come to her with good news. People didn't line up to share a joke or be friendly. When all was well, she might as well have been invisible. In a flash, she felt a moment of sympathy for Charlie. This was what he had been dealing with his whole life. Decades of it.

Lydia flipped her notebook open. 'Name?'

'Mark Kendal. Sorry. Why are you writing that down?'

Lydia looked at him for a beat before replying. 'I always write case notes.'

'But, won't that be... I dunno. Evidence? Charlie never wrote anything.'

Mark Kendal had gone from nervous to terrified.

Lydia closed the notebook. 'Tell me what's on your mind, Mark.'

'I run a phone place on Southampton Way, by the barbers.'

Lydia didn't know it, but she nodded as if she did.

'I heard that the nail place over the road is going to start selling phone cases.' Outrage overtook the fear in Mark's voice. 'I sell phone cases. That's half my business.'

'Right,' Lydia said. 'That's a shame.'

He spread his hands. 'This is my livelihood. I can't take a pay cut right now. My eldest is at university and it's crippling me. Can you stop them? Have a word?'

Lydia paused. Could she? Should she? Wasn't a free market good for the consumer? Competition giving choice and all that. Stopping price fixing. But did Charlie control who sold what in Camberwell? Was this part of the service? Lydia wished he had left a handbook. Or that she had bothered to learn the business before having him taken away. She could ask Aiden, but didn't want to go to him for everything. It looked weak. Besides, she was the new Charlie. Which meant she could do things her way. Which, in this case, meant stalling. She kept her voice even and told him she would 'look into it.'

The gratitude was embarrassing. Mark Kendal grasped her hand and seemed ready to kiss the back, before Lydia pulled away. Maybe she should watch The Godfather sooner rather than later. Maybe it would give her some pointers.

AFTER MARK HAD DEPARTED, Lydia motioned to Angel for a fresh coffee. There was a woman in a head-scarf clutching her handbag and looking like she was working up the courage to approach and Lydia needed another shot of caffeine first.

Lydia had talked to her dad about The Fork. She was keeping away from him, but they had spoken a few times on the phone and she hadn't wasted the opportunity with small talk. Henry had told her that when he had been working in the business the cafe had been neutral ground. Somewhere people could come to sort out their differences without resorting to violence. Once Charlie had taken over as head of the Family, he had adopted it, making it no longer available for folk to sort out their issues amongst themselves, but instead a place where he took troublemakers and gave them a choice. 'You're at a fork in the road, my friend,' he would tell them. And then he would lay out their choices. 'He wouldn't force anybody to do anything,' Henry had explained, but they always ended up doing the thing that Charlie wanted. 'Well, almost always.' His voice had gone very quiet.

The woman in the headscarf approached. She looked vaguely familiar, but Lydia couldn't place her. She was wearing expensive-looking yoga-pants and a drapey batwing-sleeved top in dark grey. Her face was unlined and she had perfectly threaded eyebrows and expertly applied make-up. At once, her name dropped into Lydia's mind. They had met during one of Charlie's meet-and-greets around the community, when he had been intent on showing Lydia what a big man around town he was. Sorry, when he had been training Lydia in the Crow Family business. 'Chunni,' she said. 'What can I do for you?'

Chunni dipped her chin, a blush rising to her cheeks.

More details were swimming up to the surface of Lydia's mind. Chunni ran a Pilates studio. It was an exclusive little establishment in a renovated mews property near the library, kitted out with those weird Pilates machines, the ones that look like medieval torture racks. Chunni had said that she only took three clients at a time and Lydia had wondered how much she charged the punters to make the finances work.

'I'm not sure I'm in the right place,' Chunni began. She glanced toward the door which led to both the customer toilets and the stairs to Lydia's flat. 'Are you still doing that work?'

'I'm still an investigator,' Lydia said. 'I'm not taking many clients at the moment, but I prioritise locals.' There was a vulnerable vibe coming off Chunni which Lydia definitely hadn't got the last time they had met. It was making her skin prickle with foreboding. Something was very wrong. 'Do you want to go upstairs? Talk more privately?' Over Chunni's shoulder, Lydia could see that another couple of people were waiting to speak to her. Ducking out early was not going to be a popular decision. 'One moment,' she said and rang Aiden. 'I need you at the cafe.'

HAVING ASKED Angel to tell people that Aiden Crow

was on his way and would be taking notes on Lydia's behalf, she took Chunni upstairs. It was a feeling of escape, which really didn't bode well for her prospects as the new Charlie. She was going to have to come up with a new system, a new way of handling the business, as pure avoidance wasn't going to work long term. There was enough residual respect and fear to keep things on the rails for a while, but that would run out. People's memories were irritatingly short.

Lydia made plenty of noise unlocking the front door and inviting Chunni into the flat, just in case Jason had moved from his bedroom and needed time to get out of the living room with his laptop. Chunni wouldn't be able to see him, of course, but a floating computer might raise an eyebrow.

The coast was clear and Lydia settled Chunni in the client's chair and took her place opposite. She took a pen from the mug on her desk and prepared to take notes. 'Fire away.'

Chunni was holding her handbag on her lap, she put it onto the desk and there was something about the gesture, the way the bag was angled which caught Lydia's attention. The movement hadn't seemed entirely natural.

'I'm being sued.' Chunni said. 'At least, I think I am. They haven't sent formal letters or anything, nothing from a lawyer. They say they're going to, though, and I'm worried.'

'Sued for what?'

'This man. Sean Ryan. He says he damaged his shoulder because the machine wasn't calibrated properly. He says he's in constant pain and can't do his work, so he's suing for loss of earnings and stress caused.'

It didn't seem like something that needed privacy, but perhaps Chunni was worried about word getting out that she injured her clients. To be fair, that would be bad for business. 'Has he approached you in person?'

'On the phone,' Chunni said. 'And an email.'

'May I see?'

'I will forward it to you,' Chunni said, suddenly guarded. 'I didn't bring my phone.'

Unlikely, Lydia thought. Which was curious. The 'off' feeling was growing. She would have been tempted to chalk it up to run-of-the-mill paranoia, but given recent events, Lydia thought she should pay attention. 'This sounds like something a lawyer would deal with for you.'

'But I didn't injure him. I thought you could prove that for me. Make him stop this. Follow him and record him or...' Chunni trailed off.

'You want me to scare him off?'

Chunni shrugged. 'If he sees I'm not an easy target...'

There was logic to that. And it was the sort of thing she would usually take. There was just this nagging sense of 'wrong'. And the tricky matter of payment. 'Are you asking me to do this in exchange for a favour, or are you commissioning me as an investigator. If it's the latter, here are my rates. I need a part-payment to get started.' She scribbled down some figures and pushed it across the desk.

'Payment is fine,' Chunni said. 'I don't know what kind of favour I could offer.'

63

'Okay,' Lydia said, expecting Chunni to take the piece of paper and leave. Instead, she stared at Lydia for a few moments longer, as if waiting for something else.

'Is it true that Mr Crow isn't coming back?'

'Yes,' Lydia said, hoping she was right.

AFTER CHUNNI HAD GONE, Lydia went to find Jason. He was lying on his bed with his arms crossed behind his head, eyes closed. 'I think my new client just recorded our first meeting.'

'That's weird,' he opened his eyes, blinking a couple of times like he was waking up.

'You okay?'

'Just resting,' Jason said. 'And thinking.'

'Anything I can help with?'

Jason shot her an amused look. 'I was mulling over the twin prime conjecture.'

The creepy twin girls from The Shining jumped into Lydia's head but then she remembered who she was speaking to. 'Maths?'

'Maths.' Jason confirmed. 'Are you sure? About the recording?'

'No,' Lydia shook her head. 'Just a hunch.'

LYDIA KNEW she still needed to pay a visit to Maria. Having failed to accost her outside the court, she might have to take the more dangerous step of visiting her office or home. It would be the respectful thing to do, as the head of the Crow Family and in deference to their long alliance. There was the small chance that Maria would try to kill her, of course, but hopefully that bad feeling had been put to rest. Or, at least, Maria's practical side would prevail. Lydia was the head of the Crows, now. And Maria was the head of the Silvers. They both had to act like it.

What Lydia really wanted to do was see her dad. Knowing that Alejandro was lying in cold storage in the mortuary, had shaken her more than she could understand and she wanted the comfort of her living, breathing father.

However, Lydia was rationing her contact with her dad. Mr Smith had healed him, brought back his mind from the brink of destruction. But that deterioration might not have been run-of-the-mill Alzheimer's. Her presence had always made him worse, and she and Jason had developed a theory. That her power worked like a battery, charging-up those nearby. Anybody with an ounce of magical energy, found themselves more powerful near to Lydia. Which was why Jason had become corporeal in her presence and why her father, who had spent Lydia's life suppressing and denying his Crow magic in an attempt to give her a normal life, had almost been broken by the effort. Lydia had written to him, outlining her theory. She had hoped that he would say that he would no longer try to suppress his nature. She was an adult, now. And part of the Family. He had written back, explaining that he couldn't do that to Lydia's mother. He had made a choice to live a normal life for her sake, and he wasn't going to go back on that promise. And that now that

Lydia had stepped up to Charlie, there was no going back for her.

As instructed, Lydia had burned his letter, but she could still remember the last lines, word-for-word.

I'm an old man and not just in years. My time is spent and I have not spent it flying. You are the head of the Family, now. There can only be one. I would be a distraction, an encouragement to dissent, a confusion. With a murder there can only be one winner. Burn this.

LYDIA DIDN'T KNOW if her father believed she had killed his brother, or whether he was referring to the collective noun for a group of crows. Either way, the message was clear: 'You've made your bed, now lie in it. Alone.'

At once, the walls seemed too close and Lydia had to get out of the flat. She headed out into the cool evening, striding quickly in an effort to mute her tangled feelings. She arrived at Burgess Park without consciously deciding on a destination and proceeded to walk aimlessly along the tarmac paths. She had thought that with Charlie gone she would feel a sense of freedom. Instead, she felt more trapped than ever. Wings beating against bars. Claws scrabbling on a metal floor. Caged.

Her dark thoughts were interrupted by the realisation that she was being followed.

CHAPTER SEVEN

A split-second later, Lydia felt the pull of Pearl magic. When she turned she wasn't entirely surprised to see the girl from the Pearl King's court standing by a sycamore tree, watching. She decided to take the initiative. 'Hello, again. What's your name?'

The girl still had dirty blonde hair and torn jeans, and several necklaces slung around her birdlike neck, including the one Lydia had given her on their last meeting. She picked up the lightest sense of Pearl from the girl. Just a dusting. A sheen. But the girl didn't say anything, simply kept on staring with those unnervingly light eyes. After a minute or so, Lydia turned away and continued her walk.

The girl stayed on the grass next to the path, maintaining her distance from Lydia but clearly keeping pace. They were approaching the lime kiln. It was another relic from when the area had been a hive of industry, fed by the Grand Surrey Canal. Boats had brought lime from other parts of the country, ready to be fired into quicklime before being taken to the London factories. Now it was an odd, flat-topped octagonal structure marooned in a sea of municipal parkland. Lydia stopped, as if studying the kiln. She spoke without looking at the girl. 'I thought you lot had cleared out.'

Still nothing.

'It would be better if you had,' Lydia glanced at her. 'I'm not a fan of the kidnapping.'

The girl smiled. She was missing a front tooth and a couple more were askew. When she spoke, her voice made the hairs on Lydia's neck stand up. 'You're in so much trouble.'

Lydia tilted her head. 'Is that right?'

The girl smiled wider, but didn't speak again.

After another minute of staring, Lydia had had enough. She stepped up to the girl and grasped her arm. Her hand wrapped easily around her narrow biceps and the girl turned shocked blue eyes upward. 'I think you should come with me,' Lydia said. 'Let's find you somewhere safe and warm to sleep tonight. Make sure you get a decent meal.'

The girl began to struggle like a wild animal, bucking and clawing. Lydia got her arms wrapped around her from behind and lifted her off the ground. Her legs were kicking wildly and one of them connected painfully with Lydia's knee. 'Enough,' she said, pushing a bit of Crow behind the word.

The girl stopped kicking, went limp. 'Don't take me,' she said, her voice plaintive. 'Please.'

Lydia lowered her to the ground, keeping hold of one arm. 'Why are you following me?'

The girl glared at her from underneath tangled hair. 'Was told to.'

'You're reporting back on my movements? To the king?'

The girl shrugged as if that was obvious.

'Why?'

The girl wrenched her arm out of Lydia's grip and ran. She disappeared behind the lime kiln and Lydia followed, not even sure what she was going to do when she caught the girl. Could she really force her back to The Fork for a meal? Should she? She peered into the first opening of the kiln, expecting to see the girl hiding in a corner, but it was empty. The same thing was repeated in the next couple and then Lydia was back where she started. She looked around the park. There was no way the girl could have run away from the kiln without being seen, there simply wasn't enough cover nearby. And yet, she had disappeared. To underline the fact, Lydia couldn't feel even the slightest wisp of Pearl. The girl had most definitely vanished.

FLEET CALLED. 'I've pulled the CCTV from Westminster Pier. You bring the popcorn.'

Lydia had settled into a routine with Fleet. On the nights they were both off work, she would go to his preternaturally neat flat. Fleet often cooked, or they got Pad Thai from the takeaway, and they had head-banging sex. If they had fallen into a rut, Lydia didn't mind.

She pressed the bell for his flat and waited to be

buzzed inside. 'You can use your key, you know. That's why I gave it to you.'

Lydia didn't bother to argue that the key was for emergencies only. And that had been the basis upon which she had accepted it. She deflected him with a kiss, reaching up on tiptoes and holding the back of his neck and head, feeling the tight curls of hair under her fingers as she pulled him closer.

Fleet looked slightly dazed, which was gratifying. His particular gleam, something a little bit magical, but not one of the four Families Lydia could identify, sparked a little brighter. It always hit her during the first few moments of being with Fleet and then it faded to the background as she adjusted. It wasn't alarming. Just part of Fleet. Along with the sunshine and salt scent of his skin, and his elusive smile.

'Are you hungry?' he asked, 'I can put the pasta on whenever you're ready.'

Lydia bent to unlace her boots, stepping out of them as quickly as possible. Then she towed Fleet to the bedroom. The pasta could wait.

LATER, Fleet dished up bowls of amatriciana and Lydia poured red wine. They sat on the sofa and prepared to scroll through the camera footage. There were two angles showing the street, giving good coverage of the stretch where Alejandro collapsed. The pavement was really wide at that part of the embankment, with steps down from one section to another path directly alongside the river. With the numerous benches, leafy trees and the view of the London Eye, it was a popular rest stop and there were groups of tourists and office-workers grabbing a lunchtime sandwich in the sunshine. Lydia had her notebook open next to her on the sofa, ready to jot down questions. The first one was 'why was he walking?'. It was a nice day, sure, but he was a busy man with a car service. Or, was this his habit? If so, somebody could have scoped out his schedule in order to accost him at an opportune moment. But if they knew his routine, wouldn't there have been a less public place to stage an attack?

They had the timing so didn't have to wait long before Alejandro appeared in frame. He was wearing a three-piece-suit and carrying a cane with a silver top. Anybody else would look dandyish, theatrical or old-fashioned. Alejandro looked armed. He was walking with purpose and a determined expression, not glancing around at the scenery or ambling in the sunshine. Perhaps he was considering the vote he was walking toward, or his day's business. Or, perhaps, he was aware, somehow, that he was entering the final minutes of his life.

The pavement was busy and, for a few seconds, Alejandro was swallowed by a group of people walking in the opposite direction. When he emerged, his head was down, his face hidden. Lydia couldn't see if pain or knowledge passed across it in the split second everything went wrong. It was as if he had been shot. Alejandro collapsed to the ground. Lydia replayed the moment. Alejandro didn't clutch his chest or arm or any part of his body. He just collapsed. Like his brain had stopped sending the messages to his limbs to stay strong and keep moving.

'If I was a betting man, I'd say that was a brain aneurysm.' Fleet waved his fork at the screen.

He wasn't wrong, but Lydia couldn't help think that they were seeing what they expected to see. She skipped back and watched the moment again. And again. 'That group. The ones who surround him just before. Have they been interviewed?'

Fleet shook his head, swallowing a mouthful of pasta before speaking. 'It's not considered suspicious. No need.'

'Could someone have attacked him? In that moment when we don't get a good look. I mean, he's surrounded just before he collapses, isn't that suspicious?'

'I would have bet on poisoning before the post mortem,' Fleet said. 'But there's no evidence of that. There's evidence of a-'

'Aneurysm,' Lydia finished. 'I know.'

Fleet put his empty dish onto the coffee table and picked up his wine. 'You seem angry.'

'It's Alejandro Silver,' Lydia said. 'He can't just die. Not like that. Not for no reason.' She felt a lump in her throat and picked up her own glass. Chugging wine so fast it burned.

'Sometimes people die,' Fleet said gently. 'It was too soon, of course, but he wasn't young. It happens. I'm more concerned about you.'

'I'm fine,' Lydia said automatically. 'How much more is there?'

Fleet gave her a final, worried look, and then turned

72

back to the screen, pressing play. A stream of people walked past Alejandro on the ground, and then two women in hijabs stopped. One crouched down next to Alejandro and Lydia could see her speaking, reaching out to touch his shoulder. Then the angle was obscured by a tour bus and, when that had passed, another group of people standing gawking on the street.

'What about the citizen who called the ambulance?'

'I knew you were going to ask and I asked around. No official statement was taken, but the call was recorded.' He produced his phone and scrolled for a moment. 'It was a woman. Aysha Hussain. The dispatcher talked her through CPR while she waited for the ambulance. I've put in a request for the audio file.'

'Don't we see her on here?' Lydia clicked to play the video again.

'I don't think so. That group doesn't move.'

Lydia shot him a look. 'You watched this already?'

'Just a quick scroll through. I wanted to check it was the right file and that it wouldn't be a complete waste of time.'

'Well, I appreciate you getting it for me.'

'So formal,' Fleet said, his mouth quirking into a smile. 'Is that an official thank you from the leader of the Crows?'

Lydia felt the weight of his words like a binding spell. She stiffened her spine and looked him dead in the eye. 'Is that what you want?'

Fleet's smile fell away in an instant. 'Jesus, Lyds. I was joking.'

Lydia forced her muscles to relax and she stood up,

taking her plate to the kitchen and dumping it on the side. She looked in the fridge, more for something to do than in expectation. There was a cheesecake plated up and a punnet of strawberries. She felt her stomach turn over at the thought of more food.

'Come and sit down,' Fleet said.

'I'm going to head home,' Lydia said. 'Do some work.'

'Don't leave,' Fleet stood up. 'Let's talk about it. I'm sorry I joked about your family.'

He was picking his words, clearly at a loss as to her response to his joke. It was probably an over-reaction, Lydia knew, but she hadn't realised how much she needed to keep the worlds separate. She couldn't be the head of the Crow Family when she was lying in bed with Fleet or enjoying post-coital pasta. She just couldn't.

'It's fine,' she said, reaching up on tiptoe to kiss him. 'I just want to think about all this,' she indicated the screen.

Fleet boxed up dessert while Lydia laced her boots, handing it to her at the door, with a final, thorough kiss which made her toes curl and her mind reconsider whether she really wanted to leave.

'You're not planning to speak to Maria, are you?'

'No,' Lydia lied, busying herself with the container of cheesecake to avoid looking him in the eye. There was no point in worrying Fleet more.

'You need to be careful.'

'I always am.'

74

CHAPTER EIGHT

A t lunchtime the next day, Lydia was sitting at her table in The Fork destroying Angel's signature lasagne when Aiden walked in looking worried. 'I need a word.'

She put down her fork with some regret. 'Of course you do. What's up?'

'Mr Kendal is unhappy. He says he came to you about a business issue and you haven't done anything about it.'

'The phone case guy? It's a free world.'

Aiden winced. 'He pays us to look after him.'

Lydia indicated that Aiden should sit in the chair opposite. She could do without his lanky form looming over her, blocking the sunshine streaming through the windows of the cafe. 'What do you mean he pays us? I didn't think we did that anymore.' She lowered her voice. 'The protection game.'

'No, no you're right. We don't,' Aiden said. He was

about as convincing as a nun in a strip club. 'But we do have a select few special relationships.'

Lydia pushed her plate to one side. 'What sort of relationships?'

'They pay us to help them stay ahead of the competition.'

'What exactly do you mean?'

Aiden hesitated. 'The last place that moved in nearby and started selling phone accessories closed after two weeks.'

Lydia held her hand palm-out in a 'stop' gesture. 'That's enough.'

'We closed them.'

'I got it,' Lydia said. She glanced around at the half-full cafe. 'Let's walk.'

Once they were outside, walking along a quiet side street, Lydia resumed the conversation. 'Why do we look after Mark Kendal and his pisspot little phone shop?'

Aiden shot her a guarded look. 'He supplies burners.'

'Okay,' Lydia said. 'What else?'

'That's not nothing,' Aiden said. 'You get a phone from Mark, you know you haven't been caught on some mook's CCTV, you know there's no receipt in the till showing when you bought it.'

'I'm an investigator,' Lydia said, 'I know why that's important. What else?'

'You really want to know?'

Lydia resisted the urge to stop walking and kick Aiden. Instead she nodded. 'Tell me.'

He rubbed a hand over the scruff of beard on his

chin, gazing at the pavement like it contained the secret of life. When he looked up, his expression was a mixture of fear and defiance. 'It's one of our legit businesses.'

Lydia stopped walking and stared at him.

Aiden shrugged, unable to meet her eye.

'Explain,' Lydia said eventually.

'We need places to wash funny money, so we're good friends with a few businesses in Camberwell. They use the dodgy cash, we look after them, do favours and that, and we get nice clean money in return.'

It wasn't the most important part of the story, but Lydia found her brain had snagged on the cash. 'I thought everything was digital, now. Cards and online banking.'

Aiden shrugged. 'Charlie was old fashioned.'

'You know who else likes cash? Dealers.'

Aiden shook his head. 'No drugs. Charlie made sure of that.'

'I know he wasn't a fan,' Lydia said. Although, as she spoke, she realised that he hadn't been keen on drug gangs moving into Camberwell from Peckham and Brixton. That didn't mean he wasn't running his own operation. At this point, nothing would surprise her.

They resumed walking. 'Tell me who else washes for us.'

After Aiden had listed the businesses and Lydia had asked a couple more follow-up questions, they looped around and began heading back to The Fork.

'I thought we were going somewhere,' Aiden said, as they crossed to Camberwell Grove.

'I just wanted to talk in the open air,' Lydia said. 'Less chance of being recorded or overheard.'

Aiden frowned. 'You don't think The Fork is safe? No one would dare...'

'I don't trust anything anymore,' Lydia said. 'And neither should you.'

CHARLIE CROW HAD BEEN VERY careful with the details of his business. He had rarely spoken about it on the phone and Lydia had never seen him write anything down or use a computer. Now that he was out of the picture, cooling his heels in a government facility, Lydia had checked through the house to ensure there were no nasty surprises and nothing to incriminate any of the Family, should the police come knocking. After the news from Aiden and the realisation that the criminal side to the Crow Family business was very much a going concern, Lydia let herself into the house with a fresh perspective. She was going to be more thorough this time. It was a further invasion of privacy, but she had already done far worse.

She worked systematically, room by room, using the training from her PI mentor, and the details she had picked up through experience. She had come prepared with a crow bar and chisel and she prised every dado rail and skirting away from the walls to check behind. Searching was easy when you didn't have to worry about leaving things exactly as they had been before. She emptied every drawer from every piece of furniture and kitchen unit, checking the backs and underneath.

The living room fireplace was cleanly swept, the remains of the yule log and its ash properly cleared away after the winter holiday. The fire was important. The log had to stay alight for the twelve days, or there would be bad luck. Burning the old year to make way for the new, as well as providing light at the darkest time. Lydia paused by the enormous mantelpiece, struck by the memory of Charlie leaning there, lord of all he surveyed. She could still smell wood smoke in the dead air of the unused room. Charlie had followed the traditions, but that hadn't saved him from Mr Smith and his secret department of the British government. Lydia spent her waking hours avoiding thinking about her uncle and what he was experiencing now. The guilt was too great. He had tried to kill her, but still. Family was Family.

Truthfully, Lydia had expected a greater backlash from the Crows. Certainly, she had expected more questions. It seemed, however, that Charlie had trained them not to show curiosity, to trust the leadership of the Family. She was the rightful leader, the direct descendent of Henry Crow, and the Family appeared happy to accept it. Of course, that could all be a ruse. Any one of her relatives could be biding their time, lulling her into a false sense of security before launching a coup.

Lydia ran her hands along the mantelpiece, checking for switches. There wasn't likely to be a concealed compartment or a false wall which would swing out, revealing a secret room – this was London after all and there wasn't the space – but it wasn't impossible. Upstairs, Lydia hesitated outside Charlie's bedroom door. But only for a moment. It was neat inside, with crisp white bedding like a hotel and blinds at the window. An enormous arty light fitting hovered in the middle of the room, an alien spacecraft visiting planet earth. The bedroom furniture was a dark, polished wood and Lydia checked the matching nightstands. Books, tissues, reading glasses she had never seen Charlie wear, and a small packet of photos. Lydia shook them onto the bed. There was her dad, his arm slung around another young man's shoulders. He was smiling at whoever held the camera, handsome and young with a grin that promised adventure. The other man, Lydia assumed it was Charlie, was looking off to the side, as if his attention had just been caught by something out of frame. Lydia studied the one visible eye and eyebrow, the edge of his mouth. Yes. That could be a young Charlie. There was something determined and cold in that eye. Or she was projecting.

The next photo was definitely Charlie. It was a few years later and he had filled out. He was a solid wall of muscle wearing a fitted white t-shirt and jeans and an unreadable expression in those shark eyes that Lydia knew all too well. A girl with black hair and pale skin had both arms wrapped around his narrow waist and was beaming like she had just won the lottery. She looked familiar, but Lydia didn't know why. Growing up, she had never seen her uncle with a woman. He had been married to his job. The embodiment of the road her father hadn't taken.

Lydia looked under the bed, ran her hands under the mattress and pulled the drawers out of the nightstands, checking the backs and underneath. Then she went through the storage in the dressing room, rifling through Charlie's neatly folded clothes. If he had a laptop or notebook, it would be somewhere handy so that he could use it regularly. She had been sure it would be here, in his inner sanctum. The en-suite didn't yield results, only the discovery that Charlie used herbal toothpaste, which smelled of liquorice.

Pacing the room, Lydia heard the floorboard creak as she crossed the middle of the floor. She went back over the spot, covered with a red Persian rug, taking careful steps and adjusting her weighting until she heard the creak again. It was very quiet, but there was a tiny difference in the floor, the smallest amount of flex. Rolling the rug away, Lydia scanned the polished boards. They looked neatly dovetailed, but she pulled out a pocket knife and began testing the seams of the boards. One came up. Inside was a cavity. Reaching inside, her fingers touched something soft. A cloth bag. She pulled it out and found a small notebook and a rectangular metal tin. Packed inside were bundles of money. A couple of rolls of fifties and a roll of ten-shilling notes. Spreading one out, Lydia studied its front and back a couple of times each to check she wasn't losing her mind. It was, as far as she could tell, an authentic, used ten-shilling note from the nineteen fifties.

The notebook was about the size of her hand with a hardcover and black elastic holding it shut. Inside were columns of numbers and notes which were not written in anything resembling English. Shorthand, possibly, but a quick google showed that it wasn't the official version. A code of Charlie's own devising?

Lydia sat down and went through the pages carefully, looking for anything which might refer to familiar names or businesses in Camberwell. An entry marked MKM had a string of numbers in different pens, written presumably at different times. MKM could easily be Mark Kendal mobiles. But it could be a thousand other things, as well.

Lydia packed it all back into the cloth bag for easy transportation and put the floorboard back into place. She locked the house up carefully, wondering what other surprises it still held.

LYDIA DIDN'T KNOW if it was seeing the old photographs of Charlie and her dad, but she told Aiden she wasn't available the next day and called Emma to see if she was free. By happy coincidence, Emma had a trip planned to the National Gallery and agreed to meet Lydia afterwards for a walk along the embankment.

The following afternoon, the sky was pale blue and spring sunshine made the river sparkle. It reflected off Emma's sunglasses, and the can of lager that somebody had left on a low wall, and made dappled patterns on the ground beneath the trees which lined the embankment.

They had caught up on the essentials of life and Lydia had been reassured that Archie and Maisie were thriving and that Tom, Emma's husband, was doing much better health-wise. In turn, she had filled Emma in on the last few months with the broadest of strokes.

'When you say Charlie has 'gone'. Is that a euphemism?'

'No.' Lydia took a deep breath. 'At least, I don't think so. As far as I'm aware, he's alive.'

'And you've got his job?'

'Yes. Kind of. I've delegated most of it to other people in the family. But I'm the last word. Theoretically, at least.'

'Bloody hell,' Emma said. 'That's major.'

'I'm sorry I haven't been around,' Lydia said it quickly, like ripping off a plaster. She wondered how many more times she would say these exact words to Emma and how many more times she would be forgiven before her oldest friend cut her losses.

'I need a drink,' Emma said.

'Pub?' Lydia perked up.

'Coffee.' Emma was making a beeline for a nearby booth. Standing in front of Lava Java, she glanced at the menu. 'Maisie has been waking up all week. Nothing serious, night terrors, but I'm bloody knackered.'

Night terrors sounded extremely serious. Lydia was struck, all over again, by Emma's calm competence in the face of astounding horror. Whatever depravity or danger Lydia's job revealed, the intricacies and responsibilities of parenting never ceased to impress and alarm her.

Large coffees in hand, they resumed their stroll. 'What's it like?'

'Sorry?'

'Being in charge.'

'Exhausting,' Lydia said. 'And scary. I don't know what I'm doing.'

Emma pulled a sympathetic face. 'I guess he didn't leave a handy guidebook?'

Lydia shook her head. 'Plus, I don't really want to do things the way he did. At least, not everything. He was...' She lifted the lid on her coffee cup and blew on the liquid to cool it down.

'I've heard the rumours,' Emma said.

'Exactly.'

'I don't mind you being busy,' Emma said. 'I understand. You know I've always understood your hours are weird and long and you have to disappear into cases sometimes to get them done. I get all that.'

'I know, but it's still rubbish for you. I want to be a better friend. More steady. You deserve a better friend.'

Emma pulled a wry face. 'I've got plenty of friends. I'm not sitting by the phone waiting for you to call.'

'I didn't mean that,' Lydia said. 'I know that. I just feel bad.'

'Well don't,' Emma said briskly. 'I've told you a million times. You don't need to worry about me.'

Lydia tried her coffee. Still too hot.

'I think it's more than busyness though.' Emma was watching her with a wary expression.

'What?'

'I think that sometimes, like maybe recently, you keep away from me deliberately. You lost your uncle and I know you two were close. You can talk to me, you know. You don't have to push me away.'

Emma was right, she had been close to Charlie Crow, and there was a confused soup of emotions regarding his absence. But she didn't deserve a caring, sharing session, with the sympathy and understanding she knew Emma would provide. She felt guilty and that was only right. She had betrayed Charlie. More than that, she had done the very worst thing she could do to a Crow. Worse even than killing him, she had put him in a cage.

'Do you want to talk about it now?'

'It's fine,' Lydia said. 'I'm fine. And I'm sorry I've been distant. You're right, some of it has been deliberate. I was waiting to see how things settled down. I didn't want you caught in... Anything.' Lydia kept Emma separate from the Crows, but it wouldn't take a genius to work out that she still kept in touch with her friend from school. A single unguarded conversation with her mum would do it. And if someone came looking for leverage or retribution... It didn't bear thinking about.

'You're doing your usual thing,' Emma said, annoyance clear.

'What thing?'

'Pushing everybody around you away. I don't know why you think you have to do everything on your own. It's not weak to need people.'

Well that was blatantly untrue. And not the point. 'I need to keep you safe.' She didn't add 'and your children' because she couldn't even form the words. The idea that she could be the cause of any harm coming to Maisie or Archie was, quite literally, unspeakable.

Emma regarded Lydia over her coffee cup for a long moment. 'You don't, though. I'm a grown woman. I make my own choices.'

Lydia opened her mouth to explain that it wasn't about choices or adulthood, but life and death. She encountered some very bad people in her line of work and now she was walking around with a bullseye drawn on her back. Emma, however, hadn't finished.

'And you can't seem to see the irony. The more you push everybody away, the more you keep secrets and tell half-truths, the worse off we all are. I don't expect you to be available, but I do need you to stop hiding.'

'I'm sorry,' Lydia said. She wanted to tell Emma it was for her own protection, but she also didn't want to frighten her friend. And she was afraid it would sound like a bullshit excuse, anyway.

'Don't be sorry,' Emma touched her arm. 'Talk to me.'

'I'll try,' Lydia forced a small smile. 'Old habits.'

Emma nodded. 'Good. Now, I've got to run.' She checked the time on her phone. 'School pick-up awaits.'

After hugging Emma goodbye, Lydia stopped by the booths at Westminster Pier. She recognised the man with bleached-blond hair that she had spoken to before and waited for the queue of people to clear before approaching. 'Do you remember me?'

He nodded fast. 'I was going to call.'

Lydia had just intended to check in, to keep her request fresh in the man's mind. She hadn't expected any actual information. That was the thing about investigative work. You shook a lot of trees before getting hit on the head with an apple. 'Why were you going to call? What's happened?'

'There was a woman asking about that day. Like you were.'

'A woman asked you about the day Alejandro Silver collapsed over there,' Lydia gestured to the spot, making herself absolutely clear. That was another thing she had learned over time. Don't be ambiguous when questioning a source.

He nodded eagerly. 'Yeah, yeah. She asked all about it. What he looked like. Who was with him. All that.'

'What did she look like?'

'I dunno. Dark hair?'

'When was this?'

'Monday. I was off yesterday.'

'You remember anything else about her? How was she dressed?'

'Smart. Black.'

'She was black?'

'No. Definitely white. She was wearing a black suit or something. Business. But nice.' There was a bit of leer as he recollected the woman. This was the kind of man who showed every single thought on his face. His eyes probably turned into the shape of chicken drumsticks when he was hungry.

'And she spoke posh.'

'Got it,' Lydia said. She gave the man another twenty. 'Next time, call me right away. Okay?'

CHAPTER NINE

On the way through Camberwell, Lydia couldn't shake the feeling that she was being followed. She took evasive action, stopping to pretend to look in shop windows while checking out the pedestrians and traffic in the reflections, walking in and quickly out of a deli and through a cafe she knew had two different street entrances. She didn't see anybody following, but kept up the looping walk, avoiding her usual route and doubling back at random times in the hopes of either catching sight of the surveillance or forcing them to stop. She expected to catch sight of the Pearl girl or, perhaps, someone from Mr Smith's department. She wasn't naïve enough to believe that just because she had told him she wasn't working with him any longer, that he would simply accept it. Eventually she got close enough to The Fork to walk past her dark grey Audi and she considered getting in and going for a drive. The feeling of being watched had gone, though, and she hadn't seen anything suspicious. She was being paranoid.

She could go home, now, but somehow she kept on walking, looping around and around Camberwell like a caged animal pacing the confines of its environment. Everything was different without Charlie at the helm. People spoke to her differently, people looked at her differently and everything was suddenly *her* problem. The investigator part of Lydia loved the insider information and the sense of seeing beneath the veil. But at the same time, she felt like her jacket was too tight and she couldn't take a proper breath.

Without realising, Lydia had looped around and back and was now passing St Giles Church on the main street. Not knowing why, she ducked through the entrance and into the quiet garden behind the church. Lydia wasn't religious, but she had a soft spot for this particular church and the saint it was named after. St Giles, the patron saint of the poor, destitute and the crooked. The last being the physically deformed, rather than criminal. Plus, they held a weekly jazz club in the crypt below the church with live music and a licensed bar. That was the kind of church activity Lydia could get behind.

The headstones were against the brick walls surrounding the garden and Lydia found herself walking slowly past each one, trying to read the worn inscriptions, like it was a pilgrimage to the past. This wasn't an important place to the Crows. She knew that, but still she felt something here. Something tugging at her senses, dragging her through the public garden and along the wall of memorials, looking for an unknown destination.

Most of the graves had been moved to the Camberwell cemetery, and the remaining space remade into a garden, with grass and trees and benches, but there were still a handful of memorial stones against one boundary wall and the occasional tomb dotted on the grass. Two children, around Archie and Maisie's ages were playing on top of one. She caught the lines of a nursery rhythm being chanted in victory. 'I'm the king of the castle'. It was a good mix, Lydia thought, the reminder of death in the midst of life.

And with that thought, the hairs raised on the back of Lydia's neck and she felt the unmistakable sensation of being watched. Turning slowly, Lydia cast a casual look around. The young father with the two small children wasn't looking in her direction. He was standing with one hand in his jeans pocket, head bent over his phone. There was nobody else there.

Turning back, Lydia pretended to be focused on the gravestones. She was reading the words without really meaning to when a phrase jumped out: 'Sacred in memory of Alice Elizabeth wife of John Crow of this parish who departed this life on the 14th April 1846.' She wondered how that grave had been missed in the mass exodus to the Family tomb in Camberwell Cemetery. Had this Alice Crow done something to piss off the rest of the Family? It would have to be something pretty bad to have her left out of the Family resting place for all of eternity. Or it was just a sign of how little stock the Crows put into churches and graves. The earthly remains of Crows could be anywhere, their spirits would still be high in the sky. Lydia closed her eyes and gripped her coin until she could feel them, mingling with live

Crows, borrowing their sight, feeling the air riffling through feathers and senses sharp.

Pearl. Just a trace, but Lydia felt it and it pulled her down from the freedom of the sky and back to the green earth. She turned around to scan the park again and saw Ash step from behind a tree close by. 'Feathers, Ash,' she said. 'You scared me.'

His expression didn't change for a moment and the blankness reminded her of the Pearl girl who had followed her in Burgess Park. It crossed her mind that she should perhaps be a little more careful. She was clearly too easy to find. Lydia instantly rejected the notion. She wasn't going to let anything curb her enjoyment of her city. Besides, if somebody took a hit out on her, avoiding the park wasn't going to keep her safe. They could turn up at any one of her known haunts. Or, as someone had chillingly told her once, they could just poison her food. 'What's up?'

'I've found it,' Ash said, becoming animated.

'What?'

'They've done it before.'

Lydia knew that the Pearl Family, or the core members of the family, known as the court, had taken a girl. Her name was Lucy Bunyan and one of her ancestors had signed a contract with a company which had stated they had the rights to a first-born daughter. It was creepy and definitely not legally binding, but that hadn't stopped the Pearl King from plucking the sixteen year old from Highgate Woods and keeping her prisoner until Lydia had disrupted the party. Months earlier, unbeknown to Lydia at the time, Ash had been released by the Pearls after spending twenty years in their company. Ash knew about Lucy, but she gently reminded him.

'No. Not just her,' Ash shook his head, bouncing lightly on the balls of his feet. He was still just as thin as when he had first re-entered the world, the sharp planes of his face showing that he wasn't eating enough. Or that the effects of twenty years of not eating enough were difficult to eradicate in a few months. Lydia felt a spurt of anger toward the Pearls and was relieved that she was still capable of caring. Ever since she had allowed Mr Smith to take her uncle away, she had been battling a growing numbness.

'Let's walk.' Lydia didn't want to draw unnecessary attention and she thought the motion might keep Ash calm. Instead he began pacing up and down in front of the gravestones, waving his arms as he spoke. 'I found it. I found the pattern.'

'What pattern?'

'It's been going back decades. I went to the newspaper archive in the British Library. I know everything is supposed to be online, now, but I wanted to be sure, and I found them. Kids go missing. I only searched for sixteen year olds, but there might be loads more. Different ages, I mean.'

'What makes you think it's them?'

'Every twenty years a sixteen year old goes missing from Highgate Woods.'

Lydia paused. 'All from the same place?'

Ash nodded. 'There was one, in nineteen twenty one which was Hampstead Heath and another where they didn't have a last known location, but the age and timing was right. And they were never found. None of them were ever found. Apart from Lucy.'

'And you,' Lydia said. 'You need to stay away from Highgate.'

'I told you, I've been at the library.'

Lydia thought about the girl. 'Have you seen any Pearls? They use kids. Have you been followed?'

Ash looked at Lydia with a mixture of confusion and anger. 'You think I'm weak. I'm not stupid. This happened to me. You think I wouldn't notice if I saw one of them?'

'I don't think you're stupid,' Lydia tried to placate him. She didn't want to say 'you're traumatised and are clearly not thinking clearly or looking after yourself' so she settled on 'I'm just worried about you. I want you to stay safe.'

'I'm being careful,' Ash said. 'But I won't stop. I can't.'

BACK AT THE FORK, Lydia picked up a mug of coffee from Angel and headed upstairs to work. She found Jason meditatively making a hot chocolate. He had branched out from cereal and tea and Lydia wasn't sorry. She opened the fridge and passed him the canister of whipped cream. It felt a little light, but there were three more lined up on the shelf and a catering-size bag of marshmallows she had stolen from the cafe kitchen on the countertop. In her continuing effort to stop drinking hard liquor all day every day, hot chocolate with all the trimmings was a helpful distraction.

She told him about the mysterious woman who had been asking about Alejandro at Westminster Pier.

'Maria?' Jason said.

'Sounds like it,' Lydia said. 'And something else occurred to me this afternoon.'

'Oh, right?' Jason shook the can and applied a towering spiral of cream to the mug.

'Maria has a decent motive to off Alejandro. He made her head of the Family but it's possible people weren't really treating her like the new boss. She might have figured that he needed to be out of the picture for the world to really see her as the new power. And I assume she's the heir to all his cash, too.'

Jason raised an eyebrow. 'You think she would kill her own flesh and blood?'

'I did worse.'

Jason was silent as he added mini marshmallows to the cream. Lydia didn't blame him, there was no argument. She had consigned her father's little brother to a fate worse than death. Caged. Experimented on. Tortured, maybe. Who knew what horrors he was enduring? Jason slid open a drawer and removed a packet of chocolate flakes, sticking one into the mound of cream and sugar. 'Enjoy,' he said, pushing the mug toward Lydia.

TAPPING A PENCIL ON HER NOTEBOOK, she tried to marshal her thoughts. The woman asking questions at Westminster Pier certainly sounded like Maria. The

95

question was, did this make it more or less likely that she had offed Alejandro herself?

Lydia put herself in Maria's shoes. It was an uncomfortable fit and didn't really help. Maria might investigate if she believed someone had hurt her father, but she might also ask questions if she had done the deed. Either to check that she had adequately covered her tracks and that there were no pesky witnesses who might need incentivising to keep quiet, or to give the impression of investigating Alejandro's death in order to appear innocent and clueless. Lydia opened her eyes, startled into laughter by the idea of an innocent Maria Silver. The woman had been born with a black shrivelled heart.

Jason had appeared while her eyes were shut and was sitting on the sofa, quietly tapping away on his everpresent laptop. He glanced at her. 'You're in a good mood.'

'I saw Emma,' Lydia said, deciding not to explain her attempts to get inside the mind of Maria Silver.

'That's good,' Jason nodded. 'You don't want to get too isolated. It's lonely at the top.'

'So I am discovering,' Lydia replied.

If Maria had killed her own father, she would definitely need it to look like natural causes. Not only to keep herself out of prison, but to stop retribution from other Family members. The more Lydia thought about it, the more convinced she became. Maria had shown homicidal tendencies in the past, had tried to have Lydia kidnapped and, most likely, killed. She had certainly threatened to end Lydia on more than one occasion. She was more than capable.

Lydia called Fleet and asked him to meet her in the pub. 'Crazy day, here,' Fleet replied. 'Is seven all right?'

When he walked in, Lydia was waiting at her favourite table in the corner, a pint of Fleet's preferred beer and a bag of salted peanuts in his place.

'Uh-oh,' Fleet said, after kissing her hello and sitting down.

'What?'

He gestured to the drink and snack. 'You want something.'

'I always want something when you're around.' Lydia was attempting a flirtatious tone but Fleet just frowned at her in confusion. So much for using her womanly wiles. 'If I wanted to kill somebody and make it look natural, would a brain aneurysm be a good cover?'

Fleet had his glass halfway to his mouth and he raised it in a small salute. 'There it is.'

Lydia clinked her glass against his, but refused to be distracted. 'Is there a poison that would cause an aneurysm?'

'An undetectable poison?' Fleet said, after taking a sip of his pint. 'No. Not that I have heard of, anyway. We did think of that before marking it as a non-suspicious death, you know? At the Met we pride ourselves on that kind of due diligence.'

Lydia ignored the sarcasm. 'How well do you know the pathologist? Could he have been convinced to provide a false report?'

'I don't really know him, but that would be difficult to do. It's not one person's word, there are lab techs and an assistant pathologist involved.'

'Not impossible, though?'

Fleet shrugged. 'Chain of evidence is a big deal for a reason. Mistakes happen, but less often when every stage is documented.'

'But it's hypothetically possible?'

'Very hypothetically.'

'I guess you would need access? Or the ability to bribe somebody with access?'

'At the very least.' Fleet put his glass on the table. 'First principles. Maybe the most likely explanation is the truth. Alejandro died, sadly, before his time. A previously-undiagnosed weakness leading to an aneurysm. I know you think you all have some kind of extra-special power which protects you, but it has its limits.'

'Don't lump me in with the Silvers,' Lydia said sharply.

'But you take my point,' Fleet said.

Lydia drained half her glass to avoid answering.

Another beat. 'Do you want to speak to the pathologist?'

'Yes, please. I was going to rock up to the mortuary, but I thought an official intro would be more successful. I'm sorry to ask...'

'Don't be,' Fleet said. 'I know you're sick of me saying this, but I'm on your side. Whatever you need, you can come to me.'

'I'm not sick of you saying it. Not at all.' Lydia leaned in and kissed him. Partly because she wanted to and partly because she wanted to avoid continuing the conversation. She wasn't sick of Fleet telling her that she could trust him. She just wished she could believe it.

CHAPTER TEN

Alejandro's funeral must have taken a team of people and deep pockets to organise, but no matter the planning and money which had been thrown at the event, they hadn't been able to control the weather. The day dawned warm and bright, the meteorological version of a massive 'fuck you' to what ought to have been black and raining.

'Are you sure about this?' Fleet was wearing a black suit and tie and Lydia was hit by how inappropriately attractive he was, even in funeral garb. It was distracting. She was wearing the basic black dress she put on when pretending to work in an office or posh hotel, which sat below the knee. She had a less-basic black version which sat far higher for those occasions when she needed to pick someone up. It had been a long time since she'd done honey-pot work and was glad that hadn't been off the hanger in a while. Lydia twisted her hair at the nape of her neck and fixed it with pins, matching a sensible hairstyle to the outfit. She wasn't going to have anybody saying that Crows weren't showing proper respect to the occasion.

'She suspects it wasn't natural causes and that means she probably suspects my Family. All the more reason to follow tradition. I can't be seen to snub the Silvers by not attending the funeral. And I need to speak to Maria, let her know I'm investigating and I'm her best chance of getting justice for her father. That way, she might not try to kill me.' Lydia tugged at the dress, checking that she looked properly sombre and demure.

Fleet was watching her in the mirror. 'That's not what I meant. Are you sure about this?' He gestured to them, framed together.

The boring dress was good. It might help to balance out the fact that she was walking in on the arm of DCI Fleet. Could risk be balanced that way? 'I'm sure,' she said out loud. 'I'm not hiding.'

'And that's fine,' Fleet said evenly. 'I agree, you know I do. But is this the best occasion to step out together officially?'

'Step out?' Lydia paused in the act of searching for her black court shoes. 'How old are you, again?'

He flashed a smile which made her stomach flip. 'You want to come here and say that?'

'Not if we're going to make the funeral on time,' Lydia said, not without regret. 'And that probably would start a war.'

THE TRAFFIC on Chancery Lane was halted by leather-clad motorcycle riders, parking across the busy lanes and crossing their arms, ignoring the cacophony of horns – a blaring sound which cut off abruptly as people caught sight of the funeral procession. It was led by a shining black carriage, its windows etched with silver filigree, pulled by four black horses with silver plumes and livery. The coachman had matching black and silver clothes and a top hat and the top of the carriage was covered in white flowers. Lydia wasn't one for pomp, but she had to admit it was quite beautiful.

Crawling behind the carriage were several Rolls Royce limousines in black and grey and behind those, more flashy cars including a Maserati and two Bentleys. 'Bloody hell,' Fleet said, indicating one of the cars. 'That goes for quarter of a million.'

The procession was heading to the distinctive round structure of Temple Church, which was intrinsically linked to the legal profession. It had been built by the Knights Templar, the original bankers, but the Inns of Court had moved in during the fifteen hundreds and it had been the lawyers' local one-stop for births, deaths and marriages ever since.

Having been able to duck down side streets, Lydia and Fleet arrived ahead of the procession. Once they stepped away from the bustle of Fleet Street, the court-yards and chambers of the temple area swallowed them. There were lots of people arriving at the church for the service, clad in smart black clothes and looking suitably solemn. Several people were in their justice robes or barristers' outfits, clearly fitting in the service in the midst of a busy day lawyering.

Fleet slipped his arm from around Lydia's waist and gave her a serious look. 'Last chance to back out. You don't need to prove anything to me.'

'I know that,' Lydia said. She felt a stab of uncertainty. 'Would you rather we kept things quiet? Are you worried about who will see us here?'

'Not in the slightest,' Fleet said, taking her hand.

'That's all right, then-,' Lydia broke off as she spotted a familiar face in the crowd milling outside the church. 'Wait. Is that-?'

'Chief of the Met? Yep.'

'Feathers,' Lydia breathed. She tried to slip her hand out of Fleet's and take a step to the side. There was expecting Fleet to go public and then there was making him parade his relationship with the head of the Crow Family in front of the boss of all his bosses.

Fleet squeezed her hand. 'I'm not hiding.'

They walked up to the crowd, past a couple of barristers in black court robes with bright white collars, who were carrying briefcases and navy bags with embroidered initials which looked like PE bags from primary school. Fleet spotted somebody he knew and they made small talk for a few minutes before going inside. He introduced Lydia by her first name and his acquaintance as 'Nathan from five-a-side', as if Lydia ought to know who he was talking about. She made a mental note to pay better attention to Fleet's life. They were in a committed relationship now, and she should act a bit more like a proper girlfriend. Probably.

Black marble columns reaching up to the vaulted ceiling, wooden pews lining the central aisle and a magnificent stained-glass window at the far end. So far, so-churchy, but the stone effigies on the floor of the round part of the church, like knights had decided to take a nap and then been ossified where they lay, added an eerie quality.

Neat lines of choristers dressed in white robes waited while the mourners took their seats before opening their mouths and releasing the kind of pure sound which makes every hair on the body lift. Lydia could understand why the church went in for that kind of thing. It was close to magic, and in the days before movies and the internet or even electronically amplified music, those clear voices echoing in the great vaulted space must have seemed other-worldly.

Alejandro's coffin was carried down the centre aisle on the shoulders of Silver Family members. Lydia had prepared herself for being around so many and she took shallow breaths through her nose, tasting the clean tang of metal in the back of her throat. Maria let the coffin reach its destination before making her entrance. She walked down the aisle alone wearing a sharp black dress with a pencil skirt and long sleeves, and high heels. She had swapped the enormous black sunglasses Lydia had seen her wearing as she got out of the car for an antique-looking black lace shawl which was draped over her head in the traditional Spanish style.

The church was packed, with many people standing in the round part of the structure, unable to find a seat. Lydia scanned the mourners, looking for any surprises. She found herself subconsciously looking for Charlie, as if Mr Smith and his department would have released him for the occasion. As the choir's singing and the sound of suppressed sobbing worked on her emotions, Lydia found herself blinking back tears of her own. She wouldn't allow them to fall. They weren't for Alejandro or his daughter so it would be disrespectful, but she had to produce her coin discreetly in one hand and squeeze it tightly, her other hand held in Fleet's.

Filing out into the sunshine, Fleet asked if they were going to the wake. It was in a hotel just behind the church and the mourners were streaming through the narrow streets and courts, no doubt anticipating a rejuvenating beverage and, for some, the chance to conduct a little business, cement some important relationships. A man was dead, but it would take more than that to stop the wheels of commerce and law from turning.

Lydia knew she had no right to the moral high ground on that front. She was still conducting her business, after all. Was only in attendance as she had to be. She represented the Crow Family and respect had to be given and, just as importantly, be *seen* to be given. The hotel restaurant had been booked out and there were many good-looking waiting staff weaving through the crowd with trays of drinks and canapés. There was a great deal of pale marble, gold mirrors and glittering chandeliers, as well as teal velvet seating. If you ignored all the sombre clothing, it could have been a PR event or a wedding reception. A line of well-wishers waited to pay their respects to Maria, who was still veiled in black lace and flanked by men in suits with earpieces. Lydia had to hand it to Maria, she knew how to play her part.

'Come on,' she said to Fleet, who had just picked up

two glasses of whisky from a tray and was holding one out. She knocked back the drink. 'I think we've done our duty.'

'Excuse me.' A man who was twice the width of Fleet and looked stuffed into his suit was suddenly barring Lydia's way. 'Ms Silver would like a word.'

More performance. Lydia would play along. She put her glass down on the nearest table and then she and Fleet walked past the line of people waiting to pay their respects, following the man mountain.

'We are sorry for your loss,' Fleet said when they arrived in front of the bereaved.

Maria nodded. She held out her hand to Fleet. 'DCI Fleet. Have you tried the canapés? They are divine.'

On cue, a security guard led Fleet away. Up close, Maria's eyes were hollow. Lydia felt a clutch of sympathy, while keeping her eyes on the security still standing nearby. Large men who looked like they were barely containing their urge to stomp Lydia out of existence. Lydia wondered where Maria had hired them. You could pay for violence easily enough, but not emotion. 'I'm sorry for your loss,' Lydia said.

Maria tilted her head. There was a loaded silence before she asked: 'Are you?'

The question sounded genuine and Lydia paused to give it the consideration it was due. 'I'm sorry your father is no longer with us. I preferred dealing with him.'

Maria's smile was like a skull. All teeth. 'Pretending to be candid. Is that your new thing? I should have you beaten to death.'

Her intonation didn't change for the threat and it

was all the more chilling. Maria wasn't bluffing. Lydia didn't break eye contact. 'I am here to pay my respects on behalf of the Crow Family. In recognition of the old alliance which existed between our families. And on a personal level, for the courtesy always extended to me by your father. Courtesy which seems sadly lacking today.' Lydia spread her hands, palm up. 'Which is, of course, perfectly understandable given the depth of your grief.'

At that moment Maria didn't look upset. Just furious. Which didn't mean she wasn't grieving in her own way. Lydia could relate. When she thought she had lost her own father she had wanted to burn the entire world.

'You think this,' she waved a hand, 'makes you look trustworthy? You think I don't know that you have been plotting against me and my Family?'

'That isn't true,' Lydia said.

'Do you know how my father died?'

Lydia nodded. 'Brain aneurysm.'

'That's what they say.'

'You don't believe it?'

Maria held her gaze. 'Do you?'

Lydia didn't answer. She could see the lines of tension around Maria's mouth and a flash of sadness broke through the anger in her eyes, making her seem more human than usual. One of her security staff stepped up and whispered in Maria's ear. Her gaze flicked behind Lydia and she nodded once. 'Bring him next.'

Lydia wasn't sure if she was being dismissed, as Maria was still staring over her shoulder.

'Look at them all lining up,' Maria said eventually.

'Everyone wants a favour, now. I've been head of the firm for months, nobody said shit, but now... Now they want me.'

'Change can be slow,' Lydia said. 'And people can be very old fashioned.'

'That's true,' Maria said, snapping her eyes to Lydia and seeming to collect herself. 'A lot of these old men didn't believe I was in charge. They have no choice, now. He's gone.'

Lydia nodded. She had another unexpected clutch of empathy. She felt the wind whipping around her face as she climbed The Shard, playing the stupid games to prove she was a worthy successor to Charlie.

'I think our Families should continue to work together,' Maria said. 'Whatever my personal feelings, I must acknowledge that, historically, there has been a mutually beneficial relationship.'

Maria was definitely a lawyer. Fifty words where five would suffice. 'I'm pleased to hear it,' Lydia said. 'For my part, I vow that I will find out the truth of your father's death.'

Maria's eyes widened a little.

'I will prove that I had nothing to do with it. That no Crow had anything to do with it. And, if you require, I will help you to exact justice on the person or persons responsible.' Wordiness was catching. Lydia took a deep breath and forced herself to stop speaking.

Maria's eyes had narrowed, again. She tilted her head back a fraction. 'You will bring me your findings first.' It wasn't a question.

'If I can,' Lydia said, after a moment of hesitation.

'What about your pet policeman?' Maria indicated Fleet who was watching them intently, flanked by yet more security.

'This has nothing to do with Fleet or the Met,' Lydia said. 'This is Family business.'

CHAPTER ELEVEN

The day after the funeral was a Friday and Fleet called Lydia. 'Shall we go out to eat? Or I could cook, if you're happy to come to mine.'

'Not tonight,' Lydia said. She wanted to dig into Alejandro's life for the last few months, maybe see if Jason could use his computer wizardry to dig up any secrets. 'You can come here later, though. If you want?'

'Sure.' Fleet paused. 'It would be nice to go out sometime, though.'

'Like a proper couple,' Lydia said. 'You old romantic.'

'Less of the old. Nothing wrong with a proper date. There's a Caribbean place in Vauxhall that's supposed to be good.'

'Next week, maybe. Or when things are more settled.'

Fleet paused. 'I hear what you're saying, but I think we should go tonight or this weekend. If we wait for our lives to be more settled, we're never going to go.'

Lydia found a hot chocolate on the counter, the whipped cream deflated and congealed on the brown surface. She poured it down the sink. 'Are you annoyed?'

'Not at all. But I would rather we accepted that this is how our lives are and prioritise each other now, rather than waiting for it to get easy.'

The man made a lot of sense. But Lydia didn't hold the best track record in making time for normal life. 'You know what you signed up for,' she said, keeping it light. 'I'm more about the late-night stakeouts, takeaway, sex and an unhealthy work-life balance.'

'I know,' Fleet said and she could hear the smile in his voice. 'Think about it, though. It's not like I'm asking you to take a holiday. It's just an evening out.'

'If I say yes and you book something I might have to cancel at the last minute.'

'So might I, still not a reason to not even try.'

'Well, if you're going to be all reasonable about it...' Lydia hoped that she sounded faux-annoyed rather than proper-annoyed. She felt proper-annoyed but knew she had no right to the emotion and that fact was enough to make the irritation worse. She felt as if there were pulls on her time and attention all the damn time and now Fleet was asking for more.

'Just wait until you taste the salted fish, it's supposed to be amazing with the curried goat.'

'You had better be joking.' Lydia was more of a pizza-and-a-beer kind of a girl, as Fleet well knew.

'Chicken.'

. . .

110

THAT EVENING Fleet arrived with a thin crust pizza and a bottle of red wine and hadn't argued when Lydia had said she still had a bit of work to do. She nibbled at a slice of margherita while she read yet another puff piece article about the wunderkind Alejandro Silver and his wildly successful career. Fleet was working at the other side of her desk, slumped in the client's chair with his long legs stretched out to the side. At least, Lydia assumed Fleet was working. He might have been playing Candy Crush on his phone for all she knew. She had been researching Alejandro online, going over the last few months of his life and making notes. Which were mostly just questions and blank spaces. She wasn't going to panic. All cases began like this, with random pieces floating in a big sea of 'what the hell?'. If she followed the process, she would find more pieces and, eventually, fit them all together. What was clear to her after his funeral, though, was that Maria was no longer Lydia's prime suspect. Not off the hook for his death, but no longer top of Lydia's list. She was a Silver and naturally extremely convincing, but Lydia had seen real grief in her eyes.

Alejandro had decided to enter politics the year before and, within months, had become the MP for Holborn. She broke the companionable silence to say as much to Fleet. 'How did he manage that so quickly?'

Fleet looked up from his phone. 'I have no idea.'

Lydia opened her laptop and began researching. The parliamentary seat had opened up in February when the existing MP had keeled over. Which was interesting. A Silver had got the very thing they wanted as a result of a timely death. The MP had been approaching seventy but there were pictures of her completing a five kilometre fun run the week before she died. It wasn't conclusive, of course, but it suggested a certain level of health.

A little further down the page, Lydia got her answer. It wasn't age or health related. The MP, Nadine Gormley, had been hit by a car while holidaying with her family in Greece. It was a hit and run and the case remained open.

Fleet stood up and walked to her side of the desk, leaning down to read over her shoulder. 'That's convenient.'

'That's what I was just thinking,' Lydia said. 'Don't suppose you've got a handy contact in the Greek police?'

'I can ask around. Nothing official, but someone might chat as a favour. Interpol are probably involved, too. It's an MP, after all, not-'

'A nobody,' Lydia finished.

'I wasn't going to say that,' Fleet said. 'Of course, it could be something else, something entirely unrelated to Alejandro's political career.'

'He worked criminal law,' Lydia said, echoing what Jason had suggested. 'Could be a bad guy from his past, freshly out of jail and looking for revenge.'

'I'll look at his old cases and see if anybody has been recently released.'

'I know the bill he was going to vote on that day didn't look controversial, but was there anything else scheduled that someone might want Alejandro to miss?' She was on the parliamentary website which listed all the public bills currently going through the houses. 'What are private bills?'

Fleet scanned the page. 'Things that relate to private companies, I think. They're not secret.'

Nothing jumped out to Lydia, but then anything could conceivably be enough to kill a person over. Everything important enough to make it to parliament had ramifications, even if you couldn't see them right away. Ripples spreading outward from a pebble thrown into a pool.

Fleet straightened up. 'Maybe there isn't a motive.'

Lydia was still skimming the list of bills. 'Mmm?'

'Because maybe it isn't a murder. Maybe the pathologist is right and it was a brain aneurysm.'

'I can't go back to Maria and say that. It's not going to fly.'

'Even if it's the truth?'

Lydia kept quiet. She didn't believe it was the truth. No, more than that, she *knew* it wasn't the truth. It was down there in her gut, a certainty that only grew with every piece of so-called evidence to the contrary. Alejandro Silver did not drop dead of a brain aneurysm from some undiagnosed condition. He did not. If she told Fleet, he would say that she didn't want to believe it. Or he would be defensive of the system he had dedicated his professional life to, the system he believed in. He would say that Lydia was mistrustful of his work, and that she had an inflated sense of the power of the Families. He wouldn't go so far as to say she was letting emotions cloud her judgement – the man wasn't a fool – but he might think it.

Fleet stood up and cleared their plates, then went and made coffee. When he came back, he opened his work laptop and Lydia felt a small release of tension. He might not agree with her hunch, but he would do the work. He was a good copper.

'So, motive,' Fleet said after a few minutes. 'I pulled recent releases who might have a grudge against Alejandro and there was nothing obvious. One man got out in December but he was in for white collar crime and I can't see him turning violent. Only other possibility was released the week before Alejandro died. He just served twenty-three years for killing his wife with a hammer. Found God inside, apparently.'

Lydia made a disbelieving noise.

'Quite,' Fleet said. 'But even if his piety wouldn't stop him from going after Alejandro, there are more obvious targets first. Like the brother-in-law who gave evidence. And I don't see him as the mastermind type who could organise something as controlled as this. I looked at his file and he's twice as thick as he is nasty, and has all the impulse-control problems associated with his crimes. I mean, if Alejandro had been bludgeoned in a pub then we'd have a suspect...'

'Got it,' Lydia said. 'You know I was keen on Maria for it?'

'You've changed your mind?'

Lydia decided not to reveal her moment of empathy with Maria and stuck instead to the facts. 'I haven't found anything. She was in court on the day he died and alibis don't get much better than a full room at the Old Bailey.'

'So we're back to an undetectable poison,' Fleet said.

Lydia liked the 'we' in the sentence. 'Or something less prosaic.'

'What do you mean?'

Lydia didn't want to say the word 'magic' out loud and she tried to think of an alternative. 'I was thinking about the Families,' she began. 'JRB have been trying to stir up trouble between us. This would be an excellent way to turn up the heat. Maybe I'm supposed to suspect Maria and she's supposed to go for me and, before you know it, there's a full-on war.'

'What about the Foxes? Couldn't it be one of them?'

It was no secret that Fleet didn't like or trust Paul Fox and Lydia didn't blame him. 'I doubt it, the Foxes tend to keep out of this kind of thing. And I don't see Paul trying to start a war. Too much work.'

'You're blind when it comes to him,' Fleet said. 'Your history...'

'I see perfectly well,' Lydia said. 'You don't know him the way I do.'

'Well, that's true.'

'Let's not fight,' Lydia said. 'Bigger fish.'

'So. JRB. How close did you get to a contact there?'

'Not close at all,' Lydia said. 'Shell corporations within shell corporations like a bloody Russian Doll. Best lead was the link to the Pearls.'

'You're not going there, again.' It was a statement not a question.

'Not unless I have to.'

· · · ·

STEPPING into the barbershop which hid the entrance to the Foxes' favourite drinking establishment was out of Lydia's comfort zone. It was nowhere near as scary as the first time she had done it, though. Things were very different now. Paul Fox was the head of the Fox Family and, crucially, Lydia was the head of the Crows. Still, her pulse speeded up as she pushed open the door, nodded to the barber and headed down the stairs which led to the concealed door.

One of Paul's brothers was sitting at the bar and Lydia battled the urge to walk straight out again. She had last seen him kicking her while she lay on the ground, so her second urge was to go over and stab him somewhere soft and painful.

Luckily, Paul appeared from the gloom, and wrapped his arms around her. Lydia wasn't a big hugger and Paul hadn't greeted her that way since they were an item, but she figured it was part of the show. He was marking territory with his Family and making it clear that Lydia was welcome, so she went with it. She had prepared herself for the onslaught of 'Fox' but the added proximity to his skin unleashed an extra set of pheromones into the mix. It felt like the hug went on for longer than was strictly necessary, but the sensation of being pressed up against Paul's hard chest wasn't unpleasant. Once he released her, he gazed into her eyes. 'It's good to see you here'.

She smiled her shark smile and planned a cold shower for when she got home. 'Drink?'

'Of course,' Paul signalled to somebody behind Lydia and led her to a table to sit down.

Moments later, two glasses and a bottle of Macallan arrived, courtesy of the brother Lydia had seen when she walked in. He didn't look thrilled at waiting on Lydia Crow and he would probably have preferred Paul beat him up again. After Lydia had been set upon, Paul had arranged, or more likely administered, a beating of each of the perpetrators, matching their injuries to Lydia's. And then he had banished his own father for his part in the proceedings. As apologies went, it had been pretty comprehensive. Still, the Fox sibling by the table bowed his head as if expecting further retribution.

Paul flicked his eyes and he moved away. Lydia let out her breath. She knew that she wasn't in physical danger and that the guy had been following orders from his own father, but she had no desire to chat about the weather. Or, for that matter, to have a big heart-to-heart. The past was done. He couldn't take it back and she wouldn't forget.

'I've got a proposition for you,' Paul said, uncorking the bottle and pouring two fingers into each glass. 'An alliance.'

Lydia had guessed what he was going to say, but sitting in the Den with a glass of whisky in her hand, it suddenly became very real. Could she forge a formal alliance with the Fox Family on behalf of the Crows? Should she? It was one thing to be friendly with Paul but quite another to make it official. And the Crows didn't trust the Foxes. Nobody did.

'I know our reputation,' Paul said. 'And I know we haven't been on the Crows' Christmas list for a very long time, but things have changed. We're the new generation. We don't have to be bound by the past. We can work out a new way of doing things.'

It sounded fine, but the past was still there. Was that why she kept being led to graveyards? Were her ancestors trying to remind her of her duties? That was a crazy thought. The pressure of leadership making her unstable. Already. 'I'm here because Alejandro Silver has been murdered and that is bad for all of us.'

Paul nodded approvingly. 'You're not taken in by the coroner's verdict, then?'

Lydia raised an eyebrow. 'Please. The Silvers aren't going to believe it, either. They will still be looking for retribution. I think it's important to present a united front, at least until we find enough evidence so that Maria Silver accepts the police's verdict or we find those responsible. It is also a gesture of goodwill and trust between our Families that is the first step toward a more generous and peaceful existence.'

Lydia clinked her glass against Paul's and they both drank.

'You sound different,' Paul said, head tilted back. 'You been giving lots of speeches?'

Lydia allowed herself a small, honest smile. 'It's exhausting.'

'How was the funeral?'

'Fancy,' Lydia said. 'And a bit creepy. Have you been inside Temple Church?'

He shook his head. 'I know it's where the Silvers conduct all their significant events. Christenings, memorials, weddings. Rumour has it, the main bloodline Silvers are interred underneath the church.'

'Does your Family have a church?'

Paul snorted. 'No. Not really our thing. You know the Silvers aren't really believers? The Temple Church connection was purely business.'

Lydia did know. As well as bedtime stories about the Crows, Henry had told her tales from the other Families. At the end of the sixteenth century, the Inns of Court were using the Temple Church and its environs and had invested in architecture and so on. Being men of law, and having learned from the decline of the Knights Templar who were buried deep under the church, they knew the value of a good contract and they wanted to protect their position. They petitioned King James for a charter that would ensure they could use the Temple in perpetuity and King James, being no more immune to legal persuasion than anybody else, agreed. In gratitude they gave him a gold cup which got lost years later by a broke Charles I. What wasn't in the history books, is that the Silver Family had arrived from their travels in the New World with a large cache of gold and silver and an uncanny ability to persuade others to see their point of view. They found their perfect match in the Inns of Court and quickly ingratiated themselves into the profession. Nobody knew how, but within five years of the original charter being agreed with King James, the Silvers had added an amendment; they also had use of the church in perpetuity with a special dispensation to build a Family crypt under the chancel. And there, nestled between the cherub-cheeked choristers above ground and the bones of the Knights Templars deep below, the Silver

119

Family had interred their most important ancestors ever since.

'What most people don't know,' Henry had explained. 'Is that they liked the gold cup that the Inns of Court had used, so they made a silver one for their amendment. But, being the Silvers, they didn't just give it to King James as a souvenir to be lost among Royal baubles. They made a big ceremony, where the King and the head of the Silver Family drank wine from the cup in recognition of their fealty. And then they convinced King James that the cup should remain with the Silvers, in their Family crypt as a sign of their devotion to the crown. Which meant, of course, that it was forgotten by the Crown as soon as King James passed on and the Silvers got to give a gift while never losing anything at all.'

Lydia wasn't in the habit of revealing her own knowledge, much better to find out what other people knew first, so she just said, 'I know the Inns of Court used to use the church to do their lawyer stuff back in olden times.'

Paul's expression had turned serious. He put his glass down and folded his hands. If Lydia had been dealing with anybody else she would have said he seemed suddenly nervous.

'I don't want to talk about the Silvers anymore.'

'Okay.'

He tilted his head. 'There's another way to unite our Families. Fast-track it.'

'Is that a fact?' The whisky was really good and Lydia finished her glass and poured another. She had missed the burn of it. The feeling of warmth and wellbeing. She had always had an exceedingly high tolerance and never seemed to get drunk, but four or five drinks had the pleasant effect of muting some of the buzzing in her mind and body, buzzing that she was barely aware of until the volume was turned down and a little bit of quiet space opened up.

'We should be together.'

Lydia managed not to choke on her whisky, but it was a close-run thing. 'What?'

'You heard,' Paul said calmly. 'And don't pretend to be surprised.'

'I don't think... I'm with Fleet. You know that.' There was a great deal more that Lydia could say, but invoking her prior commitment seemed the politest option.

Paul shrugged. 'It's not like you're married. And he's police.'

'I am aware,' Lydia said drily.

He sat forward suddenly, hands clasped together on the table. Lydia felt the increase in animal magnetism and the answering tension in the pit of her stomach. She wondered if he was consciously able to control it, like she could with her Crow power. Charlie had thought that the Crows had the most power and were the only ones able to train it, to harness it. He had peddled the accepted view that the other Families were vastly diluted, their powers dimmed over the decades to an echo of what they had once been. But maybe he had been wrong.

'I want you. I know you want me. I've proved that I'm loyal. What else is there?'

'You're being serious?'

'The DCI is from a different world. You must know it's not going to work out.'

'You're not in a position to comment on my relationship.' Lydia pushed herself back in her chair. She had been leaning forward, toward Paul, and that had to stop.

'I think I am. I know you.'

'You knew me, once. A long time ago.'

'Not that long. You can't trust him. And I don't want you to get hurt.'

'Funnily enough, he says exactly the same thing about you.'

CHAPTER TWELVE

Lydia hated the feeling that she was dancing to the Family's tune, but it seemed that smoothing things over with Mark Kendal would be the quickest way to appease John and, by association, the rest of the old guard. She had always thought that being at the top meant you didn't have to worry about what those below you thought or felt, but it didn't seem to be the case. And if she didn't want a revolt on her hands, she was going to have to work on her diplomacy skills.

She walked into Mark's phone shop, the door setting off a loud buzzer. Racks of phone cases hung from the walls and a metal grill was across a glass case behind the cash desk, protecting the high cost items - the iPhones and laptops – from a quick theft. She had expected to find Mark himself standing behind that desk, but he was nowhere to be seen.

'Hello?' Lydia looked around a second time, just to be sure, but the shop really wasn't big enough to hide a person. The cash desk was another glass case, this one without a grill, filled with boxes of phones and bling-tastic accessories. A multi-coloured LED sign loomed over the set-up and a desk fan turned semi-circles, making the hanging cases quiver in the draft. She waited for another minute, but Mark didn't pop up from behind the desk or walk through the front door, carrying a take-away coffee.

There wasn't an obvious door to a backroom, but after letting her eyes adjust to the rows and rows of brightly coloured cases, Lydia realised that there was an exit in the corner. It was covered in cases like the wall, rendering it almost invisible. There was a recessed handle halfway up and Lydia pulled, expecting it to be locked. Consequently, it swung open faster than she had intended and a few cases fell to the floor. Stepping over the mess, Lydia entered a room cluttered with cardboard boxes. She had to squeeze through a narrow path between towering stacks of boxes labelled with Apple, Samsung, and brands she didn't recognise. 'Mr Kendal?'

The boxes wobbled dangerously as she moved. The guy should really tidy up his store room, it was a health and safety nightmare. Turning a corner, Lydia stopped thinking. Mark Kendal was lying on the floor in a pool of dark sticky blood. His head was caved in on one side, so thoroughly and deeply that yellowish matter was visible amongst the gore. Brain, Lydia's mind supplied. That's probably a bit of Mark's brain.

Bile was in her mouth and she turned away to take a couple of breaths. She contained the urge to spit the foul taste onto the floor, it was a crime scene after all, and fished for a tissue instead. She pulled on nitrile gloves and approached the body, careful not to step in the blood. He was definitely dead, but she felt she ought to feel for a pulse, anyway. Mark Kendal's neck was cold and the flesh, as she pressed it, had a strange texture. She was no pathologist, but he had been dead for a while.

Lydia straightened up, thinking fast. Her phone was in her hand and she knew that she ought to phone the police. Instead, she took photos of the scene, working systematically around the body and the room. The urge to vomit passed as soon as she began analysing, which was a bonus. The injury was on the side of the head, not the back. That didn't rule out somebody surprising him from behind, but it made it less likely. To Lydia's untrained eye, it looked like a single, forceful blow. The murderer was either very strong or they used something very heavy. Lydia looked at the space and tried to judge whether a largish person would have had the room to get a decent arm swing. Next she tried to judge whether it had happened in this room, or whether the body had been moved after the event. The blood spread out from the head, with no drag marks or blood trail.

She crouched down and patted the body down, checking pockets and the hands for defensive wounds. The hands looked undamaged and although the finger-nails were grubby, it looked like everyday dirt rather than blood. Mark's wallet was in his front jeans pocket with a couple of credit cards, a donor card, and over a hundred in cash. Folded behind the donor card was another bank note. A ten-shilling note like the ones she had found in Charlie's bedroom. It was soft and well creased, clearly folded and refolded many times. Without thinking too much about it, Lydia pocketed the ten-shilling note, and put the rest back. Mark was lying face down and Lydia slid his wallet into the back pocket of his jeans to avoid having to reach underneath again. Once had been bad enough.

LYDIA EMERGED from the back room cautiously, but the shop was still deserted. She closed the door and wiped it down with her sleeve. There was a CCTV camera pointed at the cash desk, but a closer look showed that it had been sprayed with black paint. Whoever had been here first had already disabled it. There wasn't a back door out of the shop so Lydia had no choice but to emerge from the front, onto the street. She moved quickly and mentally crossed her fingers that nobody was paying attention.

In one hand she could feel her coin, solid and reassuring, and in the other she held her phone. Her first thought had been to phone Fleet, but her second and third thoughts had followed fast. Mark had come to her for help and now he was dead. This was connected to her family. Her first duty had to be to protect them. Besides, Mark was past helping, now. What would Charlie do?

Pushing that unhelpful thought aside, Lydia moved through Camberwell as fast as she could without running.

BACK AT THE FORK, Lydia went straight upstairs to find Jason, but the flat was empty. She sat on his bed for a few minutes, in case her presence would make him appear, but the room remained stubbornly empty. She still wanted to speak to Fleet, but before that she needed Family help. She called Aiden.

He must have been nearby, as he arrived in ten minutes. He was wearing shiny jogging trousers and a hoodie, his hair damp with sweat. 'Sorry,' he said, gesturing to himself. 'Football.'

There was something to be said for clicking your fingers and having people drop everything to obey. Especially in an emergency. Out on the terrace and with the radio playing, Lydia ran through the details.

'We need to clean it up,' Aiden said.

'I wiped everything down,' Lydia said. 'And the camera was blacked-out.'

'The body is still there, though.'

'Does that matter?' Lydia was thinking about the police investigation. They hadn't done this and she hadn't left any evidence of finding the body, so now the Met could take over. That was fine.

Aiden was frowning at her. 'You just found him?'

It hit her. Aiden thought 'found him' had been a euphemism. 'Yes! Why would I have hurt him?'

'Not my place to speculate,' Aiden said quickly.

'If I had, we have a way to clean up?'

'Well, yeah.' Aiden must have caught something in her expression, because he added, 'Emergency use only.'

Lydia paced the terrace, thinking. After turning over the issue in her mind, she realised something important. 'We should clean up, anyway.'

'Right you are,' Aiden already had his phone out. 'I'll speak to John.'

'Uncle John?' Lydia said, boggling.

'Yeah, he's got a friend of a friend. That's who we use.' He paused. 'Can I ask why? I mean, if it wasn't us?'

'It wasn't me,' Lydia said, 'but that doesn't mean it wasn't us. I still don't know what is going on with every part of the Family. I don't even know if you're telling me the truth half the time.'

Aiden opened his mouth to argue.

'Don't take it personally,' Lydia said, 'I'm not a group hugger, I don't trust easily, and most of the stuff I've found out over the last few months I don't like. Which means I'm always waiting for the next horrible surprise.'

'It wouldn't be one of us,' Aiden insisted, 'not unless you ordered it.'

He sounded certain, but he was very young and a natural follower. Lydia wasn't convinced every single Crow acted with the loyalty and unity Aiden seemed to believe. And there was a more worrying possibility. 'Okay, let's assume an outsider did this, we have a different problem. Someone murdered a local businessman with ties to us, someone of importance who was under our protection. That cannot stand.'

'Yeah,' Aiden nodded enthusiastically. 'We've gotta pay those mother-'

Lydia held up a hand and he fell silent. 'It's two problems, really. First,' she held up a finger. 'If there are whispers in the Family that I'm not a worthy leader, this isn't exactly going to make them go quiet. He wasn't a Crow, but he was supposedly under our protection. That's going to make the Family nervous. And second,' she held up another finger. 'If this was a deliberate act of aggression from outside the Family, we must assume they are looking for a reaction.'

'And they're gonna get one,' Aiden said. 'They'll see they can't fu-'

'No,' Lydia cut him off. 'If we clean it up, put the rumour out that Mr Kendal has gone on holiday or something, we stall a murder investigation and buy ourselves some time to find out who we're dealing with. And we starve them of the instant gratification. If they're watching and hoping for a public embarrassment, they'll be disappointed. And that might make them show themselves.'

'Shouldn't we be paying them back straight away? Showing that we're not to be messed with?'

'That's exactly the reaction they are looking for. It's got to be, unless it was a random robbery gone wrong from someone out of town or terminally stupid. And it didn't look that way.'

'You think they'll just call up and confess?'

'I think people are fundamentally impatient. And winning often just means being willing to wait longer than the other side.' Lydia was excellent at waiting. It was the very first thing you learned to do as a PI.

'If they want a reaction and don't get one, what if they decide to try something else?'

Lydia smiled at him. 'That's what I'm counting on.'

'WE HAVE A PROBLEM,' Aiden said, sliding into the seat opposite Lydia.

'This is getting to be a habit,' Lydia said. 'We need to be more careful.'

'Cleaning service couldn't operate. There were visitors in attendance'

'Police?'

Aiden nodded.

'Well, that's that,' Lydia leaned back in her seat. 'It's probably for the best.' She should probably keep the lying and criminality to a bare minimum. Especially given that her boyfriend was a DCI in the Met. That was a strange thought. Fleet and 'boyfriend' in the same sentence. It didn't feel right. He wasn't a boy, that was for sure.

Aiden was fidgeting, rubbing at the scruff of beard on his jaw.

'Spit it out.'

'We can't look weak.'

'You mean I can't look weak.'

Aiden swallowed. 'I've been doing your bidding. You know I'm loyal, I just think...'

'Not your job,' Lydia said. 'Leave that part to me. Speaking of which. We need to take a walk.'

Outside, Lydia waited until they were seated on a bench in Brunswick Park before continuing the conversation. She knew she was probably being paranoid, but she couldn't shake the feeling that Mr Smith was still watching her, waiting to gather fresh leverage. She was grateful to him for healing her father and always would be, but that didn't mean she wanted to jump back into his pocket. Especially now she could do real damage to her Family. She knew too much, now, to risk getting caught and that was a sobering thought.

Aiden was looking spooked, too. He rubbed at his goatee and kept putting his beanie hat on and off, as if unable to decide whether to wear it or not. His hand floated toward it for the third time. 'Touch the hat and I'll burn it,' Lydia said, and he snatched his hand away.

She waited until a couple holding greasy bags from a fast food restaurant had passed by and turned to Aiden. 'I asked you why Mark Kendal was important.'

Aiden looked down. 'I told you.'

'You said he supplied burners. But I found this.' Lydia produced the ten-shilling note and held it in front of Aiden's face. She wanted to see how much more lying Aiden was going to do.

'Old money. That's weird.'

'Yeah,' Lydia put it on the bench between them, keeping one finger resting lightly on the paper to stop it blowing away. 'You seen one of these before?'

'No,' Aiden said, and his eyes slid left. 'Why would he have that? Maybe he was into history.'

Lydia slid the note across the bench toward Aiden. 'Pick it up.'

'No!' Aiden's reaction was sudden and loud. At once he looked terrified. 'I'm sorry. Please don't.'

Lydia frowned. 'Don't what? Give you an old bank note? Tell me what the feathers is going on. Right now. I found a roll of these hidden in Charlie's house.'

Aiden's shoulders slumped. 'They're like a black spot.'

'I'm not following.'

'You know. When pirates are cursed, they have a black spot on their palm. It means they're marked for death. Or if you look into the face of the night raven, it means you'll die. Maybe not straight away, but you're marked. No escape.'

'Charlie used these to mark people?'

Aiden blinked slowly. He looked tired, but instead of making him look older, it emphasised the youth in his features. Lydia felt a lurch of sympathy. But she couldn't let up. 'I'm waiting, Aiden.'

He nodded. Resigned. 'Let's say someone had got on his bad side. Done something against the Family. Or against Charlie. You'd have a meeting with him, explain your case. And then you'd go home and find it in your pockets. Then you knew you hadn't been successful.'

'And that's it? A bit of theatre so that people knew he was going to pop round and stab them in their sleep?' Lydia felt anger at Charlie and it was a relief. The guilt she felt about handing him over to Mr Smith was never far from the surface and she craved validation that it had been justified.

'Mostly,' Aiden said, staring at the note like it was going to jump off the bench and bite him. 'If he booked a removal, he had the operator leave one. Not always, but if he wanted to send a message.'

'A removal?'

'Renovations for non-permanent work, removals for permanent.'

'Gotcha.' Bloody crime bosses and their slang. 'Why a ten-shilling note?'

'He said the Crows had always used coins but joked that it was because of inflation.' Aiden shrugged. 'I don't know. He didn't tell me everything.'

Well that was certainly true.

CHAPTER THIRTEEN

That evening, when Lydia arrived at his flat, Fleet was in a foul mood. She got two beers from the fridge and passed him one. 'Bad day?'

He put it straight onto the counter and crossed his arms. Not a good sign.

'When were you going to tell me?'

'Tell you what?'

Fleet breathed deeply, like he was trying to hold onto his temper. 'Camberwell is my manor. Did you think I wouldn't find out?'

'Give me a clue,' Lydia said, playing for time.

He stuffed his hands into his pockets and held Lydia's gaze with a look which could have stripped paint off a car.

'Is this about Mark Kendal?'

'I am practically on probation at my work. Didn't you think to give me a heads up on this one?'

'I only just heard,' Lydia said. 'What makes you

think I had prior warning? And what do you mean probation? You just got a promotion.'

Fleet didn't answer for a moment. He still looked frustrated but there was a weariness, too, like he couldn't be bothered to hold onto his anger. 'Not really. It was a sideways move,' he said eventually. 'The kind that buries me in meetings and keeps me behind a desk. I need to keep my nose clean and suck up to the brass or I'm never getting a decent case ever again.'

Lydia was stunned. 'But, why? You're brilliant at your job.'

A quick smile escaped. 'Thank you. But I'm in my boss's bad-books. Or her boss. Or both of them. It's fine, they'll get over it. I'm serving my time until they forget about punishing me or something else distracts them. But in the meantime, it would be nice to look halfway competent.'

'It's because of me, isn't it?'

Fleet's shoulders went down a notch. 'It'll be fine. Don't give it another thought.'

'You should tell them it's over. We'll go back to keeping it secret.' Lydia tried a smile. 'It'll be like old times. All that sexy sneaking around.'

'Don't try to distract me, I'm interrogating you.'

'Are you indeed?' Lydia put her hands on her hips. 'How's that going?'

Fleet sighed. 'About as well as usual.' He paused. 'Is there anything I should know?'

Lydia widened her eyes. 'About Mark Kendal? I don't know anything about it. I just heard about it from Aiden.'

'Fascinating,' Fleet said, definitely trying not to smile, now. 'And how did Aiden know?'

'It's his job to keep me informed on the local news. I don't ask about his methods.' Lydia said primly. 'Do you want to speak to him?'

Fleet looked at her for another beat before, thankfully, shaking his head. 'Did he tell you how Mr Kendal died?'

'No,' Lydia said, working hard to keep her expression neutral. 'I assumed burglary gone wrong.'

'He was bludgeoned with a heavy object. His skull was entirely compressed on the right side,'

'Oh,' Lydia's mouth went dry. At once she could smell the blood, see the brain matter exposed and tangling with his matted hair.

'Nothing was taken. And the scene looked clean, SOCO is still there, though. If anything was left, we'll find it.'

Fleet was eyeballing her in a meaningful way. He left a space and Lydia knew he was waiting for her to fill it. 'Of course you will,' she said reassuringly. She had always been so comfortable withholding details from Fleet, from everybody, really, it was as natural as breathing. This time felt different. Her stomach was cramping with guilt, but she pushed down the urge to tell him the truth. 'Shall we eat?'

LYDIA WOKE up to the sound of Fleet yelling, his voice hoarse as if he had been shouting for hours, not seconds. The light was filtering around the edges of his thick blackout curtains and she realised it was morning. Almost time for the alarm to go off. He was having a nightmare, that was clear, but Lydia hesitated. There was something more than inarticulate fear pouring from his rigid body. Light. Or something her brain was interpreting as light. The strange gleam that she had sensed from Fleet the first time she had met him, the gleam which said that somebody, maybe way back in his ancestry, had some power, but one she couldn't identify, had ignited from a gleam to a glow. No, she had seen it sparked into a glow before. This had intensified from a glow to a radiance.

Lydia didn't know what to do. Sweat was pouring down Fleet's face and his body was contorted, tendons standing out in his neck as he strained against some invisible force. She called his name, shook him by the shoulder and, in desperation, pinched his ear. Hard. When none of that woke him and he was still hoarsely shouting, the garbled sound forming into a single word 'no', she grabbed the half-full glass of water from her side of the bed and dumped it over his head.

It wasn't instant, but over the next few seconds, Fleet's yells quietened and he became conscious. His eyes focused on her face and he swallowed hard, rubbing his face with both hands and then looking at them. 'I'm wet.'

'My fault,' Lydia said. 'Sorry. Are you all right?'

'Just a bad dream.' Fleet didn't smile much but, when he did, it was like the sun coming out. The one he managed, now, was small and insincere. It was meant to reassure Lydia but all it did was give her a stomach ache.

'That wasn't a nightmare,' Lydia said.

Fleet was already getting out of bed. 'I'm going to shower.'

'What happened?' She was speaking to his back. 'That's not the first time, is it?'

'Don't worry about it,' Fleet didn't turn around, just headed into the en-suite and closed the door.

Lydia got dressed and considered stripping the bed. Then she decided that she had no desire to set a precedent for housework so she went and messed with Fleet's expensive coffee machine until it gave up the good stuff.

Fleet took his time and Lydia was wondering whether she ought to break down the door and check on him, when she heard the water shut off. She sat on the sofa and sipped her coffee, giving him space. She didn't want to admit it, but part of her was afraid. Fleet was usually unshakeable.

He emerged from the bedroom fully-dressed in a suit and tie. 'Gotta get going,' he said, kissing the top of her head and picking up the coffee for a quick sip.

'We should talk,' Lydia said.

'It's fine,' Fleet replied, pulling on his coat and patting the pockets for his keys.

Lydia had an indication of how annoying it was being in a relationship with her. Being avoidant and saying 'I'm fine' when things were clearly far from it was not helpful. She stood and walked over to Fleet, put her hand on his chest and reached out with her Crow senses. All the practice was paying off and she got a string of impressions.

'Don't,' Fleet took a step back.

'You can feel it,' Lydia said. 'Something is changing. You know I seem to power people up? People like me. I think...'

'Don't,' Fleet said, again, his face stony. 'I've got to go.'

As LYDIA HAD THOUGHT many times before, nowhere did pubs like London. She had several favourites. None of them pretentious, although one was edging that way and was saved only by its incredible twice-fried skin-on chips and comfortable seats. This pub, however, was as far from the places Lydia preferred as it was possible to get without it being an entirely different species.

Linoleum covered the floor, scratched and burned and with so much ground-in dirt the original colour was impossible to discern, and the bar was plywood, recently remodelled after the latest brawl. Figures sat alone, drinking with the grim determination of the terminally alcoholic, while a small group of old men sucked their teeth over a game of dominoes. One table was covered in glasses half-filled with beer and whisky, but nobody was sitting down. A cigarette burned in an ashtray, abandoned. This wasn't a place that cared about the indoor smoking rules.

The woman behind the bar was very thin and very tanned and had a halo of platinum curls that looked like it had been bought in a fancy-dress store. She took a last drag of her own cigarette and put the end into a mug which said 'World's Best Grandma' which had clearly been used for the purpose many times before. 'You're not welcome in here, Crow.'

'Don't be rude,' Lydia said, producing her coin and making it spin in the air. 'I'm looking for Jimmy.'

'He's not here,' the woman said, her eyes crossing as she stared at the coin as it turned lazily inches from her face.

'When did you last see him?'

'This morn-,' she broke off. 'Dunno.'

'Is there a back room?'

'Yeah. Wait... What?' The woman's eyes were glassy.

Lydia heard the scrape of a chair and knew that at least one of the drinkers was thinking about getting involved. She spoke without looking around, just raising her voice a little. 'I wouldn't if I were you.'

She plucked her coin from the air and gave the woman a wide smile. 'Thanks for your help. Is it this way?' Lydia kept moving toward the door she had spotted and ignored the movement to her right. She knew nobody would be stupid enough to take a swing at the head of the Crow Family in this shit-show little dive bar. And if she believed that wholeheartedly, she would make it true. You had to commit. If she had learned one thing, it was that.

Lydia made it to the backroom without incident and discovered another space which both time and hope had forgotten. Nicotine-stained walls, mismatched furniture and a television on one wall playing sport. The room was dominated by a pool table and three men with shaved heads and tattoos. Two of the men were in the middle of a game and the third was sitting in the corner, his feet up on a chair.

One of the pool-players gave Lydia a full up-and-down look with a leer that suggested his thought processes went on somewhere far south of his brain. 'You lost, girl?'

Lydia ignored him, fixing her attention on the man in the corner. He raised his gaze to meet hers and she felt a jolt. Not of Family power, there was no Pearl, Silver, Crow or Fox in the room, but power nonetheless. The power which came from being the biggest badass on the street and everybody knowing it. The power of being the smartest person in the room and the one with the vision. The man everybody looked to for direction, for a plan, for the big score and the smart play. In his own piss-poor small-time way, this man was a leader and Lydia could feel it. She smiled her shark smile. 'I've got a proposition for you, Jimmy.'

Jimmy Brodie, also known as The Hammer, tipped his head back a fraction, as if wanting to get a better view. He had prison tattoos on his neck and hands, faded green with age, and a thickset body which suggested bulky muscle which wasn't used quite as much as it used to be. 'Just a business deal,' Lydia said. 'Cash in exchange for an introduction.'

She knew the leering pool player had moved behind her and wasn't surprised when he spoke. 'You walk in here carrying cash? You're asking to lose it.'

'I'm not losing anything,' Lydia said, holding the boss man's gaze. 'Just looking for a certain service and happy to pay the fee.' She was working on the principle that if someone had paid a professional to take out Mr Kendal, it had to be somebody unconnected to any of the Families or, at least, someone who didn't care about the politics of the Families. Her second thought was that it was likely a local who had paid for the hit, which meant they would have sourced it locally, too. People tended to ask for recommendations for this kind of thing. It wasn't the kind of service you Googled, which meant they had probably started in the sketchiest non-Family pub in the area. Lydia reasoned that if she followed their footsteps, she ought to find the same contractor. 'So, if a girl was in the market for a reliable contractor to carry out a bit of work, who should she see?'

Jimmy's eyes had started out small and mean-looking, they had narrowed further giving the impression that he was peering through smoke. Lydia knew it was supposed to make him look even-more intimidating, but it had the opposite effect. She gave him a friendly smile and pushed a little bit of Crow into her voice. 'Quick as you like.'

'Renovation or removals?' Jimmy looked surprised after the words spilled out, as if he hadn't intended to speak.

'Removals,' Lydia said. 'And I'm crunched for time, so they need to be available to start immediately.' Whoever had killed Mr Kendal had been in the area very recently and Lydia was hoping that would further narrow down the pool of local professionals.

Jimmy nodded slowly, his eyes very slightly glazed. Lydia could hear the men behind her shifting and could feel the atmosphere in the room tighten. They were waiting for the signal from Jimmy and didn't understand why he hadn't given it yet. Lydia wondered if they had enough self-control to carry on waiting. 'Happy days,' Jimmy said, after another beat. 'He's right here. Felix, don't be shy.'

Lydia didn't look away from Jimmy and one of the men who had been playing pool moved into her field of vision. It wasn't the leering man, but his companion. A man Lydia had categorised as the least dangerous in the room, which just went to show that you could always learn something new. He had a short, neatly-trimmed beard which was just one step up from stubble, dark hair and eyes. If he didn't take plenty of holidays in the sun, he had Mediterranean heritage somewhere in his gene pool, and he had a slim-build which, now that Lydia was paying attention, could suggest martial arts. Or a reliance on long-range weapons.

'I can help you,' Felix said. 'But I must warn you, my rates are high.'

'They really are,' Jimmy said, seeming to not want to lose control of the conversation.

The leering man was sitting on the edge of the pool table, now, tapping a cigarette from a packet. The sense that she was about to be beaten up, or worse, had dissipated and Lydia wondered what secret signal she had missed. 'Can we speak in private?'

Felix looked instinctively toward Jimmy and then shrugged. 'Sure.'

He led the way down a short corridor which led not, as Lydia had been hoping, to a back yard with the good clean air of Camberwell, but to the toilet. Walking into a confined space with a hitman wasn't the most reckless thing Lydia had ever done, but it might make the top ten. She kept herself close to the door and squeezed her coin in her palm for strength.

Felix glanced at the filthy urinal, wrinkling his nose against the pungent smell, before facing Lydia. 'I know who you are.'

'Good.'

'I'm happy to do contract work, but I'm not looking for a permanent position.'

Lydia was momentarily surprised. 'That something you've been offered before?'

'Your predecessor. He liked the idea of full control over my schedule.'

That sounded like Charlie. Lydia felt cold as the full implication dawned. Charlie had been dropping enough bodies to warrant a hitman on retainer.

She pushed the thought away and straightened her spine. 'I'm after something else. A name.'

Felix's expression closed down. 'You know I can't do that.'

'I'll give you one, first,' Lydia said. 'Mark Kendal.'

Felix's face didn't so much as flicker.

'I need to know who ordered the job.'

'I don't know this name,' Felix said. 'I can't help.'

Lydia flipped her coin high into the air, making it spin slowly. Felix watched it, seemingly against his will. 'You left evidence at the scene. If you don't tell me who commissioned the job, I will make sure that evidence reaches the police.'

Felix dragged his gaze from the coin to find Lydia's

face. 'I don't leave *anything*.' His lip was curled in disgust, his eyes alight with pride.

Lydia pushed more Crow behind her words. 'Who hired you to kill Mark Kendal?'

Felix didn't want to speak, but she was dragging the words out one at a time. 'Not. Me.'

There was something there. Something in the spaces between the words that were unwillingly passing his lips. He was grimacing, now, like he was in pain, and Lydia knew that the second she relaxed her hold, he was going to lunge for her, wrap his hands around her throat and squeeze.

'Who, then? Is there another operator in town?'

Felix laughed then. 'How the fuck should I know? We're not a bloody club.'

He was lying. Not about the club aspect, but about not knowing. Lydia had other concerns, though, she could feel her hold slipping.

A sudden electronic beeping sounded. Felix pulled a phone from his pocket and frowned at the screen.

Lydia was already moving for the door, taking the moment of distraction to get out. She flew down the short corridor and shoved the bar on the fire exit at the end, praying for a back street and not a dead-end. With a rush of relief, she felt the door yield and she slammed it shut behind her. She was in a backyard with old beer barrels, wheelie bins, sodden cardboard and a collection of pint glasses on the ground overflowing with cigarette butts. It was contained by a wall with no gate, but the back windows were mercifully blind, bricked in or covered with plywood. Lydia didn't hesitate, scrambling onto a metal keg and grabbing the top of the wall to pull herself up, feet scrabbling on the brickwork. Her arms screamed in protest, but the adrenalin gave her strength and she managed to get up and over the top. She heard the fire door slam open and a furious male voice, but she was dropping down on the other side and flying far away, fast.

CHAPTER FOURTEEN

Back at the flat, Lydia was sitting at her desk. She had also been eyeing up the almost-full whisky bottle on top of her filing cabinet which had been making 'come hither' eyes at her for the last hour. It had been that kind of a day.

Her phone buzzed. Aiden. 'People are asking for a meeting.'

'When you say people...'

'John, mostly. But some others.'

Lydia got up and moved to the kitchen. She filled the kettle while Aiden spoke, realising as she did so that she wasn't thirsty for anything except alcohol. She got a beer instead and popped the cap. 'They aren't happy about...'

'Not on the phone,' Lydia warned.

'I know. I'm on my way.'

Lydia's motion sensor went off a second later and she heard Aiden's heavy footsteps in the hall. She opened the door before he could knock and led the way to the roof terrace.

With the radio playing she indicated for Aiden to speak by gesturing with her beer.

'It doesn't look good.'

'I'm aware.'

'The community knows that we were friendly with Mark. And now he's dead. That makes us look weak.' Aiden winced, as if expecting Lydia to throw something at him. 'Sorry.'

'What does John want me to do about it?'

'He wants a meeting...'

'Don't give me that. He already knows what he wants me to do and he'll have been shooting his mouth off to anyone who will listen.'

Aiden looked at the floor. 'He wants a proportionate response.'

'An eye for an eye?' Lydia sighed. That sounded right. John was nothing if not traditional. Especially since he never had to get his hands dirty. He and aunt Daisy lived in their comfortable house and enjoyed the reputation and financial safety net of the Crows without getting into the messy details. An eye for an eye sounded pretty good when you didn't have to gouge it out yourself. 'So, it's just face-saving? Not personal?'

'How do you mean?'

'Was anybody close personal friends with Mark Kendal? If someone is going to do something silly, I need to know.'

'Not that I know about,' Aiden said. 'But I'll ask around.'

. . .

FLEET CALLED on his way to the gym in a not-wonderful mood. Lydia thought she might leave some of her activities out of the 'how was your day, honey?' conversation. Pissing off a professional killer, for example.

Lydia had eaten earlier, but she offered Fleet left-over pizza, if he wanted to come round. 'I ate at the office,' Fleet said. 'And I'm heading home to crash. I wouldn't be good company tonight. Sorry.'

'No worries,' Lydia said. 'Bad day?'

'Yeah, I guess. Long, anyway. Meetings. And I've been kicked off the Mason case. Sorry, not kicked off. Reassigned.'

'To what?'

'Cross Pollination and Synergy Leveraging Solutions.' Fleet's disgusted tone let Lydia know that this was a whole new level of corporate bullshit.

Fleet seemed to find all the management and meetings far more stressful than the more-obviously dangerous parts of his job. Lydia could relate. Then a horrible thought crossed her mind. 'They're punishing you.'

'I don't think so-'

'For being with me. It's a message.'

Fleet's voice was cut out by the sound of a siren passing. Then, 'It's just the job. You get promoted and, after a while, it's all desk duty and meetings. It's not personal.'

He didn't sound totally convinced, though. 'I spoke to a captain in the Hellenic police, and she said there were no leads on the hit and run. It was a fairly busy location, not that far from the hotel where the MP was staying, but there were no witnesses.'

'None?'

'Alex Papoutsis, she's the captain, said that she had one witness originally, who said he saw a van travelling at high speed away from the area, but he recanted his statement. Said he had the wrong day.'

'Someone got to him?'

'Definitely a possibility. Although, she was telling me that hit and runs are a major problem in Greece. And they're currently classed as a misdemeanour, so there isn't a lot of budget spent on following up. If it isn't an easy solve, they usually get buried. In her experience, anyway.'

'There would have been heat on this one, though,' Lydia said. 'From the UK. Did Interpol get involved?'

'She said not really. Said it was more a case of sending on the report. Information-sharing in the spirit of inter-departmental global collaboration.'

Lydia could hear the air quotes in Fleet's voice. 'You think it was just a box-ticking exercise?'

'Exactly. I guess Interpol is as stretched as the rest of us.'

So, there was a possibility that somebody close to the MP Nadine Gormley would have a motive to kill Alejandro. If he had been involved with the hit and run in Greece and if that person knew, or suspected, him of that involvement. An image of Maria, her face obscured by black lace, her high heels and sharp skirt like weapons, jumped to the front of Lydia's mind. She saw people lining up to offer their condolences, to kiss her hand. If Alejandro had arranged a hit on an MP in order to free up a political position, how much had Maria known about his plans? How involved had she been in her father's meteoric rise? She said at the funeral that people hadn't taken her seriously before and Lydia wondered what she would have been willing to do to be seen as the rightful leader of the Silvers.

HAVING DRAINED her beer and poured a large whisky, Lydia was sitting at her desk in the growing darkness and cradled the glass. Jason was in his room, Fleet was home, and the cafe was shut up for the night. Her mobile rang with an unknown number and she answered, expecting a new prospective client or a sales call.

Mr Smith's measured tone sent a bolt of adrenaline through her body. Her first thought was that he was calling to tell her that Charlie was dead. But her second was that he wouldn't do that. Charlie would die alone and un-mourned and the Family would never even know he had passed. That was part of the punishment she had doled out. One of the many decisions in her life which had led to her sitting alone in a dark room drinking whisky. 'What do you want?'

'To help you,' Mr Smith replied. His voice set off an echo of his signature and Lydia held onto the desk to steady herself.

'How kind,' she said. 'I'm fine.'

Mr Smith made a tutting noise. 'Mr Kendal isn't fine. And I'm guessing your family isn't too pleased about his murder, either. It doesn't look good, does it?'

'I don't know what you're talking about,' Lydia said. If Mr Smith thought he could trap her into talking about protection rackets on the phone, he was delusional.

'You're out of your depth,' Mr Smith went on. 'I'm offering to throw you a rope. Let me help you. I've got the resources. I could find the person responsible for Mr Kendal's death, effect a quick resolution. Then you can go back to your family and claim all the glory. Get them back onside.'

Lydia wanted to ask him why he thought her family weren't supporting her as their leader, what rumours he had heard, but that would involve admitting that she was concerned about it. 'Why are you offering to help? Just feeling charitable? Bit of community service?'

'Maybe there's an element of that,' Mr Smith said. 'You know I'm very fond of you, but the fact is you're not cut out for this. You're an investigator. A freelancer. You're not Charlie and everybody knows it. That's dangerous. If people don't have the proper respect, there will be casualties. Poor Mr Kendal is just the start.'

Lydia's throat had gone dry. She knocked back some whisky, but when she spoke her voice still came out a little cracked. 'What would you suggest? That I retire?'

'That you let me help you. It will be our secret. I can help you hold onto your Family and hold onto your power and I won't ask anything of you that you won't be happy to give.'

'Let me think about it,' Lydia said, playing for time.

'You can reach me on this number. I suggest you do so sooner rather than later. Serius est quam cogitas.'

It was almost eight o'clock and the Pilates studio was shut. The window at the front was screened by a jungle of house plants, but there were no electric lights showing beyond, and the front door was locked. Lydia had assumed they would stay open in the evening. Surely people had to fit in workouts after office hours? And with such a small space, they could hardly cram in enough business to stay afloat without working all the hours of the day.

Lydia rapped on the glass of the front door. She was about to call Chunni when a door at the back of the studio opened, spilling light across the polished wooden floor. Chunni crossed the studio and unlocked the front door. She apologised for keeping Lydia waiting.

'I was catching up on emails. Come in.'

As soon as Lydia crossed the threshold, she felt it.

'My office is out back,' Chunni was weaving through the machines to the doorway. 'It's a bit small, I'm afraid, but you know London rent.'

'You live here?' Lydia asked.

'Would you like tea?' Chunni began listing types of fruit and herbal tea and Lydia tuned out, concentrating instead on her other senses.

The back room stretched the definition. When Chunni had said 'a bit small' she meant 'a cupboard with a kettle'. There was a single upright chair which had a closed laptop on the seat. Lydia stood in the doorway watching Chunni fussing with little paper sachets, then she moved away to walk around the studio. 'Where do your clients change?'

'On the right.'

Lydia set off, not asking for permission. A plain door led to a flight of stairs. On the first landing there was a door to a toilet and a changing room. Looking inside there was a single stall and basin. The changing room had a light wooden bench and a row of hooks on the wall. It smelled of feet, despite the reed diffuser in the corner. The feeling was stronger on the stairs and weaker in the changing room. Carrying on up to the next floor, Lydia knew she was getting closer. The building reminded her of The Fork but instead of a half-glass door inscribed with 'Crow Investigations', she was met with a plain door, swinging hastily shut, and the smell of cooking food.

Chunni was coming up the stairs behind her and Lydia raised her voice to ask, 'Who is up here?'

She knocked on the door and then opened it. There was resistance, but Lydia shoved and it yielded.

An extremely petite woman with a waterfall of fine pale blonde hair was turning to run and Lydia caught her arm.

'Don't!' Chunni was there, grabbing at Lydia from behind. 'Leave her alone!'

Lydia let go of the blonde's arm. She suddenly realised that both women were frightened. Of her. Which was a strange feeling. 'I'm not going to hurt you,' she said, raising her hands in a gesture of peace. 'I just want to talk.'

'We haven't done anything,' the blonde woman said and, if Lydia had been in any doubt, the sound of her voice clinched it. She was Pearl.

'You came to me,' Lydia looked at Chunni over her

156

shoulder. 'I'm here to help because you asked me to.'
The blonde woman took the opportunity to retreat into
the single-purpose room. It had the exposed brick walls
and industrial light fittings of the studio downstairs, but
with an unfolded sofa bed in front of the television and a
sleek fitted kitchen against one wall. 'Why don't we sit
down and you can tell me what's going on. Why are you
so frightened?'

Chunni let go of Lydia and crossed to meet the
blonde woman, taking her hand. 'This is my wife,
Heather.'

'Okay.' Lydia concentrated on making herself look as
friendly and non-threatening as possible. It wasn't something she had ever had to work at before and it felt
bizarre. She was a short woman with moderate fighting
skills, which had only ever been used in self-defence.
She had no language or experience for reassuring
women that she wasn't going to hurt them. In a flash she
realised this was how good men must feel all the time.
'Let me help.'

Chunni and Heather exchanged a glance.

'Is it the case you brought to me?' Lydia tried, when
nothing was forthcoming. Still nothing.

'I'm sorry,' Chunni said, her voice very small.

The penny dropped. 'There is nobody suing you, is
there? You just wanted to speak to me.'

A hesitation. Then an imperceptible nod.

'Why?'

Another shared glance. Heather was so pale she
looked as if she might vomit. Lydia felt sympathy but a
surge of impatience was there, too. She considered

157

pushing a little. A bit of Crow whammy to move things along. She was busy. And Chunni had lied to her. 'I'm waiting,' Lydia said, mildly enough.

'We heard you had taken over,' Chunni said hesitantly. 'And Charlie hadn't been bothered about me and Heather, but we didn't know if you would be different. I wanted to meet you. To see what you were like.'

For a split second, Lydia thought Chunni meant 'to check if you were homophobic' but then she realised the more obvious concern. 'You thought I might not approve of a Pearl-owned business in Camberwell?'

A quick nod. 'Charlie didn't care. He said business was business.'

'Why do you think I would feel differently?'

'My mum said it used to be a rule,' Heather said. Her voice was quiet but with a beautiful tone. Lydia could feel the pull of the Pearl, the urge to lean in and listen closer, and she consciously stiffened her muscles to hold herself in check. 'She said it wasn't allowed and that if Jack Crow was still alive, he'd have strung us up outside The Old Hermit and nobody would have said a word.'

Lydia had only the vaguest memories of her grandfather, but she could see why that rumour had taken hold. She remembered glittering black eyes and a hooked nose below a sweep of white hair. In that moment, another memory chased behind the image. Her father, looking very tired and very scared, speaking quietly and quickly in the kitchen on the old corded phone which had hung on the wall. Her angle was sharp, as if Lydia were down on the floor. 'No, I can't,' her father was saying. A deep breath. Then: 'I won't.' Why had that memory surfaced?

Had he been speaking to her grandfather? Lydia brought herself back to the present. 'Is that why you recorded me?'

Pure terror flashed across Chunni's face.

'It's all right,' Lydia said briskly, trying not to enjoy her reaction. 'I just want you to delete the footage. And never do it again, obviously.' She didn't want people waltzing into her office and taking clandestine recordings. Chunni *should* be sorry for that. She fixed them both with a hard stare. 'I help people. Especially those that live in Camberwell. But you don't need to lie to me.' She waited a beat before adding: 'It's a bad idea.'

'I'm sorry,' Heather whispered. 'We're sorry.'

'It's already deleted,' Chunni was saying. 'I swear.'

Lydia looked at the women. They seemed cowed, but how much of that was an act to get them off the hook and out of trouble? Suddenly it felt very important to Lydia to be sure these women wouldn't cross her again. She needed to make an example of them, something which could act as a warning to others. She hated the idea that Mr Smith might have had a point. She was Lydia Crow and she couldn't have ordinary people disrespecting her. Not without repercussions. Aiden had been warning her that she had to show strength or people wouldn't maintain the proper respect for the Family and now this. Lydia didn't want to be like Charlie, but she wondered what he would do. An image of Big Neil tied to a chair in the lock-up, beaten and bloody flashed into her mind.

Chunni and Heather must have seen something cross her face as they began babbling further apologies.

Lydia held up her hand to silence them. She produced her coin and spun it in the air, drawing their attention. 'Lydia Crow knew that you had betrayed her trust and she came to your home and she hurt you both in ways that you can't even think about without feeling sick.'

The colour drained from Chunni and Heather's faces, leaving dark hollows around their eyes. 'You will tell anybody who will listen not to cross Lydia Crow. That she knows when you are lying. And that her little sparrows are everywhere. Seeing everything.' A tiny moan escaped from Heather's lips.

Lydia waited a beat to make sure the message had sunk in and then plucked her coin from the air. 'I'll see myself out.'

CHAPTER FIFTEEN

'What time is it?' Fleet's voice, thick with sleep. Lydia opened her eyes and met darkness. Her eyes adjusted slowly as her brain kicked into gear. Her phone was ringing. She rolled over and retrieved it from the floor, stabbing at the answer button. 'Yes?'

There was heavy breathing, the rumble of traffic. 'It's me. I just wanted to say 'goodbye'. I wanted to say-'

'Ash? Where are you?' Lydia was sitting up, now, the phone pressed against her ear. 'Are you okay?'

'Thank you for everything.'

'Feathers!'

Fleet was sitting up, too, and he rubbed a hand over his face, stubble rasping in the sudden quiet. 'What's up?'

'He said 'goodbye'.' Lydia got up and began to pull on her clothes. 'Hell Hawk. What is he doing, now?'

Fleet swung his legs from under the duvet.

'It's okay,' Lydia said. 'You go back to sleep. I'm pretty sure I know where Ash will be.' She was using her

161

phone to access Ash's mobile GPS as she spoke. Jason had installed the software and she wasn't sure if it was entirely legal, so she didn't elaborate further.

'I'll come with you,' Fleet said, clicking on his bedside light. 'Give me a second.'

It was almost five as Lydia drove to Highgate, Fleet yawning extravagantly in the passenger seat. Sunrise wasn't for another hour and the streetlights were still lit, but there was the suggestion of light in the sky. Dew covered the parked cars and colours emerged murkily in the early morning twilight.

'You think he'll be here?'

'Where else?' Lydia took the Archway Gate into the woods.

'Is this a good idea?' Fleet caught her hand, stopping her. 'Should we try calling?'

Lydia understood his reticence. She didn't particularly want to go wandering among the half-lit trees, either. The sense of Pearl was suffusing her mind, pulling her into the darkest part of the forest. It was an inducement and a warning. 'He's vulnerable,' Lydia said. 'I can't leave him.'

Fleet tilted his head back, as if the sky would give him an alternative answer. When it didn't, he sighed and resumed walking. Their feet crunched on the ground and Lydia stopped every few paces to listen. She wanted to call out to Ash, but it felt foolhardy. She knew where he would be anyway, so she picked her way back to the place where Lucy Bunyan had disappeared.

The small clearing held the still shape of Ash as if it was built for him. He was on the ground, hands scrabbling in the dirt and a stream of low guttural noises coming from his throat, like an animal. He looked up as they approached and Lydia caught the flash of wild eyes. His stringy hair hung like foliage around a face which gleamed white in the dim light. He was even thinner than the last time she had seen him and his bony wrists protruded sharply from filthy shirt cuffs. His hands looked black and Lydia realised that they were caked with dirt and blood. He shook his head, as if denying their existence, and then turned back to his self-imposed task of digging in the earth with his bare hands.

'Ash,' Lydia began, keeping her voice low and calm. 'We're here to help.'

He didn't stop his frenzied action or even appear to hear Lydia.

'All right there, mate,' Fleet tried. 'Come along now, let's get you somewhere warm. Get something to eat and drink.' It was his copper voice. Soothing and authoritative all in one go and Lydia was impressed at Ash's ability to completely ignore it.

She took a step closer and a twig broke under her Dr Marten with a loud crack. Ash looked up at that, his nose lifted to the air as if he needed to use senses other than sight. Lydia could relate. The stink of Pearl was strong in the clearing, but the trees were behaving so far. The sense of Pearl was like perfume hanging in an empty room, but Lydia wanted to get them all far away before the Pearls returned. 'Come on, Ash. It's not safe

163

for us here.' She put a hand on his shoulder and he reared back as if burned.

'It's okay.'

Ash seemed to focus on Lydia's face for the first time. Sweat was pouring down his forehead and he blinked hard. 'Lydia?'

'That's right, it's me.' She held out a hand. 'Come with me, now. I'll get you sorted out. You can stay at my place, get some rest.'

Ash's eyes cleared for a fraction of a second and he sat back on his heels. Then a keening sound reverberated around the clearing. For a moment Lydia wasn't sure if it was the wind in the trees or a small animal caught in the jaws of a trap. Then she realised it was coming from Ash. Tears sheeted down his face and his mouth widened as the high keening became a howl.

'Shush, shush,' Lydia couldn't stop herself, she put a hand over his mouth. 'Ash. Quiet. You've got to be quiet.'

He spoke against her hand. 'I want them to come.'

'No, you don't.'

'I do. I want them to take me back. Why won't they take me back?' He fell back to the ground, fingers scraping desperately through the dirt. 'I'm here. Let me in. I want to come home. Let me in.'

Ash moved into the air. Fleet had his arms wrapped around his body and was hoisting him from the ground. 'We've got to go,' he said to Lydia over Ash's bucking shoulder. He had his arms pinned and Lydia caught hold of his flailing legs. They managed to get out of the clearing and Ash stopped struggling. Fleet stopped and readjusted his hold so that Ash was half-walking, one arm around Fleet's neck. 'Your place or mine?'

Ash was Lydia's problem. 'Mine.'

ONCE ASH WAS prone on her sofa and Fleet had left for work, Lydia asked Jason to keep watch so that she could get some sleep. After an hour's nap which felt like falling down a deep hole, she sat at her desk and poured caffeine down her throat until she felt halfway awake. She watched Ash's chest rise and fall as he slept, his face pale and hollow and somehow still tense, even in the depths of sleep. Jason had gone into the kitchen, but she couldn't hear the sounds of breakfast. It was possible that he had disappeared. She tried to remember if that was happening more often these days and realised that she wouldn't know. She hadn't been home enough. And she had been distracted.

Lydia leaned back in her chair and fought the desire to go back to sleep. There was a tiredness that wasn't just physical. She missed her client work. Or, more accurately, she missed the feeling that her life was her own. She had more power than she had ever had in her life, but the strings attached had wrapped around her life and her soul and they were getting tighter every day. Ash keening in the forest felt like an omen. A visitation from another realm. And a warning of what would happen if her spirit got any more twisted.

He woke up at midday and Lydia coaxed him to drink some soup. Ash had refused anything except water, babbling about keeping his body 'pure and clear' and Lydia had been forced to use a little Crow persuasion. 'You've got to eat,' she said, as he sipped from a mug, eyes anguished as if she was making him drink poison.

After he had drained the mug, she gave him the choice of juice, milk, hot chocolate or lemonade. Anything with calories, basically.

'Water.'

'Feathers, Ash. You're wasting away.'

'I can't,' he said. 'Just water. Please. They won't take me back if I'm not pure.'

Lydia swore loudly. 'You weren't exactly treating your body like a temple when they took you before. Weren't you drunk?'

'I was young,' Ash said, sadly. 'That counts for a lot.'

'But why do you want to go back? I thought you wanted revenge? I thought you wanted to make sure they didn't take anybody else?'

Ash started crying silently, which was worse in the domestic quiet of the flat than it had been in the woods. The pain radiating from him was infecting the air, making tears prick behind Lydia's eyelids and a lump form in her throat. 'I can't help it,' he managed after a while. 'I miss it. I miss them. I don't belong here anymore. I ache all over and the longing is like a pit I can't fill. I have no appetite, human food tastes like filth. Like dead things.'

'Go vegetarian. Be a vegan. Clean eating and all that,' Lydia tried.

'Plants die when they are picked. Fruit spoils from the moment it breaks from the tree. I can taste it. The

166

rot.' He heaved suddenly and the tomato soup so carefully sipped came gushing out, over his shirt and jeans, splashing onto the carpet.

WHEN FLEET ARRIVED after work that night, he was bearing gifts. Takeaway noodles, wonton soup and a bottle of red. Lydia wasn't long back from dropping Ash at his childhood home and she filled Fleet in on the day while he poured two large glasses and she fetched cutlery and kitchen roll.

'I feel like I should have gone in and spoken to his parents but he's a grown up.'

'You're not responsible for him.'

Lydia pointed her fork at him. 'You can't talk. What about that guy from that refugee case? You still check up on him.'

'That's different,' Fleet said. 'And it's not like I keep tabs on every single person I arrest.' He took a swig of wine. 'And this isn't your fault. You helped him get out of hospital. You gave him answers. You believed his story when nobody else would.'

Lydia wasn't going to let herself off that easily. 'I let him down.'

They ate in silence for a few minutes. Fleet wasn't attacking his food with his usual gusto and he finished his glass of wine quickly, pouring himself another glass and topping up Lydia's before she had taken more than a couple of sips. 'I need to tell you something.'

Hell Hawk. Lydia put down her fork. 'What's wrong?'

'I've been given an official warning at work. They talked about suspension, so I should be grateful, really.'

It took Lydia a beat to realise that, for once, Fleet's trouble wasn't her fault. 'What do you mean? Why?'

'I got into an argument.'

'That's not...'

'And I lamped Butler.'

Lydia knew the name. Fleet had complained about his laziness and general incompetence many times. 'He probably deserved it. It's not like you to get violent, though. Must have been a bad argument.'

'He was being a dick,' Fleet said. 'And I've been a bit tense recently. Part of me was waiting for a reason.'

Lydia wanted to say she had noticed, but it felt like kicking a man when he was down. She settled on: 'You've been unhappy at work, I know.'

'Well, I'm off my only remaining cases, now.' He forced a smile. 'I'll be able to take it easy for a few weeks.'

'Was it really enough to get a formal reprimand?'

Fleet shrugged. 'Maybe not in usual circumstances. Butler was pushing me first so it wasn't one-sided, but I'm under a cloud at the moment.'

Lydia was horrified. 'Because you're with me?'

Fleet flashed a wry smile. 'Probably. They'll get over it, though.'

'We should go covert again.' Lydia attempted a leer. 'I don't mind being your dirty little secret.'

'No,' Fleet reached and cupped her cheek. 'I told you. I'm all in. I'm not fucking this up again.'

She leaned into his hand. The warmth of his skin

and feel of his strong fingers against her face sent feelings to other parts of her body and she moved closer, as Fleet did the same. Their lips met and his hand slipped to the back of her neck, tangling in her hair. Her brain momentarily shorting out in the most enjoyable way.

'Stop distracting me,' Lydia broke from the kiss, mock severe. 'And I'm serious. I don't want to ruin your career. You don't have to choose.'

'I do,' Fleet said, his face still close, eyes warm. 'And I choose us.'

She could smell the fresh ozone of the sea and feel sunshine on her skin as she leaned closer.

AFTER A PLEASANT HOUR of choosing each other, Lydia stretched on the bed, feeling the deep relaxation in her muscles.

'Shall I warm up the food?'

'There's ice cream,' Lydia said. 'Get two spoons.'

She watched Fleet pull on boxer shorts and enjoyed the view as he crossed the room. There was a scar on his right shoulder blade and she made a mental note to ask him about it. They should know everything about each other, now. No secrets. Lydia felt a spurt of fear. She had no idea if such a thing was possible, but she knew she wanted to try.

When he returned with the ice cream and cutlery, she was sitting up against pillows. 'Tell me what happened at work.'

'I already did,' Fleet peeled the lid open and passed the carton and a spoon.

'You hit a colleague in the office. That's very much not like you.'

'I hit him in the face,' Fleet said, trying to keep things light.

'DCI Ignatius Fleet,' Lydia waved her spoon threateningly, 'tell me what happened.'

'He has been asking for it for weeks, making little comments. Insults. And it's been worse since Alejandro... He's been indicating that you will be next.'

'What the hell?'

'It's my fault for reacting. He's like a child and I gave him attention. He's the needy sort.'

'So he's been saying things about me?' Now the pieces clicked into place. Someone had insulted Lydia and Fleet had defended her honour. 'I don't care about that and neither should you.' Lydia stopped. It wasn't like Fleet to care about the opinions of an idiot. He was the most evolved, controlled, *grown-up* man she had ever known. 'What aren't you telling me?'

Fleet took the carton and excavated a spoonful of ice cream. 'I don't want to talk about it. I'm embarrassed by my behaviour.'

Lydia took the carton back and set it on the bedside table. She took one of Fleet's hands in her own and waited for him to elaborate.

After a moment he let out a sigh which seemed to come from deep within. 'It wasn't just about you. He suggested that my career progression wasn't down to ability.'

Lydia inhaled sharply.

Fleet smiled at her expression. 'Not affirmative

action, although I think he meant that, too. More that I was playing both sides of the law and that gave me information. An edge. He suggested that the reason I made so many collars was because I was responsible for half the crimes. Or that I knew the people responsible.'

Lydia swore. 'He was asking to be smacked, then.'

Fleet shook his head. 'I played into his hands. He accused me of being a criminal and I committed assault. Not my smartest comeback.'

CHAPTER SIXTEEN

Lydia was on her roof terrace, enjoying the weak morning sunshine on her face. It had rained in the night and the air was still damp and chilly, but jeans, boots and a thick hoodie were keeping her comfortable and the mug of strong coffee was sparking her synapses. Jason had been near the railing, looking down into the street but then had shimmered for a moment and disappeared. Lydia was waiting to see if he was going to reappear. That sometimes happened, especially if he had disappeared on purpose, and she was determined not to jump if it did.

'Boo!' A voice right next to her ear. Lydia jolted but managed not to yell out.

'You're not funny,' she said, twisting to glare at the ghost.

'I'm bored.' Jason shoved at the rolled sleeves on his baggy grey suit. 'I can't seem to settle to anything.'

Lydia knew he was restless. Leaving the building

might not have been fun for either of them, but it had opened a door in Jason's world. A door that seemed to taunt him.

'What are you doing, anyway? You've been staring into space for twenty minutes.'

'Trying to think,' Lydia said, taking a sip of her coffee. 'Trying and failing.'

'About what? Alejandro?'

Lydia nodded. 'I feel like he was involved in the hit on Nadine Gormley, but there's no evidence to link him to it. And how did he pay for it? He's the head of the Silvers, though, maybe he took it from the firm?'

'Why would he have an MP killed?' Jason asked. 'Just to open up a vacancy? That seems extreme.'

'Yeah, but it's a one-in, one-out kind of a job. And he was in a hurry.'

'Jesus,' Jason shuddered. 'I had no idea they could be that ruthless.'

Lydia skipped over that. Jason hadn't wanted to know the details of his own murder, which had occurred on the day of his wedding to Amy Silver. A match which had been distinctly unpopular with the rest of the Family. And she was going to respect his wishes and keep her mouth shut, unless he expressly requested the information. Sometimes ignorance was, well not exactly bliss, but survival. She distracted him. 'And that's probably expensive, right? I don't know the going rate for a hit, but it can't be cheap. But you know the firm. The size of the offices, the amount of money that place must generate. I thought the whole Family was richer than God.'

Jason frowned, thinking. 'It depends on where the bulk of the accessible cash is, though. If his private wealth is tied up in assets like property, he wouldn't have loads on hand. And he couldn't just take it out of the business, that would leave a trail. More likely he borrowed it or was being bank-rolled by an invested third party.'

'But he must have a ton of money in his personal accounts. Or under his mattress.'

'I don't know,' Jason said. 'The hit might only have been part of it. He went from nothing to MP really fast. Is that normal?'

Lydia's grasp of politics was minimal. 'No idea.'

'Me neither, but it seems possible that some bribery was involved. Maybe the costs mounted up. Or maybe it wasn't just cash that was needed.'

'Favours?' Lydia understood back-scratching. A lot of the Crow empire had been built on it. 'Someone wanted him in in power so that he could do bigger, better favours.' It niggled, though. Who was powerful enough to manipulate the head of the Silvers? Who would dare?

They went indoors and Jason drifted to the sofa to pick up his laptop.

The alarm on the pressure pad she had under the carpet in the hallway sounded. 'That'll be Fleet. Better make yourself scarce.'

'Because you're going to get naked in here?'

Lydia tried very hard to pretend he hadn't just said that. Having a sex life in a haunted building was entirely contingent on her ability to conveniently forget that she lived with a ghost who could appear in any room at any time.

'No JOY with getting hold of the pathologist, he's on holiday,' Fleet said, after kissing Lydia 'hello'. He took off his coat and threw it onto the sofa so recently vacated by Jason and his computer.

'Hell Hawk.'

'Yep. See, other professionals take time off.'

'Hilarious,' Lydia replied. 'When is he back?'

'A month.'

'That's a long holiday.'

'He made an extremely thorough report before he left,' Fleet said patiently. 'You've seen the extremely thorough report. Is it really that important to speak to him?'

'Something doesn't feel right.' Lydia had been going back over the day in the hospital mortuary; the smell of chemicals and death, the bright lighting. She hadn't been in the viewing room for very long, but she had seen Alejandro on the table. His hair had been swept back off his face and his features had looked waxy and weird, both familiar and completely wrong. All impressions completely in-line with seeing a dead body. It wasn't her first, after all.

She closed her eyes. What else? His arms had been by his sides, palms facing up. A sheet covering most of his body. The pathologist in his gown, looping his mask around his ears and talking to Fleet, barely glancing in her direction. The technician had come in, then. He had been late. Lydia could see the scene in her mind's eye and remember her revulsion. She wondered if she would ever get used to the smell of mortuaries. There hadn't been the tang of Silver and she had put that down to being in the other room, separated from Alejandro by a wall and thick glass.

'My boss had a word.' Fleet sounded tense and Lydia opened her eyes to look at him.

'About the case?'

'About me trying to get hold of the pathologist, yes. I don't know who told her, but she wasn't best pleased.'

'Because it isn't your case?'

'That. And the fact that it isn't a case at all.'

'Right,' Lydia turned away. It wasn't her concern that the Met seemed hell-bent on filing this as unsuspicious. Good for their stats, she supposed.

'That's odd, though,' Fleet said. 'I mean, I'm in the dog house, but it still seems weirdly petty. Not something she would usually get bothered about.'

'What are you saying?'

Fleet held her gaze. 'I'm starting to come around to your way of thinking. Maybe this wasn't natural. Or even if it was, there is something going on. Something is definitely not right.'

As THE DOORS closed on Michael Corleone and the credits began to roll, Lydia glanced at Fleet. His head was back on the sofa and his chest rose and fell gently.

Jason was sitting on the floor on her other side, his back against the sofa.

'I'm not sure that helped,' Lydia said. 'He killed the heads of the other families at the end. I'm not sure mass murder is entirely practical.'

'Don't rule it out,' Jason said, glancing over his shoulder.

'You think I'm too weak?'

'No, definitely not.'

'But?'

'I think there's a different lesson. About teamwork.'

Lydia wasn't a team player, she knew that. That's why she had settled on PI as her career of choice. It meant working alone almost all of the time. Long hours sitting alone for surveillance. Not speaking to another human being for days at a time. Watching from the outside and not having to join in. Bliss. 'You think I should get closer to Aiden and the rest?'

'I don't know,' Jason said, his voice serious. 'But did you notice the heads of the family at the end when they got whacked? They got them when they were alone.'

'You really know how to ruin film night, you know?' Lydia reached down and kissed the top of Jason's cool head. 'I'm going to bed.'

'Lightweight,' Jason said, and pressed the remote to start The Godfather Part Two.

THE NEXT DAY Fleet left early for work. Lydia was still in bed when he called. 'Meet me at the park.'

Burgess Park was their place and Lydia knew she

would find Fleet at the Bridge to Nowhere. What she didn't know was why he had a face like thunder. 'I thought we should speak outside,' he said, not moving to kiss her 'hello'.

'Sounds serious,' Lydia.

'Mark Kendal,' Fleet said.

Lydia waited, wondering what was coming next.

'Jesus, Lydia, you were there and you didn't even tell me.'

Ah. 'What makes you say that?'

'I asked you straight and you lied to my face.'

'What are you talking about?'

'CCTV on the street covers the front. We reviewed the footage from the day he died and will be tracing all the customers in and out that day.'

Hell Hawk. 'Am I going to be brought in?'

Fleet waited a beat, watching her. Then shook his head. 'So it was you. I wasn't sure.'

'I didn't kill him.'

'Well that's something.' Fleet rubbed a hand over his face. 'It was a quiet afternoon. Not many customers and nobody at all after four.'

Lydia had been preparing to explain why she hadn't told Fleet about finding the body, but his words derailed her. 'You thought I did it?'

'The CCTV is council-owned and we got it quickly. I watched the lot and there were a couple of weird outages. The screen goes fuzzy for a minute at four forty-six and again eight minutes later.'

'And you assumed that was me?'

'Well, I remember something similar happening to

the CCTV when that Russian hitman who threatened you died in hospital. I was following a hunch that it was a Crow thing and that made me think of you... A hunch that you just confirmed.'

'Right,' Lydia said, stalling for time. 'Very smart. You really do have excellent investigative instincts.'

Fleet raised an eyebrow in a way that meant flattery was not going to help. 'That time with the Russian, I'm assuming that was your Uncle Charlie? And I figured you would have told me if it could possibly be... Wait. Is your uncle back?'

'No. Of course not.' Lydia tasted feathers at the back of her throat and felt a shiver run up her back, cold talons tapping on bone. She hoped it was just the thought of it and not a premonition.

'Right. Well that's what I thought. So, if it's not Charlie, it had to be the other powerful Crow I know.'

'You thought I might have killed that man?'

Fleet shrugged. 'If he attacked you, maybe. Or you had a really good reason. Or you'd just popped by for a friendly chat. I don't know.'

Lydia didn't know whether to be horrified or flattered. It was one thing for the good folk of Camberwell to have a healthy respect for her authority as the head of the Crows and quite another for Fleet to be so casual about her ability to murder another human being. Suspected ability. Whatever.

'Don't take it the wrong way,' Fleet said. 'I just meant that I trust your judgement. If things got violent, there was a good reason.'

'But you know that I didn't do it? You believe me?'

'Of course I believe you,' Fleet said, but his eyes slid left. Another moment. 'Would you tell me if you had? Do you trust me?'

'Of course,' Lydia said, but she wasn't sure if she was telling the truth.

CHAPTER SEVENTEEN

Accessing the Silver Family's final resting place definitely fell under the heading 'poor taste'. Worse than that, it was the kind of action that could start a war between the families. Or, at the very least, give Maria a reason to kill Lydia. Of course, Maria already seemed keen on that idea, so it probably wasn't going to make things any worse than they already were.

Lydia needed a wingman, someone to cause a distraction so that she could slip downstairs in the Temple Church. She had been going to ask Aiden, but she wasn't sure of his abilities. Or whether she was ready to trust him. Fleet was out for two reasons. First off, if he used his badge to gain access, it might get back to his bosses and she didn't want to make his work life any more difficult than it already was. And secondly, she was pretty sure he was still angry about the Mark Kendal lying incident. It didn't seem like the right time to ask for a dodgy favour.

The Silver Family crypt was underneath the main

church, but that was all she had been able to find out online. It wasn't like they advertised how to access it.

Paul Fox was waiting outside the side entrance to the church and he greeted her with his customary, 'Hello, Little Bird.'

Lydia nodded 'hello', not even bothering to tell Paul not to call her 'Little Bird'. She wasn't looking forward to going underground and didn't have the bandwidth for anything else. 'I don't know what to expect in there. You might need to distract the priest. Minister? Whatever. I was thinking you could ask about having a wedding and that should get him talking.'

'Is this your way of saying you've been reconsidering my proposal?' Paul's tone was teasing, but his eyes were serious.

'No,' Lydia said quickly. 'I think our alliance should remain purely platonic.'

'I don't think you mean that,' Paul said. 'You're lying to yourself.'

'I've changed my mind. I don't need your help, thank you.'

Paul held up his hands. 'Truce. I won't mention it again. Not today, anyway.'

Lydia hesitated. Now they were here, it seemed a shame not to go in together. She pushed her emotions to the side. This was business. And she didn't want Paul to have the satisfaction of thinking that he had rattled her. 'Fine. You distract whoever needs distracting and I'll find the crypt.'

'I think I should come with you,' Paul said. 'You might need a hand.'

'I don't see how we can both sneak backstage.' Lydia stopped. 'Is it called backstage in a church? That doesn't sound right.'

'You're nervous,' Paul said.

'Obviously,' Lydia said. She could feel the sharp tang of Silver just standing this close to the church. Residue from the sheer number of Silver Family gatherings on the premises, or the effect of the bodies in the crypt below her feet. Which was creepy. Lydia didn't scare easily, but the prospect of opening a coffin to look at a recently deceased Alejandro Silver was a little daunting. 'If I don't need you to run interference, I will welcome your help in the crypt. Happy?'

Paul nodded. 'Ecstatic.' He slung an arm around her shoulders as they walked through the door.

Lydia was going to object, but she guessed it would look natural if they were posing as an engaged couple. She tried her best to ignore the warmth of his body against hers, the Fox magic clouding her mind and igniting her nerve-endings.

Sunlight danced through the stained-glass windows and lit up dust motes in the air. Lydia took shallow breaths and concentrated on the incense and wood polish notes. There were a few visitors sitting in separate, silent contemplation, and a group of tourists in the round section of the church, gawping at the Templar effigies on the floor.

There was a white-robed figure at the chancel end of the building and to his left, a thick wooden door set in an arched doorway. 'Ready?' Lydia broke away from Paul and walked up the aisle, looking around as if admiring the architecture. Paul followed her and took her hand. 'Follow me,' he whispered close to her ear, his warm breath making her shiver.

Lydia had planned for Paul to approach the minister and engage him in conversation while she slipped through the door, but he seemed hellbent on ignoring that perfectly good set-up. He pulled her straight up the aisle to the chancel. They were close enough that Lydia could see the priest's white hair and thin-rimmed reading glasses. He was bent over a large book, The Bible, presumably, and didn't look up as they approached. Paul pulled her by the hand to the doorway and within a matter of seconds they were on the other side. Lydia held her breath, expecting shouting or for it to be yanked open and an irate priest to ask them what the bloody hell they thought they were playing at. Paul was moving through the chamber, which seemed to be a kind of dressing room with old hymnals piled in one corner and a rack of robes.

'How-?'

Paul shook his head. They passed through another door and found a short stone passage. At the end was a thick external-looking door and to the left was a narrow opening with a stone arch and steps leading down. It looked like something from a castle and at the same time too prosaic and accessible a route to lead to a crypt, but it was definitely the right direction so Lydia started down, holding the rough stone wall to keep her balance as the steps wound tightly downward. As they descended, Lydia felt the air getting cooler, although the chill of the stone beneath her fingertips cooled her blood further.

At the bottom of the stairs another opening led into a small stone room. An incongruously modern door was set into the far wall along with several red and white health and safety notices which warned of everything from toxic fumes to uneven flooring. A channel ran along the stone floor and disappeared under the innocuous pine door.

'How did you do that? He didn't seem to see us.'

Paul was examining the lock on the door and he looked sideways at Lydia. 'Foxes are good at not being noticed if we don't want to be.'

Lydia reached for her small roll of picks from her inside jacket pocket, but Paul already had a pick and a bump key and was working on the mechanism with an impressive focused calm. Again, she hadn't seen him move. One moment he had been studying the lock and the next he was halfway to springing it. At once, Lydia appreciated that the Fox's reputation for stealth wasn't just a way of avoiding the more overtly prejudiced term of 'sly'. The man had skills.

Behind the modern door there were more steps down and then a short passage with a low barrel ceiling and a black iron gate. It had a lock but was hanging very slightly open which was somehow immensely creepy, like an unseen presence had just gone through. Behind this was a short flight of stone steps which then opened out into a wide vaulted passage. The air was noticeably cooler and drier down here and there was a stillness that came from being in the presence of the dead. Or it was the psychic residue of grief and religion. Lydia could taste Silver in the back of her throat and in her nasal passages and its cold, clean odour made her shiver.

They moved forward, alert and ready for the sight of tombs or shelves of coffins or whatever it was you found in ancient creepy crypts. The space was impossible to calculate, the short pillars, shadowy recesses which could lead to a new section or passage or just a dead end, confusing the eye. It looked like the start of a labyrinth, a place you could wander for days, lost. The low ceiling was a reminder of the weight of the earth above and Lydia took a deep breath to steady herself.

Paul whistled quietly. 'Is that what I think it is?'

Ahead, Lydia saw something gleaming in the semi-dark. The Silver Family cup was placed in a recess in the stone. Lydia reflexively grabbed Paul's arm, bracing herself for the onslaught of Silver she had experienced the last time she had encountered the relic. That had been in Alejandro's office when he had deliberately exposed her to the cup to gauge her reaction. She had lost her lunch on his office carpet.

Strangely, nothing happened. The base level hum of Silver remained constant, even as she moved cautiously closer.

'Sneaky bastards,' Paul said. 'I suppose they swapped it for a replica.' The Families placed their relics into the British Museum as part of the 1943 truce. The Crow Family had kept their real coins back, so they couldn't really cast stones.

'This is one, too,' Lydia said, close enough, now, to reach out a finger and touch the intricately moulded surface of the cup. 'It's a fake.'

Paul shot her a calculating look. 'How do you know?'

'I've met the real deal before,' Lydia said. 'And this is not it.'

They moved further into the crypt, finding a room with large, sealed tombs with ancient engravings, which dated back to the sixteen-hundreds. Down here, away from the elements, they were well preserved and perfectly readable. Another chamber had shelves carved into bare rock, each holding smaller sealed stone caskets. A warehouse of the important dead.

'Here,' Paul said from another section. He was temporarily obscured by a pillar. 'This is the more recent stuff. I've found Alejandro's great-grandparents.'

Lydia joined Paul next to an array of stone tombs. Each was topped with a smooth marble top, the engraving crisp and new. The last two were blank, presumably waiting for their residents to move in. Paul was leaning over another. 'Here he is,' Paul said. 'Alejandro.'

'What about Maria's mother?'

'Not here,' Paul said. 'Not that I've seen. Perhaps you have to be main bloodline to make it down here. Or she wasn't considered important enough?'

Lydia shrugged. 'I blame the patriarchy.'

The tomb was recently sealed with a line of caulking visible underneath the slight overhang of the marble top. Paul produced a chisel and a small hammer from inside his jacket and Lydia eyed him as he got onto the floor to study the seal. 'Have you done this before?'

'He'll be embalmed so there shouldn't be much odour,' Paul said. 'You ready?'

'Wait,' Lydia put a hand on his shoulder. Grave desecration. It was a big step. And seeing the fake Silver cup had given her a better idea. She put her hands onto the marble surface and closed her eyes. Nothing.

'What are you doing?'

'Feeling for him. I can sense the Family powers.'

Paul seemed to take this information in his stride. 'Even when we're dead?'

'It's much fainter, but, yeah. Especially if it was strong in life. Alejandro gave off quite the signal.'

Paul leered up at her from his reclined position on the stone floor. 'Why do I suddenly feel jealous?'

'Because you're a weirdo.' Lydia moved over to another of the caskets and placed her hands on the marble. Instantly, the background level of 'Silver' increased, like she had turned the dial on a radio. It was clear and sharp.

As an experiment, she went back to one of the oldest tombs and placed her hands on the stone. It took a few seconds of concentration, but then she felt it. A metallic taste on her tongue. She closed her eyes and felt the Silver sense intensify. She saw the warm glow of a flickering candle, reflected in the polished surface of a silver plate. There was roast meat, spilling its juices across the burnished surface, and the anticipation of a hot meal. A warm fur wrapped around her shoulders. The sound of a crackling fire.

Lydia opened her eyes and returned to the cold chamber. She felt wetness on her face and realised she was crying. She had been warm and safe and she wanted to go back to that place. It took an effort to move her hands from the stone but she managed it. Paul was behind her, his arms encircling her and she allowed herself to lean back, drawing warmth and strength from his presence. The sadness ebbed away as she came fully back to herself and the present. She was leaning back against Paul Fox, his body warm and solid against hers. She shifted, suddenly embarrassed, and scrubbed at her cheeks with her hands. When she could trust herself to speak she said: 'Definitely Silvers in there. Doesn't matter that they've been dead for centuries, I can still feel them.'

She walked back to Alejandro's resting place and tried again. Even with her palms pressed firmly against the marble surface and her eyes shut against distractions and every part of her reaching out in the dark, all she got was a vast emptiness where Silver ought to be. There was nothing. She opened her eyes and found Paul regarding her, his eyes unreadable in the dim light. 'I would lay money that the body inside here is not a member of the Silver Family.'

Paul tilted his chin up. 'Fair bet it's not Alejandro, then?'

'I would say the chances are absolutely zero.'

CHAPTER EIGHTEEN

The restaurant was a modern European place just off Carnaby Street in Soho. Fleet said that a proper date ought to be somewhere different to their usual haunts and Lydia didn't disagree. Eating out in Camberwell was no longer a private affair and she could just imagine the bowing and scraping from whichever pub or restaurant she chose. Charlie had loved all of that, but it made Lydia shrink inside her skin.

Lydia had arrived on time, which was something of a miracle, but Fleet had texted to say he was running late. She crunched a breadstick, admired the colourful op-art mural which took up the entire side wall of the restaurant and tried to get herself into a date frame of mind. Which made her wonder if she had ever been on a proper date. She had had hook-ups and relationships, but never done the romantic date thing. Was that normal for the times or utterly tragic? Lydia couldn't decide.

At that moment, Paul Fox slid into the seat opposite. It was as if she had conjured her ex just by thinking about her relationship history. She was facing the main body of the restaurant but he had managed to get this close without her seeing his approach. Not for the first time, she wondered about the extent of the Fox Family powers.

'You look very nice tonight,' Paul said, getting an eyeful. 'Special occasion?'

Lydia was wearing her standard uniform of jeans, Dr Martens and a black top, although the top was thinner and silkier than usual, with a lower neckline than she wore day-to-day. It was hardly a cocktail dress. She gave him her best dead-eye stare and ignored the warm feeling that had ignited low in her stomach. It was just pheromones. Animal lust. Biology. It meant nothing.

'Sorry to crash the party,' Paul leaned back in his chair, not even pretending to look regretful.

'What do you want?'

'Straight to business, is it? No soft soap, no little dance? Not even a drink?'

Lydia waited, not speaking. She resisted the urge to look around to see if Fleet had arrived. She didn't want to show any weakness.

'He's not here,' Paul said, as irritatingly able to read her mind as ever. 'Loverboy is late. I do hope that isn't a bad sign. Are things cooling off between the two of you?'

'Leave Fleet out of it,' Lydia said. 'Do you have news for me?'

'As it happens, I do. People like to talk, and I've been doing the rounds. I heard that Alejandro Silver was in the market for a bit of credit. He needed the kind of cash you don't get from a bank.'

'I know about that,' Lydia said, relieved and disappointed in equal measure, 'but I appreciate you coming to me with it. Anything else?'

Paul smiled. 'I take it you also know about Operation Bergamot?'

Lydia kept her features neutral.

'I mean, I'm sure you do. Alejandro was observed having cosy chats with a high-ranking officer on three occasions. It took quite a bit of persuasion and no small cost to find out he was the focus of a police operation. You'll know all about it, already, of course. It's a big deal for the Met and you've got a direct line to the police. At least, I assume that's the appeal of the DCI. Not that he isn't tall and handsome.' Paul's gaze flicked over her shoulder. 'Speak of the devil.'

Fleet was wearing a dark wool coat with a three-piece suit underneath. He looked like a grown-up with a proper job and a pension plan. Which Lydia found extremely hot. Next to Fleet, Paul looked even more like a thug from the wrong side of the tracks. Which Lydia also found extremely hot. Both men were sizing each other up like they wanted to get physical. Which was complicated. And, right now, she was battling the urge to throw her drink at Fleet. Also complicated.

She stood up and kissed Fleet on the cheek, refusing to give Paul Fox the satisfaction of seeing that he had her rattled. 'Paul was just leaving. He brought us some information about Alejandro so we're very grateful.' To Paul she said: 'Thank you. I owe you one.'

He didn't take the hint to leave, watching Fleet carefully instead as he spoke. 'I was just telling Lydia about

Operation Bergamot. I was surprised she didn't already know about it.'

Fleet visibly flinched and Lydia felt it like a blow to the stomach.

'Yeah, I thought as much. Makes me wonder how much she can trust you.' Paul leaned into Lydia and spoke close to her ear. 'Watch out for him.'

'Have a nice evening,' Lydia said. 'Give my regards to your brothers. I hope they're keeping the aggravated assaults to a bare minimum.'

Paul bared his teeth. 'We've paid for that.'

'Thank you for stopping by,' Fleet said, slinging a protective arm around Lydia's shoulders. She moved away and took her seat. When she chanced a look at Paul, he was back in laconic mode, a smile playing on his lips. She hated to think what conclusions he was busy drawing behind that relaxed exterior.

'Well, good night, kids. Don't stay up too late. You're both out of your territory, here.'

'Is that a threat?' Fleet was still standing and Lydia could see tension written into every muscle.

'Of course not, DCI Fleet,' Paul said, emphasis on the DCI. 'But you might want to think about being more honest with your girlfriend. She's too smart to stay with a liar for long.' Paul didn't look at Lydia again, just stared at Fleet for a beat. When Fleet didn't respond, he nodded like it was exactly the response he expected and he was perfectly satisfied, then turned on his heel and left.

Fleet sat down, shooting the cuffs of his shirt and

folding his hands on the table. 'You want to tell me why Paul Fox is joining our dates, now?'

'Really?' Lydia dug her fingernails into her palm to stop herself from raising her voice. 'That's what you want to lead with?'

'What?' Fleet's brows lowered.

'Operation Bergamot.'

He had the decency to look abashed. 'I was going to tell you about that tonight.'

'Before or after dinner?'

'After, ideally. This is supposed to be us having a normal evening like a normal couple.'

'We're not a normal couple,' Lydia said, standing up. 'I'm not normal.'

'Don't be like that.' Fleet was frowning in earnest, now, and he wasn't able to keep the frustration out of his voice.

'I'm going home,' Lydia said. 'I'm not hungry, anyway.'

THE NEXT MORNING Lydia found herself wide awake before six, watching the patterns of light on her bedroom ceiling. She got up and dressed in stretchy clothes on the basis that walking wasn't going to be enough to release the tension she felt and she was going to have to try running. The situation was truly drastic.

Outside The Fork the street was deserted. The line of parked cars were damp with dew and Lydia stretched before setting off at a brisk walk, arms swinging to warm up. She was so intent on moving that it was a second before her conscious mind caught up with an anomaly that her unconscious instincts had logged. One of the cars wasn't covered in condensation. Which mean that it was warm.

She didn't break stride, continuing to the corner at the end of the street without looking around. Once around the corner, she stopped and waited. A moment later a man appeared. He flicked a glance at Lydia and then continued past. He was wearing a suit and Lydia got the very slightest feeling of motion sickness as he passed. 'Good effort,' Lydia said. 'But you were too hasty to follow.'

The man stopped. 'Excuse me?'

'You've been made,' Lydia said. 'Don't waste my time. Call your boss and tell him I want a word.'

The man feigned confusion very convincingly and if Lydia hadn't been able to catch the faint trace of salted sea air that meant he had been in recent contact with Mr Smith, Lydia might have started to doubt her instincts. 'I still have his number so I can call him. Or I can go to the safe house near his office. I'm giving you the chance to take control of the situation and save a little face. If you're very quick, I might not even tell him I spotted your follow.'

The man glowered and pulled out a phone. He thumbed a text and then walked away.

The Mercedes pulled up silently. Even if Lydia hadn't recognised it as Mr Smith's, she would have guessed 'spy' or 'top-level arms dealer'. The back door opened and she got in.

Mr Smith looked the same. His signature was the

same, too, and with mere seconds to prepare for it, Lydia was battling a wave of motion sickness as she settled into the leather seat.

'You look well,' Mr Smith said.

'I thought we were done.' Lydia felt the urge to ask after Charlie and she held her breath until she had it under control.

Mr Smith inclined his head slightly. 'This is something new.'

'I can't help you,' Lydia said. She looked him in the eye. 'I won't help you. So you can stop having me followed. It's a waste of your precious resources.'

'This isn't about you helping me,' Mr Smith said. 'Very much the opposite.'

'Is that right?'

'I'm keeping you under surveillance for your own protection.'

'I doubt that,' Lydia said.

'Wouldn't you like people to know that you didn't kill Alejandro Silver?'

'He's not dead,' Lydia said and enjoyed the look of surprise on Mr Smith's face. It confirmed her suspicion that Alejandro's body hadn't simply been moved elsewhere. 'Something you already knew, of course.'

He smoothed his expression quickly. 'What makes you say that?'

'He isn't in the crypt. And I'm guessing the whole performance is something to do with Operation Bergamot.'

'Ah,' he said, his eyes widening just a small amount at her use of 'Bergamot'. The police database spewed out random words to assign to operations and there was no way she would have been able to guess it or work it out. 'I assume your DCI spilled the beans. Very careless of him. Very unprofessional.'

Lydia ignored the stab of emotion that elicited. Mr Smith wanted her to accept his help, to rely on him, and she would use that to keep him talking. 'I assume the pathologist won't be coming back from his holiday. Unless the trip was part of a bribe? And you must have had a spare body. Swapped in the ambulance? Were the paramedics your employees or was that some more bribery? I saw the corpse in the mortuary and it looked exactly like Alejandro. That's impressive.'

Mr Smith smiled. 'The perks of government work. Ample resources.'

'And he's in hiding now? What from?'

'There was a SOCA operation which was focused on political corruption. Alejandro Silver got swept up in it after his astonishing rise.'

Serious and Organised Crime weren't part of the Met, but they worked together. The fear that Fleet had been keeping information about the Alejandro case from her rose in her throat. 'Swept up how?'

'He had help, obviously, but where the cash came from for that help and who exactly benefited was of interest. Alejandro didn't want a scandal. It would damage his family's reputation, harm their firm, and, besides, he wasn't keen on being dragged through court on the other side of the dock.'

'Can't say I blame him.'

'SOCA offered immunity. Witness protection.'

Lydia snorted. She couldn't imagine Alejandro hiding. What would they do? Set him up with a warehouse job and a little terraced house somewhere up north? Call him Nigel and give him a Ford Focus and a membership to the local leisure centre. No.

'In exchange, he had to gather evidence against the people who had helped him. That's where I came in.'

Lydia stopped trying to picture Alejandro out of London living a normal life and focused on Mr Smith. 'Why?'

'SOCA was interested in political links to arms dealers and drug barons, very bad people Interpol have been chasing around the globe, and they found Alejandro because of a suspicious death in Greece which was linked to a known assassin.'

'The MP,' Lydia said. 'Nadine Gormley.'

'Exactly so,' Mr Smith said. 'But that turned out to be by-the-by.'

'How so?'

'Alejandro Silver wasn't being bankrolled by someone on Interpol's list. He had been to our old friends JRB for help.'

That brought up several questions, but Lydia settled on, 'How do you know that?'

He glanced down, picked an imaginary piece of lint off his immaculate suit, and offered something else. 'You once said to me that you thought JRB were trying to stir up trouble between the Families.'

'There have always been people who would like to see the Families destroy each other. Either because they fear us or because of the potential reward.'

'A war would have casualties, but it would leave bounty strewn across London, just waiting for somebody else to step in and collect. There have always been those who live from the flotsam of wrecks. I'm interested in the ones that tinker with the lighthouse.'

Lydia followed the metaphor, but wished he would stop talking about the sea. It made her nausea worse. She thought she could hear gulls and the sound of waves crashing. Mr Smith was watching her closely, like he knew she was feeling unwell. It struck Lydia that he may have learned a great deal from Charlie by this point. That he probably knew exactly the effect he was having.

'They don't even need to be destroyed,' he continued. 'Just mistrustful of each other, killing each other one at a time. It makes them vulnerable, open to infiltration and deals from outside agencies.'

Lydia glared at him. 'Something you have already taken advantage of.'

He smiled and Lydia felt her body lurch as if the deck she was standing on had lurched with the roll of a big wave. Not a deck. Not a boat, she reminded herself. She was in a car.

'I am here for you,' he said. 'I have no wish to see you destroyed by Maria Silver.'

'We just established that Alejandro is still alive.'

'And who else believes that? Unless he turns up and does a little dance in Trafalgar Square, you and your Family are chief suspects in his death.'

Lydia didn't reply.

'I can protect you. You are vulnerable and everybody knows it, it's only a matter of time before one of the other

Families makes a move on you. Or perhaps the threat will come from within. You just don't have Charlie's killer instinct and everybody knows it. You've seen what my department can do. Let me help you. I don't want to see you harmed.'

'Because you're hoping to use me as an asset in the future.' Lydia couldn't keep the bitterness out of her voice.

'That's part of it, of course,' Mr Smith said. 'My motives aren't really important at this point, though, are they?'

He was right. Lydia had bigger problems and if he was offering to help with one of the biggest, she would be a fool to turn him down. She felt chased down, though. Hemmed in. And that made her cranky. Plus, she had never fancied herself as particularly clever. 'I'll handle Maria Silver on my own. Tell your goons to stop following me. We made a deal and now I'm out. I'm not Alejandro or Charlie and I won't be your puppet.'

CHAPTER NINETEEN

Lydia stood on the pavement and watched the Mercedes peel away. She had the sinking feeling that she had just rejected an offer she couldn't afford to refuse. She turned back to The Fork, trying to stop her thoughts from spiralling downward. She hated that Mr Smith was getting under her skin. He was playing mind games, calling her weak because he wanted her to react, to put her faith in him. Somehow knowing that it was a strategy didn't make it less effective. She was afraid that there was truth to his words. Maybe she couldn't protect her Family, let alone the people of Camberwell?

Refusing to wallow, Lydia paused by the entrance and dialled Ash. She would check in on him. If she could prove she had truly saved Ash, maybe she wasn't a lost cause. And if the Pearls were still watching her, she should show them that she was still keeping an eye on Ash.

It wasn't a promising start. Lydia met Ash at one of the benches on Camberwell Green and he looked just as thin and jumpy as the last time she had seen him. He was clearly still struggling to eat and she would lay money that he was hardly sleeping, either. Jason had been making hot chocolate again, and Lydia had decanted it into two travel mugs. She passed one to Ash and wondered if this was anything close to the way Emma must feel all the time. The worry and responsibility for another human life. The gnawing sense that she should be able to fix him if only she tried harder.

'Thank you for meeting me,' she began, but Ash waved a hand. He was staring at a girl who was running to pick up a fallen soft toy from the path. She had a passing resemblance to the Pearl girl who had been following Lydia, but the similarity was broken when she skipped back to her mum and older brother.

'What do you need?' Ash said, still watching the family.

'I just wanted to check on you. How are you doing?'

Ash twitched. 'I've been in the library. Catching up on the news from the last twenty years. I thought it might distract me.'

'Has it?'

'I still miss them. Have you heard anything? Are you here because they have taken somebody?' He looked at Lydia and his expression was a strange mix of hope and revulsion.

'Not as far as I know. Have you tried to contact them again?'

He shook his head. 'Not really. Only in my dreams.'

Well that was creepy. 'Have you remembered more about your time underground?' She felt bad using Ash for information, but she had to protect her Family and the more she knew about the Pearls the better. Especially since they didn't seem to have forgotten about her. 'Is that okay? I know it might be hard...'

'I don't mind,' Ash said, shrugging. 'I want to talk about them, it feels the most real thing in my life and I can't talk to anybody else about it. Obviously.'

His eyes had lit up and Lydia hoped he was going to manage to stay calm.

'The king suggested they were trapped underground and I know they use kids as their eyes and ears aboveground. I wondered if that tallied with your experience? Do you remember any of them ever leaving? Did they talk about being trapped?'

Ash had wrapped his hands around the travel mug. 'Time was weird, as you know, but they were always in the court.' His face scrunched in concentration for a moment and then he shook his head. 'No. They never left to my knowledge. The king, anyway, I can't be sure about every single Pearl.'

'That's helpful, thank you,' Lydia said.

Ash was staring into space. 'I don't think they left. They were content. Happy.'

'That's-'

'They didn't talk about mundane matters,' Ash broke in. 'I sort of forgot about all of this, honestly.'

'All of what?'

'The world. London. Normal life.'

LYDIA WALKED WITH ASH, wanting to check that he

really was okay after talking about the Pearls. He said that he was heading to an appointment with an acupuncturist, 'mum and dad are getting desperate', but that he was attending the outpatients clinic at the Maudsley every week, too. Lydia was glad he was still getting help, but her heart clenched at the size of the problem.

'I know I'm not stable,' he said, glancing at her. 'I'm not so far gone that I don't know that. I know I can't keep going to the woods. I'm hoping they'll put me back on the antipsychotics. The antidepressants just aren't enough. They don't touch it. The feelings.'

Ash was speaking more quickly, now, and Lydia could see he was getting agitated.

'I can't stop thinking about them. I can't stop missing them. I just feel like I've been hollowed out, you know?'

'I know,' Lydia said, steering him across the main road. 'It'll get better, you've got to give it time.'

They took the cut-through road, Medlar Street, and walked under the railway and past an unwelcoming carpark with rolls of barbed wire. There was a cold wind, reminding Lydia that winter hadn't entirely given way to spring, and she zipped up her jacket. At that moment, Ash stopped speaking and stood stock still. He let out a strangled noise and fell to the ground. The colour fled from his cheeks, leaving him cadaverous and blue-lipped. His eyes were wide open and terrified. He seemed conscious but he clearly wasn't breathing. Kneeling on the cold pavement, Lydia hoisted his upper half onto her lap, cradling his head and calling his name. 'Breathe, Ash,' she said. 'Take a breath.'

She could feel Pearl magic pouring off him and

looked around automatically. They were alone and Ash still hadn't taken a breath. How long could you go without oxygen before brain damage set in? First aid training told her to lie him down, tilt his chin back and breathe air into his lungs. Crow training told her that she had to fight the Pearl mojo or no amount of CPR was going to help. 'Ash, you're okay, they can't hurt you. Breathe, Ash.' She kept saying his name, trying to calm his panic. His eyes rolled back, so all she could see was the whites and then they closed.

Lydia leaned down and whispered into his ear. 'Leave him alone.'

She could hear trees rustling, wind blowing through branches and leaves even though there were none nearby. It sounded like laughter. 'Stop it,' she said out loud.

She could see the trees, now. They were twisted and strange-looking, laden with brown-cased fruit and the sweet smell of rot filled her nostrils, obliterating the clean scent of pearls. Lydia closed her eyes and reached out in the darkness. She could hear wings beating, but they were faint and far away. The trees were loud and creaking. Roots were running underneath the earth, below the paving slabs and concrete and the rubble of old buildings. Ancient roots which still connected, roots which still remembered.

Her coin was between her fingers and, following her instincts and with her eyes tightly shut, she felt for Ash's face and forced his mouth open, putting the coin on his tongue. Immediately his head jerked and he took an enormous breath, like a man surfacing from deep water.

Lydia's eyes flew open. 'Don't swallow it,' she said, hoping it wasn't too late. Ash's eyelids fluttered and then closed again. He dragged in heaving breaths and on one of the exhales her coin dropped out into her waiting palm.

With her eyes open, Lydia could see the trees, again. They were translucent and ghostly, overlaid on the pavement and buildings and parked cars of the side street and they fanned the flames of panic which were licking at the edges of her mind, clouding her thoughts and making her heart race. She was surrounded by trees. She hadn't walked into the dark forest, but the Pearls had sent the forest to her. She focused on Ash's face, trying to block out the sound of wood creaking and leaves moving. 'We need to move,' she said. 'Now.'

Ash's eyes opened and he looked at her with a strange expression. It was his face, but suddenly looked nothing like Ash. The fine muscles around his eyes and mouth had settled into something unfamiliar. Something mocking. A second before he spoke, Lydia realised who had taken possession of Ash. The Pearl King. The words were definitely not Ash's.

'Do you know where you are, child?'

'I'm in my manor,' Lydia said, staring deep into Ash's eyes. She wanted the creature who was looking back to feel her gaze. 'Camberwell is the Crows' roost and you are not welcome here.'

'This was once an orchard.' Ash's voice sounded different. His vocal cords, the king's intonation and accent. 'Medlar trees as far as the eye could see. Do you know this fruit? The medlar. It is well-named for you, I think. Very appropriate. You are a meddler, Lydia Crow, and we tire of your interference.'

The sound of creaking tree branches, rustling leaves, and buds bursting into blossom was getting louder by the second. Lydia ignored it all and kept her focus on Ash's face. 'Why don't you talk to me in person? This,' she indicated Ash's prone body, 'is beneath your dignity.'

'This boy is my servant and I will use him however I choose, whenever I choose.'

'No need to be tetchy,' Lydia said, trying to annoy the king. If she could annoy the king, she could distract the king and maybe that would give her an opening. At the same time, she was trying to reach out for the sound of wings, a thousand tiny hearts beating, the feel of a warm air current lifting her up. It was difficult while blind terror threatened to engulf her, and Ash's face grew ever-paler, but she tried. She pictured black wings closing over their bodies, shielding them and squeezed her coin in one hand, focusing her energy. There were vibrations in the air and Lydia felt a warmth around her, as if a shelter had cut the cool breeze.

Ash was still white, though, and gasping for breath. His face was still wrong, his expression not his own. Lydia felt a surge of hate for the king and she pushed, trying to usurp the presence that was squatting inside Ash or using him as their own personal puppet. The voice, which was stronger than ought to have been possible from Ash's weakened body, said: 'You were warned. You must not speak of us.'

Ash began to cry and Lydia knew he had returned to himself. The shelter she had pulled over them, formed of invisible wings, was holding back the trees which still reached out twisted branches, but she could sense the roots underneath the ground rising. They had to move. She wasn't going to be able to protect them for much longer.

Lydia forced herself up and pulled Ash to his feet. 'Come on,' she said, towing him for a few paces before he found his feet and began to run with her. They stumbled down the street, dodging the ghostly trees. Lydia tried to keep her balance while holding onto Ash and concentrating to keep the wings closed around them like armour. There was a single stunted trunk growing from a square space in the pavement and it took Lydia a second to realize that it was a real tree and not one of the ghosts brought back by the king. A remnant of the orchard which had once stood here. Lydia paused and closed her eyes, bringing the Crow energy into the front of her mind and then down her arms and into her fingers. She let her anger over Ash's treatment and her fear for him rise up, and then she imagined the king was standing in place of the twisted piece of ancient wood. Her hands were either very hot or very cold, she could not tell. There was a burning sensation which quickly turned to a numbness. She touched the tree, letting the feeling flow out of her fingers. It burst into flames.

The ghost trees vanished in an instant. The rustle of leaves and creaking of branches disappeared and the sounds of the city flooded back. A siren wailed in the distance, like the siren call of home. Lydia and Ash walked out of Medlar Street, breathing hard, and joined the parade of shops and barbers and cafes and the people crowding the pavement. A man was playing steel drums with a hat on the floor and a sign which said, optimistically, 'thank you', and a pit bull on a lead trotted over to sniff at Lydia's leg. Some people might hark to the good old days, when Camberwell was a bucolic idyll with fields stretching as far as the eye could see and orchards thick with sticky fruit, but, on balance, Lydia preferred this version. Still, they needed to get off the streets.

LUCKILY, The Fork wasn't far and they made it without further incident. Ash's colour was better and he made it up the stairs to the flat in good time, despite seeming to be unable to stop saying 'I'm sorry' in a low monotone.

'Just a bit further,' Lydia said, chivvying him all the way. 'Keep going, almost there.'

Not a natural cheerleader, Lydia felt exhausted from the strain of staying calm. The Pearl King had reached out and manipulated Ash as easily as slipping on a coat. Lydia knew how it felt to have another soul inside herself having given Jason a lift on numerous occasions. It wasn't pleasant. The thought of that soul taking over was unbearable. Lydia was preoccupied with these thoughts and it took her a second to realize that Ash had stopped his quiet chant. She turned in time to see him move suddenly and violently, knocking her to the floor and sitting on her chest, knees pinning her shoulders. His hands wrapped around her throat and his eyes rolled back in his head, showing all white.

The Crow energy was there without her having to

think and she used it to throw Ash off, swivelling as he fell to the side and reversing their positions. 'Stop it,' she said, pinning him in place. One arm got free and went straight for her neck in a jabbing blow she only just avoided. 'Stop!'

His body was jerking, straining to throw her. Lydia wasn't sure how long she could hold him in place, even with the Crow power flowing and his emaciated frame. He was being powered by something older and stronger than them both. A connection from far beneath the earth in the Pearl Court. 'Sod it,' Lydia said and punched Ash in the side of the head.

CHAPTER TWENTY

Lydia used duct tape to secure Ash to the chair she usually used for clients. It was a basic upright and her main concern was that he would tip it and break something if he decided to struggle. He was still woozy from the punch to the head and she was getting seriously worried that he had a concussion. How did you know how hard to hit a person? How much was too much? When to stop? Cursing Charlie for not giving her training in the elements that really matter, Lydia held a cold flannel to the back of Ash's neck.

His eyes fluttered open. 'Lydia?'

'I'm sorry I had to hit you,' Lydia said. 'You weren't going to stop.'

'Did I hurt you?' The shadows under Ash's eyes were darker than ever, his skin so pale it was translucent and she could see the veins underneath. His voice was just a quiet croak.

'What the hell is going on?' Jason appeared next to

Lydia and she dropped the duct tape. It landed on its edge and rolled underneath the desk.

'Not now,' Lydia said, careful not to look in Jason's direction. Ash seemed pretty out of it but Lydia didn't want to alarm him any further by talking to a ghost.

'What happened to him?' Jason stared at Ash with naked horror. 'He looks half-dead. And are you into kinky stuff, now?'

'I'm going to sort this out,' Lydia said, leaning down and looking into Ash's eyes. 'Everything is going to be okay. I'm sorry I've restrained you. It's for your own protection. Now that we know the king can speak and act through your body, we can't take any chances.' She turned away, glancing at Jason as she moved to check that he had understood.

'Holy shit,' Jason said. 'They can do that? Use a human being like a glove puppet.'

'Apparently,' Lydia said, still not looking properly at Jason. She focused on Ash. 'Can you feel them now?'

Ash closed his eyes, his brow creasing. 'No.'

'Good,' Lydia wiped his face with the flannel. 'You thirsty?'

She moved away to get a glass of water, Jason following. 'What are you going to do?'

'I don't know,' Lydia said quietly, filling the glass. 'He needs to eat and drink and rest. He's exhausted and probably concussed.'

'Where's Fleet?'

'At work. And he doesn't need to know about this until later. I need to get things under control first.'

'He could help. You shouldn't be alone. What if Ash gets free? Tries to hurt you again?'

'Fleet shouldn't be a party to this. He's still police.'

'Lydia,' Jason said. 'Don't be stubborn. You don't have to do everything on your own.'

'I'm not on my own,' she said, smiling at Jason. 'I've got you.'

Back in the office, Ash was as slumped as it was possible for a man to be while firmly taped to an upright chair. She had wound the tape around his chest for extra security and it gave him the unfortunate appearance of Hannibal Lecter strapped to the trolley in a strait jacket.

'Water,' Lydia said. 'Take it slowly.'

Ash lifted his head slowly, as if it physically hurt. His eyes rolled, the whites showing, but then he seemed to focus. Lydia bent down and held the glass to his lips, tilting it so that he could drink. Ash's mouth stretched in a wide smile which looked all wrong. Before Lydia could react, he had bitten down on the glass. It broke and blood spurted from his cut lips. Lydia jerked back as Ash snapped at her, blood flowing. It wasn't Ash looking through the hazel eyes. He crunched the glass, his jaws moving methodically. His Adam's apple bobbed as he swallowed the mouthful of glass.

Lydia's throat had gone dry with fear but she managed to speak. 'If you hurt him, I won't answer your questions.'

Ash grinned, the blood flowing faster as his mouth stretched, opening the wounds. 'What makes you think I have questions for you, child?'

'What else could you want?' Lydia tried to modulate

her voice, to sound reasonable. She had to get the king onside before he hurt Ash any further. 'I want a truce. No more watching me, no more intimidation. If you kill me, another Crow will take over and, honestly, I'm the most reasonable one in the Family. Besides, there'll be a whole blood vendetta thing. Eye for an eye and all that. Let's come to a mutually beneficial agreement now.'

'Agreement?' The king spoke in a tone of genuine confusion. Lydia didn't know if that was because they didn't know the word or because they couldn't believe a mere human would dare to use it.

'One leader to another.'

Ash's bloodied lips curled in disgust. 'I do not recognise your authority.'

Okay. Lydia swallowed. Tried a different tack. 'I am aware that I disrespected you and I regret my actions.'

The King, through Ash, laughed and Lydia fought the urge to be sick. The sound was otherworldly and it made every part of Lydia want to curl up in safe space far, far away. 'I imagine that's true.'

'But I can offer you a gift in recompense for my part in the loss of your latest guest.'

'A new toy?' Ash's eyes gleamed.

'Yes. In exchange for a conversation. If we pool our knowledge, it will be mutually advantageous. We have a common enemy, I believe.'

'I find that hard to believe,' the king said. Despite using Ash's vocal cords and mouth, the king's voice was recognisable. At least it was to Lydia, who could feel the Pearl magic flowing with every sound.

'Until recently I was being blackmailed by a government department and I wondered if you or a member of your family might be having a similar problem.'

'These are the concerns of the upper world. They are not mine.'

She tried a different tack. 'Alejandro Silver isn't really dead. He made some sort of deal with JRB, but—'

Ash's face went slack and Lydia thought that king had severed their connection. Then a thin hiss escaped his lips. 'You are unwise to mention that name in my presence.'

'I mean no disrespect, your majesty.' Deference did not come naturally to Lydia, but she was willing to try.

'What is the gift you offer?'

Lydia didn't look at Jason, couldn't bear to see the shock she knew would follow her words. 'Ash. I will bring him to you. Or you can bring him yourself, I guess. But I will smooth his disappearance with the police. I won't come looking.'

Ash's expression changed. It appeared they were thinking, and when Ash spoke it was still with the regal intonation of the Pearl King. 'I believe my small friend told you this once. I like dead things.'

Ash's head twisted and there was a loud crack.

Lydia stumbled back, dimly aware of panicked swearing from a horrified Jason. Lydia forced herself into action and felt for a pulse on Ash's neck. There wasn't one.

'I should call an ambulance,' Lydia said. 'Do CPR.' She began pulling at the tape around his chest. She needed to get Ash onto the floor to do CPR.

'Too late,' Jason said. 'He's gone.'

Lydia knew he was right. Ash was utterly still. And the crack that she had heard, with the unnatural angle of his neck. He was dead. He had been killed. Instantly.

'What are we going to do?'

'You're right. He's gone.'

'But this is our home,' Jason said. 'He's in our home, taped to a chair.' If he needed to breathe, Jason would be hyperventilating. As it was, he was floating a foot above the carpet and vibrating.

'Stay calm,' Lydia grabbed his arm and squeezed, trying to anchor Jason in the room.

'I can't believe how quickly... He was alive just a moment ago. He was talking.'

'Can you see him?' Lydia said as the thought struck her. 'His spirit?'

Jason shook his head. 'He's not here. There's nothing. He's just gone. One moment he was here and the next moment...'

'It's okay,' Lydia said, swallowing her nausea. 'Why don't you put the kettle on.'

'What about the police?'

'I'm going to sort it,' she patted Jason's arm. 'I need a tea. For the shock.'

Jason's vibrating marginally eased as he visibly pulled himself together. 'Of course. Right. I'll do that.'

As soon as Jason moved into the kitchen, she picked up her mobile from her desk.

'Yo, boss.' Aiden answered with his customary enthusiasm.

Lydia was unable to tear her gaze from Ash's lolling head so she turned away. That was worse, it was as if she could feel the dead man looking at her, could imagine his head lifting on its broken neck and the mouth opening. She turned to face the chair again, her eyes pricking with tears at the sight of Ash's lifeless body.

'I've got a small problem.'

AIDEN'S INFORMATION turned out to be very good. Two women wearing pink tabards emblazoned with 'Claire's Cleaning' logos, arrived thirty minutes later. 'You should go out,' one of them said, without preamble.

'I'd rather stay,' Lydia said, not even sure if that was true.

The woman shrugged. 'You're the boss, but the chemicals are very strong.'

Part of Lydia's mind had been trying to work out how they were going to get a body out of her flat without attracting attention. Not to mention manoeuvre a grown man, admittedly a very thin one, when they were about the same height as Lydia. One of the women was built like an Olympic wrestler, but still. Bodies were heavy when they were dead.

Her phone rang. Aiden. 'We should talk. I'm downstairs.'

The women had little wheelie suitcases, matching the pink of their tabards. One of the them unzipped hers and pulled out folded plastic sheeting which they began to lay out on the floor. At once, Lydia decided that delegation was a very important skill. 'I'll leave you to it,' she muttered, backing to the door.

'Three hours,' the first woman said.

Lydia didn't go far. She felt a strange pull to be nearby while Ash's mortal remains were being handled. She owed him that much. Downstairs in The Fork, she took one of the paperback books from the free shelf and sat at her usual table. Moments later, Angel arrived at the table. Today, her dreads were tied up behind a bright pink scarf and she was only sixty-per-cent managing to conceal her habitual scowl. Since Lydia had taken over in Charlie's place, Angel was clearly trying to be less surly, but old habits died hard. Truth be known, Lydia didn't want her to change. But she couldn't work out how to tell Angel that without losing face. She was pretty sure Angel would lose any respect for her whatsoever if she tried. While it was nice not having to pay for food and coffee and having Angel appear when summoned, Lydia felt an ache at the formality that existed between them now. 'Coffee, please,' Lydia said. She added a sandwich to the order, although she wasn't hungry in the slightest. 'And if anybody asks, I've been here all morning. Spread the word.'

'Is someone going to ask?'

Lydia held her gaze until Angel looked away. 'Coffee coming up. You want that sandwich toasted?'

Alibi in place, Lydia tried to read the book she had picked up. A fat airport thriller with dog-eared pages and a tattered front cover. She sipped her coffee and read the same page several times, picking at the cheese toastie and forcing herself to chew and swallow. Ash's lifeless body, his neck cruelly twisted and his eyes wide and unseeing, kept leapfrogging to the front of her mind. It was an image that wouldn't stay away, no matter how many times she shoved it back into the darkness. Something Charlie had said to her once played in a loop: 'You try to save everyone, you save no one.' She couldn't protect Ash from the Pearls. They felt impunity to reach into her home and kill a man in front of her. She hadn't protected Mark Kendal, a man who ought to be untouchable under the protection of the mighty Crows. Her closest ally, the man who shared her bed, was keeping secrets, and her own family questioned her methods and strategy. Maybe Mr Smith was right. Maybe she was too weak to be the head of the Family.

CHAPTER TWENTY-ONE

That night, Lydia switched off her phone. Fleet had messaged, asking to talk, but she felt physically and emotionally wrecked. The flat was immaculately clean with no sign of the duct tape, any kind of struggle or Ash himself. The air was thick with pine-scented bleach and the synthetic floral of air freshener. Lydia opened the windows and stripped, putting every item of clothing into the washing machine. Then she took a long shower, scrubbing at her skin and underneath her nails. She didn't want to be in the flat but she didn't want to be anywhere else, either. She checked on Jason, who looked as upset as she was. 'How could they do that?' he asked, eyes hollow.

She didn't know if he meant morally or physically or both. 'I don't know. Are you all right?'

Jason shrugged, his outline vibrating slightly. 'Not really. But at least he's at peace, now. He's not here.'

That was something, Lydia supposed. Just not enough.

. . .

THE NEXT DAY, Lydia got up early. Her first thought was to start the day with a slug of whisky, something she had been pretty good at not doing for the last few months. With great reluctance, she decided to make another attempt at running, instead. She laced up her trainers and headed out into a damp spring morning. It was a half-hearted effort with Lydia's whole body feeling heavier than usual. She slowed as she approached home, the same dark thoughts swirling. Fleet was waiting for her outside the cafe. She was sweaty, thirsty and not in the mood for more lies. 'We're not open yet.'

'Can we talk?'

He looked wretched and Lydia felt a clutch of empathy. Still. She couldn't shake the fear that she couldn't trust him. He was police. She was the head of the Crows. It was a conflict that couldn't be resolved.

'Please,' Fleet said. 'Can we go upstairs?'

LYDIA WENT into the flat first, making plenty of noise to warn Jason. She downed a glass of water standing at the kitchen sink and refilled it before joining Fleet in the office. He was standing in the middle of the room, looking worried and absolutely exhausted.

Lydia wondered if he had slept at all and then she reminded herself that she didn't care. She leaned against her desk and crossed her arms. 'I've been very slow on the uptake. In my defence, I've always had a blind spot when it comes to you.'

'What are you talking about?'

'Did they offer you a deal?'

'Who?' Fleet looked mystified, but Lydia knew he was a good liar. He was police, after all, and it was part of the training.

'Your boss. Or your boss's boss. Was it for a promotion or more casework or a better salary? I hope it was all three.'

'What Paul said...' Fleet began. 'I only found out that day. I was going to tell you at the restaurant but he got there first. I swear. He knew more than I did, too. I was only given the bare minimum. You know I'm not flavour of the month with the top brass.'

Lydia wanted to believe Fleet, but she also knew that was part of the problem. She couldn't afford mistakes any more. The stakes were too high to risk trusting the wrong person and, there and then, she realised she would have to go back to her old habit of not trusting anybody at all. That was fine. 'What did they tell you?'

'That there's a task force looking at organised crime. It's been focusing on the Silver Family since last year when Alejandro first started to make a move into politics. I think he made a few bigwigs nervous and they put the pressure on and that filtered down through management. You know how it works.'

'Sure,' Lydia said.

'I didn't know,' Fleet said, again.

'Why did they tell you about it? Are you part of it?'

'Not part of it. They did have questions, though. About Maria Silver. And you.'

'What did you tell them?'

227

'Only what they already know. Your history with Maria. They have the details from the Yas Bishop case, but I gave them the truth so that they know what she's capable of.'

Maria had killed Yas Bishop, one of the only people linked to JRB, and Lydia had made sure she had been jailed for it. Unfortunately, the conviction hadn't stuck.

'Who is running the operation? Did they believe you?'

Fleet shrugged. 'Kate Harmon. Haven't encountered her before and she wasn't giving anything away.'

'Does that mean you're under suspicion, too?'

'I don't think so,' Fleet said. 'She's just doing her job. We're not really supposed to talk about open cases, not even with other police, unless we're part of the team. You have to put in a request for information through the system.'

'Coppers talk though, right?'

Fleet smiled tightly. 'Right.'

Lydia thought for a moment longer. Fleet reached for her and she stepped away, wanting to keep a clear head.

'You have to believe me,' Fleet said. 'I had no idea until yesterday. I would have told you.'

Lydia looked at him properly. He looked anguished and his eyes telegraphed sincerity. But the doubt remained.

'I chose you,' he was saying. 'I'm on your side first. I swear.' His eyes lit up with an idea. 'Use your power on me.'

'What?'

'I've seen you ask questions. People go all glazed and they answer you. Do that to me. Then you'll know I'm telling the truth.'

Lydia was already shaking her head. 'I wouldn't do that to you. I don't...'

'I want you to do it,' Fleet took her hands, ducking his head to look directly into her eyes. 'I need you to trust me and we're both old enough and experienced enough to know that sometimes trust needs hard proof. I let you down before and I swore to you that I would never do that again. I know that's true, but you don't. I'll prove it to you every day for the rest of my life if you'll let me, but this way is quicker.'

Lydia hesitated for another moment and then nodded her head. She wanted to trust Fleet and he was right, this was a shortcut to that trust. The fact that he was willing for her to use her power on him was almost enough to banish every last scrap of doubt. Almost wasn't going to cut it, though.

She pulled her hands away and produced her coin, making it hover in the air between their bodies. Fleet's eyes widened slightly but he didn't move away. 'Look into my eyes.'

'Is that important?' Fleet said, doing as he was told.

'It's quicker,' Lydia said, wondering why he didn't have the glazed obedience she expected. She pushed a bit of Crow whammy behind her next words. 'Stand on one leg.'

Fleet's lips quirked up at the corners. 'Are you messing with me?'

Well, that *was* odd. The unusual gleam that she had

sensed from Fleet when they first met was just part of him, now. Just as familiar and reassuring as his brown eyes and the deep timbre of his voice. Which was probably why it took a moment longer than it ought to have for Lydia to realise that it was getting stronger.

She could hear waves on sand, wind blowing through palm leaves and taste salt on her lips. Lydia blinked, trying to clear her mind.

'What are you doing?'

'Nothing,' Fleet said. 'I'm waiting for you to do your thing.'

Lydia shoved everything she had behind her words. 'Did you know about the operation involving Alejandro Silver before today?'

'No,' Fleet said instantly. She could see that he was trying not to smile.

'This is very weird,' Lydia said, trying harder. 'It doesn't seem to be working-'

In that moment, Fleet let out a strangled sound. His whole body stiffened and his eyes took on the glazed look she was used to seeing in people when she used her Crow magic to gain control.

'Right,' Lydia said out loud, trying not to sound as rattled as she felt. She had pushed hard to get Fleet into a suggestive state and now she wondered whether to pull the throttle back a little. She realised that she had no idea whether this kind of control was damaging for people. If she used too much for too long, would she kill off brain cells?

She had no desire to turn her significant other into a drooling vegetable, but before she could pull back on her power, Fleet lurched violently and almost fell over. He took a jerky step forward to catch his balance and blinked hard. 'What was that?' His voice was normal and slightly pissed-off. 'You didn't say it would hurt.'

'I didn't think it did. No one has ever said so before. I'm sorry,' Lydia reached up and plucked her coin from the air between them, pocketing it quickly before reaching for Fleet. 'Are you okay?'

'Did you get carried away?' His colour was already returning to normal and the tension left his features.

'I might have used more than usual, it didn't seem to be affecting you. You should sit down.'

'I'm fine. It only hurt for a moment.'

'Where? All over, or-'

Fleet took her hand and put it against his chest.

'That's never happened before. I swear I didn't know that would happen.'

'It's okay,' Fleet dipped his head. 'I'm okay.'

Lydia was close enough that she could see a sheen of sweat on his forehead and his skin had an ashy tone. 'Does it still hurt?'

'No. I just feel a bit wiped out. It was like something was clutching my heart. Squeezing it so hard that it stopped beating.'

'Feathers,' Lydia took a step away, but Fleet increased his grip on her hand, keeping in in place.

'It's all right. It's beating again, now. No harm done.'

'We don't know that,' Lydia pulled away successfully this time. 'We should go to hospital, get you checked over.'

Fleet smiled, but Lydia could see it wasn't at full

231

wattage. He wasn't feeling as fine as he pretended. 'Sit down, at least,' she grabbed his hand and pulled him to the bedroom. 'Or lie down.'

'I might need a few minutes,' he said, trying to keep things light.

'Stop it,' Lydia said. 'I'm worried. And you should rest.'

Fleet sat on the bed. 'I really am fine.'

Lydia climbed onto his lap and pressed herself against Fleet. His arms moved around to bring her closer and they kissed. After a moment, Fleet stopped. 'Okay,' he said and Lydia could see the pain on his face. 'Maybe I will rest. Just for a moment. And then you can try again.'

'I don't think so,' Lydia said. 'It didn't work on you.'

Fleet was clearly relieved and just as clearly trying to hide the fact. 'But I want you to know I'm telling the truth about the operation. I really didn't know before.'

'I believe you,' Lydia said. 'The fact that you wanted me to interrogate you and are willing for me to try again. That's enough.'

Fleet's eyes were searching her own. 'Is it?'

Lydia didn't know how else to say 'yes' so she kissed him.

LATER, curled up with Fleet, her back against his chest and his arms around her, Lydia felt the very last of her doubt ebb away. She could feel his gleam and the beating of his heart and every sense, both magical and animal, told her that Fleet was hers. She thought about what Emma had said about isolating herself. She thought about Maria. Furious and alone, surrounded by security she paid to protect her. She twisted around to face Fleet and put a hand on his cheek. 'I'm sorry I didn't tell you about Mark Kendal.'

'I can understand why you didn't,' he said after a moment.

'I'm all in,' Lydia said. 'From now on.'

Fleet's warm smile filled her soul with light. 'Me, too.'

'Which means I've got to tell you something bad.'

'Okay,' Fleet said, looking at her steadily.

'Ash is dead,' Lydia managed to get the words out and then she felt something break inside. 'It's my fault. I thought the king might take him back. He wanted to go back, wasn't coping with normal life. And I thought I could get the king onside. Maybe develop them as an ally. For the good of my Family. The greater good. But he killed him.' She was fully crying by the time she got to end of her confession, the words coming between gasps and hiccups. 'It's my fault.'

Fleet held her and stroked her hair. 'It's not your fault. You didn't kill him. You tried to help him.'

'I was going to give him to the king. I thought better someone who wanted to be with them than an unwilling child.'

'And if the king had taken him, he would be alive. You didn't hurt him, Lyds. You're not a killer.'

Lydia closed her eyes and breathed in the comforting scent of Fleet and allowed herself to be comforted. Just a moment. 'What if that's the problem?'

CHAPTER TWENTY-TWO

L ydia had fallen asleep in Fleet's arms, waking up with a line of drool connecting her cheek to his chest. 'Sorry,' she said, lifting her head and wiping his skin with her hand.

'I don't mind,' Fleet said, sounding sleepy. 'I told you I was all in.'

'I didn't realise that included dribble. Good to know.'

Lydia kissed him and then untangled herself to get dressed.

Fleet propped himself up on one elbow. 'What's happening?'

'You should meet my parents.'

'Is this another test?' Fleet said, starting to pull on his clothes.

'No. Just something that normal couples do.'

ONCE FULLY DRESSED, Lydia settled into the driving

seat and pointed the Audi toward the suburbs. She stabbed at the radio a few times before switching it off.

'Are you nervous?'

'I've never brought anybody home.'

'That can't be true,' Fleet said, but he looked pleased.

The idea of her teenage self rocking up at the parental abode with Paul Fox made her snort with laughter. It was possible that the nerves were getting to her. She felt giddy.

Her mother opened the door with a tea towel over one shoulder and a distracted expression. It cleared to one of pure joy the moment she saw Lydia. 'Hello, love. This is a nice surprise.'

'This is Fleet,' Lydia said. 'My...' She hesitated over the word 'boyfriend'. It just seemed ridiculous.

'Come on in,' her mother said, mercifully glossing over the moment.

Seeing Fleet in her childhood home was something Lydia had been trying to prepare herself for on the drive over. She had expected it to look all wrong. She couldn't picture her London copper in the living room where she had played board games and watched TV after school and gossiped with Emma. Instead, Fleet shook her dad's hand and began chatting about the snooker which was, inevitably, playing in the corner.

Lydia caught up with her mum in the kitchen and helped her bring in mugs of tea and a plate of sliced fruit cake. 'Switch that off,' her mother said, nodding at the television. 'Guests.'

Henry Crow smiled conspiratorially at Fleet and hit the mute button.

'So, you're a detective, Ignatius?' Lydia's mother offered Fleet some cake.

'Call me Fleet,' Fleet said. He chatted with her parents about his work and his upbringing before the conversation moved onto roadworks and urban regeneration, and Henry and Susan's recent discovery of cruises as the ultimate holiday.

'The food was incredible and you're away from everything.'

'Do you want a walk before we head back?' Lydia asked her dad.

Susan Crow looked at the rain-soaked window and took the hint. She kissed Lydia goodbye and hugged Fleet. 'You two must come for dinner next time. I'll do a roast.'

'That would be wonderful, thank you.' Fleet picked up Lydia's jacket and held it out to her.

At the pavement, Fleet said: 'I'll wait in the car. Give you time to catch up with your dad.'

Lydia was going to agree, but she stamped on the instinct. 'Come with us.'

Henry raised his eyebrows but didn't say anything.

'That's all right,' Fleet said, 'you go ahead.' He took the car keys and got into the passenger side to wait.

Walking with Henry Crow through the kind of drizzling rain which didn't seem to be falling from the sky but, nonetheless, soaked through clothes with a tenacious inevitability, Lydia tried to work out where to begin. She started with her topmost worry, the fear that her presence would make him ill again. 'I'm sorry to be here in person. I know we need to be careful, but I wanted to see you.'

Henry shook his head. 'It's a precaution. We don't know anything for sure. It could be that your man has fixed the problem permanently. Besides,' Henry tilted his head. 'You're an adult, now. I don't have to hide. That should make a difference.'

'You're joining the life again?'

'No,' her dad smiled sadly. 'Your mother would kill me. But I've given all this a lot of thought. It's about balance, right? If seeing you powers me up, I just need to make sure I siphon some away every time we meet.' Henry looked around the deserted street and then clapped his hands loudly. When he brought them apart his coin appeared between them, hanging in thin air entirely motionless. He let it hang there for a few seconds and Lydia could see the strain on his face. Then he clapped his hands together again and the coin was gone.

She swallowed hard. 'Is that going to work?'

'I hope so,' Henry said, visibly paler than he had been a minute before. 'What's the alternative? That I never see my only daughter? Just telephone calls for the rest of my life.'

'There are worse fates,' Lydia said and they resumed their sedate pace along the pavement.

'Well, it's my decision. You have nothing to feel guilty about. None of this is your fault.'

'I'm not sure about that,' Lydia said, thinking about

238

Charlie. She still didn't know what her father suspected about that, let alone his opinion.

'I wanted you to have a choice,' Henry said. 'And you did. I was groomed to take over after your grandfather. He was a bastard and liked to pit us kids against each other. Said the competition between me and Charlie would make us stronger. But what I really learned, was the stuff he never said. I learned by watching and I know one thing for sure. You can't lead the family on your own. And you can't let people stew over grudges. You've got to keep everyone together.'

They walked a little further and Lydia tried to formulate a way to tell her father everything that had happened. Charlie. The deal she made with Mr Smith which he didn't seem keen to let drop. Alejandro's faked death. The fact that Maria Silver was still after her blood. Mark Kendal, killed on her watch. Ash.

'Talk to me,' her father said. 'There's one big question in your mind. What is it?'

Lydia spoke without thinking. 'What if I'm not good for the Family? Bringing people together isn't my strong suit.'

'You seem to be working on it,' Henry said. 'Bringing your man around here is a start.'

'You don't disapprove?'

'It doesn't matter what I think. He'll be a tough sell to the rest of the Family, but they'll come round.'

'I'm not so sure,' Lydia said.

'Make them. You're the boss.'

'I'm not sure I ought to be,' Lydia said.

'Don't mistake bad things happening for bad leadership. Bad things happen all the time, especially in our line of business. That's not on you.'

More than anything, Lydia wanted to believe him. 'But two people have died.'

'You think things would have been better under Charlie?'

'No, but-'

'Only take responsibility for what you can control. Unless you pulled the trigger yourself, you didn't kill anyone. Besides,' Henry said. 'Death isn't the worst thing.'

LYDIA SETTLED into the passenger seat, enjoying the new sense of calm that had enveloped her the moment her parents had welcomed Fleet. He had offered to drive back and it was nice to know that she could close her eyes, put her feet up on the dash and enjoy the release of tension. Beckenham was only half an hour's drive, but she hadn't realised how much she had needed to get out of Camberwell, even for a few hours. Maybe her parents were onto something with the cruise idea. 'Maybe not a cruise, but I could consider a holiday,' she said out loud.

Fleet stopped at traffic lights and looked across with a fondness that made Lydia's breath catch in her chest. 'I'll hold you to that.'

At Denmark Hill, Fleet slowed to navigate some roadworks close to Kings College Hospital. He was musing on something Henry had said to him while Lydia had been in the kitchen. 'I think he was quoting poetry. And then he said something about angels.'

'Oh, you know,' Lydia said, delighted that her father had been waxing lyrical on his favourite poet. 'The famous Blake quote from when he had that vision on Peckham Rye?'

'No,' Fleet gestured for a woman on a bicycle to finish crossing in front of the car, before moving off. 'Vision, huh?'

'Yeah, Dad always said it wasn't angels, but Crows. Even though that would be black wings so I couldn't really see it. I mean, Blake says he saw 'bright angelic wings bespangling every bough like stars'. It doesn't track.'

'You don't see much bespangling these days,' Fleet glanced at her, smiling. Then his expression changed and he yanked the steering wheel to the right. In that moment, time seemed to slow. Lydia seemed to have plenty of time to see the side window shatter and then the car was spinning, the street scene outside blurring into something incomprehensible. The tyres were screeching on the wet road and someone was swearing loudly.

A loud crunching sound and then the car wasn't moving any longer. They were facing the wrong way down the road, a people-carrier was stopped so close to them that Lydia could see the woman gripping the steering wheel with shock in her eyes. There was a small child in the front seat, crying. The woman's mouth was opening and closing and Lydia wondered what she was saying. Further away, the sounds of brakes being slammed. It seemed very quiet, suddenly, and Lydia wasn't sure if her hearing had been damaged. Fleet was holding his shoulder, slumped over and eyes closed, blood on his face. For a single, heart-stopping second, Lydia thought he was dead, but then his eyes opened and he looked at her. 'Are you all right?' His voice was groggy and his eyes were trying to shut again.

'I'm not hurt.' Lydia couldn't feel any pain at all, even as she moved to unclip her seatbelt. Probably the adrenaline, but she filed worrying about her own possible injuries to 'later'. Fleet looked bad. She reached across and unclipped his seat belt. 'We need to get out.'

'No,' Fleet said. 'We don't know if they're still out there.' He was more alert, now, and peering through the windscreen.

'Who is out where? We need to get out.' Maybe she had seen too many films, but Lydia had the distinct impression that they needed to vacate the crashed vehicle before it turned into a fiery ball of death.

'Whoever just shot me,' Fleet said, and then he passed out.

CHAPTER TWENTY-THREE

Lydia had never felt a fear like it. She could hear voices, car doors slamming, and feel the rush of air as someone pulled open the passenger side door, but she was focused on Fleet. His breath was coming in shallow gasps, and his eyes fluttered like he was going to pass out. She put her hands on his face. 'Fleet, stay awake.'

He didn't comply. The moment he passed out, his hand fell away from his shoulder and blood gushed out, soaking his shirt and jacket in seconds. Lydia pressed her own hand to it to staunch the flow, but blood was leaking between her fingers. She needed a pad of material. Clean material. And she needed to lie Fleet back so that she could tilt up his chin if he needed resuscitation. She could climb on top of him, maybe hit the recline lever to get the seat back, but what if he had other injuries and she made them worse?

It felt like hours, trying to make simple decisions. Which should she prioritise? Should she go around to the other side of the car and try to drag him out? There could be a shooter waiting for her to do exactly that, waiting for the opportunity to finish the job. And always there, threatening to overwhelm her, was the fear. Don't let him die. Don't let him die. Don't let him die.

A flash of fluorescent yellow through the driver side window and another blast of air, as the door opened. Lydia felt a rush of relief. The professionals had arrived.

LYDIA DIDN'T WANT to leave Fleet's side, but she was persuaded into the adjoining bay in A&E while the trauma surgeon assessed Fleet's shoulder wound. The nurse who accomplished this feat was even shorter than Lydia but she had the kind of authority Lydia could only dream of and she was powerless to resist. 'I need to check you over, hen, and the faster you let me do my job, the sooner you can see your pal.'

Lydia knew when she was beaten and allowed the Scottish powerhouse in navy scrubs to run down a checklist of questions while she palpated Lydia's abdomen, took her blood pressure, shone a light into her eyes and asked her to look left and right. The last bit was the worst and Lydia bit the inside of her mouth to stop herself squeaking with the sudden sharp pains.

The nurse nodded and made a mark on the chart. 'Soft tissue damage in the neck and shoulder, very common in a car accident, I'm afraid.'

'We didn't hit anything,' Lydia said.

'It's the sudden stop. You'll be needing to take it easy for a few days.'

A police officer popped her head around the curtain. 'Sorry. I can come back.'

'I'm done here,' the nurse said. To Lydia she added: 'No alcohol tonight, Ibuprofen for the pain, ice the area if you get any swelling, and come straight back in if you experience any nausea or dizziness.'

Lydia sat up and swung her legs off the examination table.

'I need to ask you some questions,' the officer said. 'If you're up to it.'

'Fire away,' Lydia said and then winced. Poor choice of words. Part of her brain, the tiniest portion which wasn't fully taken up with fear for Fleet, had been running over the incident. She hadn't seen a shooter and, while she was far from an expert, she thought it must have come from somewhere high up.

'This is a firearm incident and is being taken extremely seriously. The Emergency Response Team are conducting a thorough search of the area and I must insist that you do not leave this part of the building without speaking to either myself or another officer.'

'Have you found anything?'

'We are in the very early stages of our investigation, but I want to assure you that your safety is a priority. We believe an individual fired on your car from an upper floor or roof of a building nearby. Can you think of any reason why your vehicle would have been a target?'

Lydia widened her eyes slightly. 'No. Absolutely not.'

FLEET WAS PROPPED up on white pillows, face turned away from the door. His arm was strapped across his chest and covered in bandages. Lydia could see an intravenous line into the back of his hand but nothing else, which she took as a good sign.

He turned his head as she approached.

'Hey you,' Lydia said.

'No grapes?'

Lydia was too tense to attempt a smile. 'What have they said? Shouldn't you be lying down?'

'I'm just waiting for this to be taken out,' he indicated the IV. 'And the discharge paperwork. Can you take me home?'

'Of course,' Lydia said and kissed him lightly on the lips. 'It seems a bit quick.'

'It was barely a graze. Nothing important got damaged.'

'How is the pain?'

He gave her a loopy smile. 'Great right now. But I'm not gonna lie, it's going to suck when the opiates wear off.' He was slurring very slightly and Lydia wondered what they had given him. 'I'm warning you now, I'm going to be pathetic.'

That did make Lydia smile. 'You saved my life. You get to be as feeble as you like.'

Fleet gazed at her fondly. 'I love you.'

At that moment a man with a clipboard appeared, he nodded at Lydia and then told Fleet that he would have to wait for the final sign off, but that he could take his IV out if Fleet wanted.

'I do want,' Fleet said, nodding with the exaggerated

care of the slightly high. 'Thank you.'

Lydia took the opportunity to head outside. The police were still very much in evidence, so she changed plan and went to the vending machine in the corridor instead. It was quiet, and once an elderly man being pushed in a wheelchair by an orderly had disappeared around the corner, Lydia used a burner phone to call the number she had for Mr Smith. A woman answered with 'Elias Electrics, how can I help you?' Bloody secret service. 'I need to see Mr Smith urgently. This is Lydia Crow.'

'There is nobody here with that name,' the woman said.

'Just pass on the message,' Lydia said and finished the call. Then she went back inside to collect Fleet.

LYDIA'S CAR had been taken by the police so she called a taxi to get her and Fleet back to The Fork. 'My flat is nicer,' Fleet said, and Lydia was relieved. He must be feeling more like himself if he was complaining about her domestic standards.

'Feel free to go home,' Lydia said. 'But if you want the Lydia Crow nursing experience, you're going to have to deal with my unwashed bedding.'

Fleet raised an eyebrow. 'Nursing, eh? Sounds good.'

'Don't get excited,' Lydia said, paying the driver.

SHE HAD JUST SETTLED Fleet into her bed when her burner phone rang. She closed the bedroom door and moved into the living room to answer it. 'You want a meeting?' Mr Smith asked.

'I want you to come to The Fork and explain yourself,' Lydia said. 'Someone just tried to kill me.'

'I don't think that's such a-'

'Fleet was shot,' Lydia said. 'I'm not leaving him alone.'

A short silence. 'Ten minutes.'

GOOD AS HIS WORD, Mr Smith texted the burner phone nine minutes later to say he was outside the cafe. Lydia asked Jason to keep an eye on Fleet, who had already dozed off.

'They wouldn't have let him out if he wasn't okay,' Jason said. 'But of course I'll watch him.'

The sky had darkened in the short time they had been back and the streetlights were illuminated, casting an orange glow on the wet pavement. Mr Smith was standing outside his Mercedes, hands folded. 'I understand DCI Fleet wasn't seriously injured.'

Lydia ignored that. 'What do you know? Is this about Alejandro and Operation Bergamot? Why am I being targeted?'

'The first part of the operation failed, but the back-up portion yielded promising results. Alejandro offered information on a bill that was coming to Parliament before it was made public. He also offered his vote and a seat on the lucrative advisory position that would open up as a result of that bill being passed. It was intended to gather evidence of corruption by a particular individual and to discover the identity of that individual's managing associate or associates.'

'You can speak in English, you know,' Lydia said, irritated out of silence. 'You got him to dangle something juicy in front of his shady contact and stuck him with a wire.'

Mr Smith inclined his head. 'Quite so.'

Lydia waited for him to elaborate. She didn't want to have to prompt him, but Mr Smith had been being an enigmatic dick for far longer than Lydia. She was never going to win the conversational battle. 'Just tell me,' she said, pushing a little bit of Crow behind her words, just for fun.

Mr Smith's nostrils flared, like he could smell something bad. 'There's no need for that. I'm here to help. Mr Silver's contact was a conduit to a person who conducts business through many aliases and runs their funds through shell corporations.'

'Including our old pals, JRB?'

Mr Smith nodded. 'We didn't get anything useful recorded and Mr Silver made it clear that he would not be testifying in open court. He did discover some details about the contract which had been taken out on Ms Gormley, details we were able to cross-reference to be fairly certain that the job was carried out by the person at the centre of Operation Bergamot.'

'The person? I thought this was about political corruption or terrorism or arms dealing.'

'It's about all of those things, but there is an individual who has been making trouble internationally. Hence the multi-organisation operation and Interpol. I was brought in as an expert on the Families,' he inclined his head slightly, 'but that was only after Alejandro was linked.'

'So, it's not about JRB or the Silvers.' Or the Crows, is what Lydia meant, but didn't say.

'Only tangentially and recently. This Operation has been going on for the last two years. Maybe longer. Even I'm not privy to all of the intel.'

Lydia could see his annoyance at that.

'And when I say 'making trouble' I mean killing key people at inopportune moments around the world.'

'This is about an assassin?' Lydia took a moment to let that settle in. 'Why would they be after me?'

'We don't know that they are,' Mr Smith said. 'I'm inclined to think not. It is more likely that the attempt on your life today was more tangentially linked. Which doesn't mean you shouldn't consider my previous offer. Let me protect you.'

Lydia ignored that. 'You mean, that Maria sent someone to have a pop because she thinks I killed her father? So it wouldn't be happening if it wasn't for your stupid operation. Fleet got shot. Did I mention that?'

'Don't be dramatic. It was just a graze. Not even a through-and-through. He'll be fine. And don't pretend Maria wasn't looking to off you before the operation. You can't blame us for the bad blood between you.'

Lydia forced herself to be quiet, to think. She took a calming breath and squeezed her coin in her palm. 'So what was the back-up part of your grand plan?'

'The public nature of Alejandro's disappearance.'

'The funeral?'

'All of it. Having him die, not disappear. We wanted to see if it would bring the operative to London.'

'Why would it? You had just done their job for them? Saved them a trip?'

'They would have to check he was really dead. And also that it wasn't another operative. Professional pride.'

'That seems far from reliable. Why would they care?'

'Reputation, then. At the level this person is working, there is no margin for error and no room for competition. And, beyond that, there is a chance the assassin may have further targets in the city. If they were commissioned to hit one of the Family heads, it's possible they were commissioned to get them all.'

Lydia went cold. 'So today's attempt could have been your assassin. Make up your mind.'

Mr Smith smiled. 'Anything's possible between heaven and earth.'

Something else snagged Lydia's attention. Which was good because it stopped her from punching him. 'You keep saying 'they'. How much detail do you have on the killer?'

'Very little. We don't have a gender as witness reports are extremely scarce. We have a man in Buenos Aires who swears he saw a beautiful blonde leaving the hotel after a prominent union leader took his own life in his suite. And we have another report of an unknown man with a short beard and brown hair seen driving away from the scene where the head of the Colombian cartel was gunned down as he left his mistress's apartment.'

'Why didn't you tell me this last time we spoke?'

'I work on a need to know basis,' Mr Smith said. 'You know how it is.'

'And getting shot at qualifies me for clearance. I guess it's my lucky day.'

'I'd say so,' Mr Smith said. 'The assassin we are looking for doesn't tend to miss.'

BACK UPSTAIRS, Lydia held a whispered conversation with Jason in the living room and then went into the bedroom as quietly as possible, not wanting to wake up Fleet. She got into bed with him and lay awake, watching headlights on the ceiling. She knew there was a pressure sensor outside her flat, heavy-duty locks on the building and a watchful ghost in attendance, but her mind wouldn't stop racing.

A couple of hours later, Lydia hadn't slept. She thought she was keeping still and quiet but she felt Fleet stir. 'Can't sleep?'

'How's the pain?' Lydia sat up, reaching for the packet of paracetamol.

'Not too bad,' Fleet said, grunting slightly as he shifted position. 'How about you?'

'I'm fine,' Lydia said. And it was true. Her neck felt a bit stiff and sore, but it paled into insignificance when she thought about how close Fleet had come to being seriously hurt. Or worse. She propped herself up on one elbow to look at him in the dim light filtering through the curtains. Alive and whole. Sleepy-eyed and with a rough scruff of stubble.

'Do you ever wonder about your father?'

'Not really,' Fleet said.

'Not ever?'

Fleet was quiet for a while and Lydia wondered if he was drifting back to sleep. 'Why are you asking?'

'There's something about you,' she began, trying to pick her words carefully. 'Something different.'

'I should hope so,' he said, pulling her down with his good arm and kissing her lips.

After a few pleasant moments of that, Lydia holding her weight off his body for fear of hurting his shoulder, she tried a different tack. 'What do you think makes you such a good copper?'

Fleet frowned. 'Training? Hard work? Ability to not punch people when they're being annoying.' He smiled. 'Most of the time.'

Lydia shook her head gently. 'You have really good instincts.'

'Thank you. I think?' Fleet's frown deepened. 'Why do I feel you are leading up to saying something I don't want to hear?'

'That guy at work. The idiot. He wasn't wrong about your success rate.' She held up her hands. 'Wrong about the reason for it, of course, but I was just thinking... Do you ever get a feeling about something before it happens?'

'Of course, all the time. Everybody does. We've got those evolutionary survival instincts that mean we take in loads of information subconsciously and make decisions quickly before we've consciously noticed. I read a book about it once.'

'Right. But more than that, do you ever have a strong feeling about how something is going to play out. And then everything happens the way you expected?'

'I don't know,' Fleet looked properly wary now. 'Maybe sometimes. But that's experience. I know what's going to happen with some cases because it's happened a hundred times before. Criminals aren't that inventive. They make the same mistakes. They say the same things. I've just been doing this job a long time.'

'And when you're out and about, you sometimes react really quickly. Before even the tiny signs have happened. Like today.'

'That was luck,' Fleet said. 'And I must have seen something. It goes with the job. Coppers are all the same. The good ones, anyway. You develop a sixth sense for trouble.'

Lydia knew he wanted to drop it, but she couldn't. 'I didn't see anything. If you hadn't steered when you did, one of us would have been killed.'

'Unless it was a warning shot,' Fleet said. 'Or we might not have been the targets.'

He was playing devil's advocate, Lydia knew, but she wasn't going to be derailed. 'How did you know to move when you did?'

'The gunshot was a clue,' Fleet said, his voice sleepy now.

'That wasn't how it happened,' Lydia said. 'You wrenched the steering wheel and then the glass shattered. How did you know there was a sniper?'

Lydia stared at his shadowed face, looking for an answer, but Fleet had slipped back to sleep.

CHAPTER TWENTY-FOUR

Lydia walked through the downstairs of Charlie's house, closing blinds and lighting candles. She had considered holding the gathering at The Fork, but wanted to make it clear that this was a private family party with a small 'f' on the word 'family'. It was also a gathering of the inner circle of the capital-f Family, too, but it felt important to emphasise the blood ties foremost.

Angel had made two large pans of lasagne and dropped them off earlier with detailed instructions. Even Lydia couldn't mess up reheating them in Charlie's state-of-the-art oven. She had taken a delivery of garlic and rosemary focaccia, six bottles of wine and a raspberry and ricotta cheesecake from the Italian deli. Fleet was in the kitchen, dressing salad leaves in a glass serving bowl. He was only able to use one arm so it was taking longer than it might have done, but Lydia left him to it. Telling her tough-as-nails copper that he wasn't capable of applying olive oil to some vegetation wouldn't be great for his self-esteem.

The guests arrived right on time and there was much kissing and hugging. Daisy and John brought wine and Aiden staggered under a flower arrangement of unwieldy proportions.

'No gifts necessary,' Lydia said. 'This is just a family meal. Nothing formal.'

She directed the guests to the living room for drinks and then heard the front door open again. She had invited both of her parents, though she hadn't been sure they would come, but there they were. Her mother looked well-rested and surprisingly relaxed, wearing a fitted black dress and her signature red lipstick. Her father was in a suit, something she hadn't seen for a few years and, together, they looked more like heirs to a crime family than she had ever seen. John went pale as Henry Crow walked into the house and greeted everyone and his colour didn't improve when he kissed Lydia and congratulated her on her successful climb of The Shard. It was a public declaration of approval and John would have to be a fool – or sick of life – to challenge her authority now.

After drinks, Lydia led the way to the kitchen where the big table was set.

'What is he doing here?' John said as soon as he caught sight of Fleet, who was chopping peppers, a tea towel over one shoulder.

'We're together. And he's part of the family,' Lydia said.

'Did I miss the wedding?' Daisy said in an acidic tone.

'The man took a bullet for me,' Lydia indicated Fleet's bandaged shoulder. 'And I have just informed you that he is part of this family. Anybody got anything else to say about it?' She looked around, making eye contact. Nobody did.

Lydia told them to sit at the table while she dished up. 'I'll help,' Daisy said, pushing her chair back.

'No, sit down.' Daisy froze halfway out of her seat and Lydia attempted to sound less authoritarian. 'Relax! You can pour the wine.'

In the kitchen, Fleet put a steadying hand on the small of her back. Lydia leaned against him briefly and then tackled the lasagne, dishing out squares while trying not to think about the weirdness of the atmosphere. This shouldn't be odd. They were family. She had been kept separate from the Family business while growing up, but she had still enjoyed family parties and outings, had still been doted on by uncles and aunts, had played with cousins. A memory of Maddie, dead-eyed in the dim light of her living room with her hands wrapped around Lydia's throat, jumped into her mind. Lydia pushed it away.

'Dig in,' she said brightly, slinging plates in front of people and then carrying across the second pan of lasagne which was still half-full. 'Help yourself to seconds when you're ready.'

Slowly, conversation began to flow. Henry talked to Aiden about snooker and Aiden gazed at him in frank hero worship. John asked Fleet about his shoulder as a way to segue into his own litany of physical complaints; his dodgy ankle, his slipped disc, the time he got shingles. Daisy drank wine steadily and hardly spoke, but you couldn't have everything.

Once plates were cleared and people were sitting back in their chairs making the kind of satisfied noises that indicated a good meal had been devoured, Lydia took a ten-shilling note out of her pocket and put it on the table. Instantly, the conversation stopped, all eyes drawn to the money.

'You all know there is someone taking pot shots at this family.' Lydia looked around the table. 'Someone killed Mark Kendal and I found one of these in his wallet. And this week, someone took a literal pot shot at my car. If Fleet hadn't acted as quickly as he did, I might have been seriously hurt. Maybe even killed.'

Lydia glanced at her mother who hadn't been able to stop a small gasp. She had a hand up to her mouth and her eyes were wide with horror. Henry put an arm around her shoulders, pulling her close. 'It's okay,' Lydia said, taking her mother's hand and giving it a squeeze. 'I'm fine. Thanks to Fleet.' She let that settle in for another moment.

'Thank you,' Susan said to a clearly embarrassed Fleet.

She hated to worry her parents, but any member of the Crow Family who still had a problem with her boyfriend would have to stay very quiet about it indeed. 'I don't know who to blame, yet.'

'Maria Silver would be top of the list,' Aiden said. 'Surely?'

'I'm not jumping to conclusions. Alejandro was mixed up in a government operation and I have it on good authority that there is a rogue assassin currently on the loose. You're right, though,' she nodded to Aiden and he sat up a little straighter, 'Maria Silver is not my biggest fan.'

'What do you want us to do?' Aiden asked.

'I want you to all be on your guard, that's sensible, but I don't want any retribution. No eye for an eye bullshit,' Lydia looked at John as she said the last part. 'But I'm going to sort this out, make sure there is no more unpleasantness.' She tapped the ten-shilling note. 'I'm taking this to Maria, but before I give it to her, I'm going to give her the chance to ally with us. I need you all to understand something very important. Our quarrel is not with the Silvers. Or the Foxes. Or even the Pearls. In fact, if we don't join with the other Families, put aside past problems and learn to work together, we're going to be picked off one by one. There's a government department that would like to use our power, and there is JRB. All I know for sure is that they want us at each other's throats, weak and squabbling like little children. I'm proposing we don't play into their hands.'

'What makes you think she'll even hear you out?' John said. 'Charlie told me what she did to you after you got her arrested.'

'I have some information which is extremely pertinent to the Silver Family. She's going to want to hear what I have to say about her father.'

'What about Alejandro?'

Lydia smiled her shark smile. 'He's not dead.'

After the family had left, Lydia prepared to head to her meeting with Maria.

'Please don't go,' Fleet's voice was gentle, but very serious. 'I'm asking you.'

'I'm sorry,' Lydia said. 'You heard my rousing speech. Now I've got to follow through.'

What Lydia didn't say was that she couldn't stop seeing Chunni and Heather's frightened faces and Ash's lifeless one. She was head of the Crow Family, but she wasn't Charlie Crow. Or Grandpa Crow. If there was a chance Maria Silver was walking around believing that her own father was dead when he was very much alive, Lydia was going to take her the truth. She might be a murderous witch with a cold dead heart, but she was also a human being. And Lydia had seen real grief in her face. She had to tell her the truth.

'Then, I'm coming with you.' Fleet picked his coat up from the chair.

'You don't have to do that.'

'Maybe the presence of the Met will stop it from escalating.'

'And maybe it will do exactly the opposite. If Maria thinks I'm trying something when she told me to come alone...'

'When people say 'come alone' they usually mean you harm.'

'Or they're frightened. Or value their privacy,' Lydia countered. 'Some people find it hard to trust.'

Fleet gave her a long look. 'Tell me honestly, is that what you think is going on in this situation?'

Lydia didn't meet his gaze. 'Maybe.'

'It doesn't matter,' Fleet said. 'I've told you, I'm all in. I'm not a copper first, I'm yours. Whatever that means and wherever it takes me. We're in this together from now on and I'm not going to let you keep me at arm's length.' Fleet was breathing a little harder by the time he'd finished his speech and his eyes were shining a little.

'Well, then,' Lydia said lightly. 'Let's go.'

THE MEETING WAS in neutral territory, at least, but Lydia didn't disagree with Fleet's assessment of the plan. It was a clusterfuck. 'At least it's not a multi-storey car park,' Lydia said. 'She can't be planning anything especially bad in a hotel.'

Fleet gave Lydia the look she deserved. Maria Silver had booked the sky bar at one of the nicest hotels in the City but that didn't mean she wasn't planning to stab Lydia over cocktails.

'I'm bringing good news,' Lydia said. 'It could be the making of us. A bright new day.'

Whoever had decorated the hotel had been overly fond of shining black glass and glittering gold decorations. The effect was luxurious but with an undertone of sleaze. Probably not what they were going for, but Lydia would be the first to admit that she might be wrong. Interior décor was not her strong suit, and five-hundred-quid-a-night hotels not her natural environment. Weirdly, Fleet looked perfectly at home. She commented on it as they rode the lift to the top floor. 'You always seem at ease, how do you manage that?'

He flashed her a smile. 'Because I always am.'

A uniformed member of staff stopped them as they entered the bar. 'This is a private function. There's a bar open on floor seven or the Milanese Restaurant on-'

'We're invited,' Lydia said, and one of Maria's security staff nodded them through.

Maria was standing on the terrace, looking out at the twinkling lights of the city. She turned as they approached. 'You said you have information for me. I'm listening.'

'We should sit down,' Lydia said.

Maria raised an eyebrow but she indicated chairs arranged around a table. Lydia waited for Maria to sit before taking a seat opposite. Fleet remained standing behind Lydia, like a bodyguard. Lydia was glad his jacket hid his bandaged shoulder. She didn't think there was going to be a physical confrontation but, in her experience, it was best not to show any weakness around Maria. With that in mind, Lydia launched straight into her prepared speech.

'I know you don't like me, but I hope you will accept that I am genuinely trying to help. Mainly because it helps me, of course, but also because I think you should know the truth.'

Maria folded her hands in her lap. Her expression didn't change and she didn't speak.

Lydia ploughed on. 'I don't think your father is dead. It definitely isn't his body in the Silver crypt.' She wondered if Maria would be more convinced if she explained that she hadn't been able to sense 'Silver' or whether she would be revealing her secret for no real gain. 'And the Silver cup is a fake, too.'

The only sign that Maria was listening was the very slight tilt of her head. That and the fact that she hadn't smacked Lydia in the face. Yet. 'Can you think of a reason he might have wanted to disappear? It's okay if you don't want to tell me, but I want you to think about it.'

'Why are you bringing this to me?' Maria asked.

'I told you. Whatever has happened between us in the past, I think you ought to know.'

Maria smiled. 'What makes you think I don't already know? How typically egotistical of a Crow to believe she knows more about Silver business than I do.'

Lydia waited a moment, trying to work out if Maria was bluffing. She was incredibly poised if that was the case, but she was the head of the Silver Family. Poise was her birth right. When it became apparent that Maria wasn't going to fill the silence, Lydia said, 'If you know he isn't dead, why have you been putting the word out that I did it? Why send a sniper to kill me?'

A barely perceptible frown creased Maria's brow before she shrugged. 'Opportunity.'

Fleet stepped forward. 'You just admitted to attempted murder, Ms Silver. As you are aware, booking a professional killer is the same as-'

Maria didn't so much as glance at Fleet. Instead, she addressed Lydia. 'You brought your pet policeman. How sweet.'

'And now we're leaving.' Lydia stood up.

'I don't think so,' Maria said. 'We haven't had our drinks, yet.'

'I came to tell you that I believe your father is alive. I was under the mistaken belief that your actions were driven by grief.'

'And you wanted to save your own skin.'

'I have no problem staying alive,' Lydia said. She gestured to herself. 'Look. Here I am. An attempt by a pro and I'm still breathing. I came to deliver the information because I thought it was the right thing to do. Morally. We have our personal differences, but we belong to ancient and respectable Families. I, for one, intend to act like it.'

Maria narrowed her eyes. 'A grubby little Crow trying to get the moral high ground. Have you any idea how ridiculous you appear? I'm the establishment, I'm the law.'

'Very well,' Lydia said. 'If you want to keep it personal, I will behave unprofessionally from now on.'

'Is that supposed to frighten me?'

'That depends. How do you feel about your father's cowardice becoming public knowledge? It's my understanding that he made a deal with the secret service in order to protect himself from JRB. The great Alejandro Silver borrowing money from a company associated with the Pearls. And then, worse for a lawyer, finding out that he had made a deal which made him into a puppet. He had to vote the way JRB demanded, among other less-savoury favours. So to get away from JRB he got into bed with the secret service, and agreed to act as their stooge, instead. In return, they faked his death. He wanted to protect the good name of the Silver Family and the firm, and to keep his daughter from being tarred by the same brush.' Lydia shrugged. 'Wherever your father is, I'm willing to bet he can't come home. A dead man can't be a politician or a lawyer or the head of a Family. It's over for him. The only thing keeping him going is that he kept your reputation clean. You really want to destroy that?'

Maria's lips were in a thin line. 'What do you suggest?'

'That you cancel the hit against me, for starters.'

Maria tilted her head. 'I misspoke earlier. I haven't the faintest idea what you mean.'

Lydia wasn't sure what game Maria was playing and whether or not she believed her. She had the sense Maria had been surprised when she had mentioned the sniper, but then she was a Silver and as twisted as a corkscrew.

'Besides,' Maria said with a chilling smile. 'If I wanted to remove you I wouldn't be so careless as to hire a contractor and leave a trail. I would undertake the matter personally.'

Well *that* had the ring of truth. 'Regardless, you've come for me in the past. And you've made threats. I'm willing to move on, for the sake of both our Families. I'm offering you a free pass just this once, but I will never be so lenient again.'

Maria's mouth snapped shut. Her gaze went to Fleet.

'Don't look at him.' Lydia waited until Maria's eyes were staring into her own and then she drew on the

Crow power, the thousands of black feathers and fluttering hearts. She held them lightly, not showing her coin or pushing Maria in any particular direction, just holding the power there so that it filled the room with the sound of beating wings. 'I know that your Family cup has gone. I know that Alejandro is in hiding. Ally with me or I will destroy you.'

CHAPTER TWENTY-FIVE

L ater that night, Lydia was still wired from the meeting with Maria and felt sure she wasn't going to fall asleep anytime soon. She disentangled from Fleet in order to reach for her phone and checked the news, more by reflex than anything else. She kept expecting to see a story about Ash's disappearance, maybe a tearful plea by his parents, but nothing had appeared, yet. Lydia blinked and turned her phone face down. She thought that she had successfully pushed her feelings about Ash deep inside and then locked them in a box for good measure, but the thought of his parents losing their son all over again made her throat hurt. Fleet turned over in his sleep and Lydia got up and tiptoed out to her office, so as not to wake him up. He was recovering very well, but he needed to rest.

Sitting at her desk, the lamp pooling light on the messy surface, Lydia began looking through the latest batch of correspondence shoved through Charlie's letterbox. She had picked it up during the family meal prep and brought it back and now she needed something mindless to occupy her. Flyers. Insurance renewal. A handwritten thank-you note sent from Australia. Lydia fetched the whisky and treated herself to a slug straight from the bottle. Begging letter for a loan. Catalogue. An offer on a case of wine. Invitation to a charity ball. Wedding invitation. A heavy cream envelope with nothing on the front, not even Charlie's name. Lydia used her pen knife to slit the thick paper. Inside, there was a sheet of Silver and Silver note paper with a typed date, time and address, and the words: 'This is goodbye, old friend.' It was an office building in Canary Wharf, not a place she recognised, and the date was the following day. Lydia looked at her watch. Well, the same day, now.

FLEET WAS NOT happy and not only because Lydia was changing the dressing on his shoulder wound. He hissed a breath between his teeth as Lydia dabbed a little too hard with the antiseptic. 'I don't understand why you think it's Alejandro. Why would he leave a note at Charlie's house? He knows he's gone.'

'But he doesn't know the details,' Lydia argued. 'I've spread the word that he's taken a long holiday. Most assume that means he's dead, but Alejandro might think it means he's also taken a deal with the government. I mean, he might be hoping that Charlie has done the same thing as him. Misery loves company, after all.'

'But...'

'And he might be reaching out to the house on the

assumption that Charlie is hiding out there, or checking on it. He might not think there's a high chance of getting in touch with Charlie, but if he doesn't have any options... Or maybe he left notes like this in a hundred other dead drops. Who knows how many little secrets Charlie and Alejandro shared over the years.'

'Fine, but I still don't see why he would get in touch, now. Especially since he's supposed to be dead.'

Lydia stuck the fresh dressing onto the wound and smoothed down the edges to make sure it was stuck firmly. 'They've been allies for a long time. Alejandro might just want the chance to say goodbye before he gets moved abroad or whatever the leaders of Operation Bergamot have planned for him. Or he might have a plan to get out of his situation.'

'Or he might be hoping to lure you to an isolated location.' Fleet pulled his shirt back on and began to button it.

'Alejandro has always allied with the Crows. He's not going to hurt me. Besides, this invitation is meant for my uncle, not me.'

'Alejandro's not necessarily acting of his own free will. Wasn't he used by the government op to gather evidence?'

'Well, Charlie's not going to turn up, so Charlie can't accidentally give him any incriminating evidence. I'm going to attend, it's the respectful thing to do.'

'Respect, huh?' Fleet tilted his head.

Lydia kissed him lightly. 'That, and the possibility that he might be persuaded to tell us what he found for Operation Bergamot about JRB.'

CANARY WHARF in east London was the second business and financial district after the City. The Mayflower had sailed from the docks nearby, and the East India Quay celebrated trading routes and enterprise. Back in the day, it would have smelled of tobacco and sugar, imported from the newly colonised America, but now it smelled of exhaust fumes and money. Shining skyscrapers housing thousands of offices, concrete-and-glass outdoor seating areas and vast underground carparks. Plus, the ubiquitous ground floor cafes and restaurants, willing and able to feed the stock market monkeys and besuited banking serfs. Plenty of bright young things in sharp suits would be making a killing, Lydia was sure, but many more would be working high-stress positions for a few years before burning out on salaries that seemed good until you factored in London-living, with a precious few at the top of the tree, multiplying their wealth until they were untouchable.

The meeting was set for eight in the evening and the address was on the twelfth floor of a shiny office block with a sculpted concrete concourse with a large lily pond, and a central atrium which was supposed to show off the buildings' 'design forward' sensibilities. At least, that was what the website told Lydia when she scoped it out. It also had at least six floors of offices-to-let, so it seemed that not everybody was lining up to buy.

There was a large reception area and a bank of lifts on the wall beyond. It was deserted, which wasn't a surprise at this time of day. Lydia couldn't see much in the way of security, but Fleet went over to the desk and flashed his badge. 'Floor twelve, need to take a look.'

'It's empty,' the neat young man said. His name badge said 'Mitch' and he had the kind of starter-moustache Lydia associated with fifteen-year-old boys. If he was the guard for the night, they definitely weren't anticipating much trouble.

'That's right, son,' Fleet said. 'And I need to take a quick look at it. Problem?'

The man slid laminated guest passes across the desk. 'Elevator two.'

'Lift,' Fleet muttered as they walked away. 'We're still in bloody London, aren't we?'

They were half an hour early for the meeting to give them time to check out the location beforehand. Plus, you never knew what you might see if you turned up before the party had officially started.

The lift moved smoothly upward and Fleet leaned against the bar against the back wall. Suddenly, he straightened. The lift had stopped and the doors began to slide open but Fleet had already started moving, he lunged in front of Lydia, managing to shove her to the side of the lift and stab the button to close the doors at almost the same time. Lydia didn't have time to process what had happened, let alone ask him what was happening when her head seemed to explode. She threw out an instinctive blast of energy through the gap in the lift doors but her ears were ringing and she had no idea if she hit anybody.

And then the doors were closing again and the lift was moving down. Lydia was about to ask Fleet what had happened, she just needed to wait for the ringing in her ears to stop, when she realised that Fleet was moving in slow motion. No, he was falling in slow motion, his good hand clutching his bad shoulder and an expression of pain on his face.

'Fleet!' Lydia was falling with Fleet, unable to bear his weight, but she hoped that she was cushioning his fall at least.

'I'm okay,' he said grimacing. He moved his jacket aside and Lydia saw a small red stain blooming on his white shirt. He had ripped open his shoulder wound when he had stretched to hit the lift button and push Lydia.

'What the hell was that...' Lydia trailed off as she noticed a dent in lift wall, at chest height. 'Did someone just shoot at us?'

'I need to call it in,' Fleet was saying as the lift descended.

Lydia couldn't take her eyes off the bullet lodged in the metal wall of the lift. It had been so close. If Fleet hadn't moved so quickly one of them would definitely have been hit. She felt weak and fuzzy from the discharge of energy, too. Like three bad hangovers arriving all at once.

The doors opened on the ground floor and it was surreally quiet. The security guard behind the desk still looked far too young for the job and the place was still mercifully empty.

'He might be on his way down,' Fleet was saying. 'This is a public safety issue.'

'I doubt it,' Lydia said. 'He only wants to kill me.'

But Fleet was already moving behind the desk, taking control of the situation in a very Fleet manner. 'There's been an incident on floor twelve, how many people are currently in the building?'

The guard's eyes grew wide as he pushed away from the desk to stand. 'Not many. Ten maybe on floor four, they work late there. Nowhere that high. They're not in use.'

Lydia joined Fleet behind the desk. There were a couple of monitors, the screens showing feeds from the building's cameras. The images changed every few seconds.

'Show me floor twelve,' Fleet said, pointing at the screens.

'I don't know how,' the guard said in a panicky voice. 'They're just on a loop like that and I watch them. I'm not usually on my own—'

'Sit down,' Fleet said, 'put your head between your knees.' He put his hand on the guard's shoulder and pushed him gently back into his chair. 'You're all right. Breathe.'

At that moment, the image on the far-right monitor changed. It showed an empty office floor, deserted apart from a figure lying on the floor. Lydia leaned in, studying the grainy image. It looked like a man, one arm flung out to the side. A very still man.

Fleet had seen it, too. 'Okay.' He had his mobile out and was calling in.

'I'm going up,' Lydia said, already moving. That wild blast of energy. She had hit someone.

'Not a good idea. Back up is on its way. We need to secure the building. Make sure the civilians are safe.'

'Your back up is on the way,' Lydia said. 'I need a look at the guy before they arrive.' What she didn't say but knew Fleet had observed was this; the man wasn't about to shoot anybody else.

Still, not wanting to be over-confident, Lydia took a different lift to the floor below and then used the stairs to approach the twelfth. And she didn't complain when Fleet insisted on coming with her. She was pretty sure her attacker was dead or unconscious, but there was a chance he was still dangerous.

'I'm guessing this isn't protocol,' Lydia said, getting out at the eleventh floor and taking the stairs.

'No. But you're right. They're unlikely to start attacking random office workers.'

They fell silent as they approached the door to the twelfth floor. The staircase was disturbingly open with lots of glass panels and mood lighting set along each step. Lydia pressed against the wall as she approached the opening to the office floor. She wished there was a nice solid door she could hide behind, maybe with a handy-dandy viewing panel to peek through. Instead, she crept forward, trying to see into the space without showing herself.

Acres of grey industrial carpet broken up with pillars and a few glass boxes which would presumably function as not-at-all-private offices. Even without cubicles and ringing phones, the place was a soul-sucking hellscape.

A hellscape with a dead man on the floor near to the bank of lifts. The way the man was lying and the fallen gun, a foot or so away from his outstretched arm, made it very clear that he was no longer a threat to anybody. Fleet put his good arm in front of Lydia, shaking his head, and making the approach in a wide circle. Once he was close enough, he kicked the gun further away from the body.

'He's dead,' Lydia said quietly. She knew she ought to feel bad, but she was flooded with relief that the man with the gun who had just shot at them was no longer a threat.

Fleet shot her an exasperated look, but she saw his shoulders relax as he got a better look at the body.

Up close, there was no question. Lydia had expected the man to be dead, so it wasn't much of a shock. What did surprise her, however, was that she recognised him.

'Felix,' Lydia said. 'He's a professional.'

Fleet had crossed to the gun he had kicked away and was crouched down, examining it without touching. 'A professional who has been watching too many mob films,' he said. 'He's wrapped the grip with tape.'

'To prevent fingerprints?'

Fleet nodded, still looking. 'That's the idea. Outdated now we've got DNA matching.'

Lydia pulled on nitrile gloves, stepping closer to the body. Then she stopped. Fleet was shaking his head, as if he wanted to deny something, and then he sank to the ground.

She crossed to him, instead. 'What's wrong?'

'I moved before the lift doors opened,' he said. 'I think that precognition thing, that instinct you were talking about. I think it happened again.'

'And thank feathers it did. You saved my life again.'

'I didn't,' Fleet said, looking up at her.

'Don't be modest,' Lydia said. 'You pushed me out of the line of fire. There's a bullet embedded in that lift wall that was meant for-'

'No,' Fleet was shaking his head. 'I saw it happen. That's never happened before. I've had feelings. Hunches. You know the kind of thing. And, yeah, I moved the steering wheel before I'd consciously recognised there was a reason to, but this was different. I saw it happen. When we were in the lift. The doors opened and he was there,' Fleet glanced at Felix. 'He shot me. Here'. Fleet put a hand in the middle of his chest, over his heart. And then the colour drained from his face.

'Put your head between your knees,' Lydia said, but Fleet was way ahead of her.

She spoke to the back of his neck. 'Why would he want to kill you?'

Fleet said something incomprehensible in reply.

She patted down Felix's body until she found his phone. It required a thumb print to unlock and Lydia lifted Felix's lifeless hand and pressed the relevant digit on the button before she could think about it too much. Once unlocked, she navigated to the call history and pressed to redial the last number.

'Yes?' Mr Smith said. 'Is it done?'

CHAPTER TWENTY-SIX

Lydia had left Fleet in the office building before the police turned up. Time was of the essence and she couldn't afford to get stuck. Lydia didn't know how quickly Mr Smith would find out what had happened and she wanted to speak to him while she knew more than he did. He would probably have guessed that something had gone awry, but there was a small window when he, hopefully, didn't have all the details.

'He'll guess that you know he set us up,' Fleet said. 'It's too dangerous.'

'He wants me to run to him,' Lydia said with more certainty than she felt. 'He wants me to make a new deal, to work for him. If I dangle what he most wants, he'll believe me because he *wants* to believe.'

Fleet hadn't looked convinced but he had wished her luck.

Lydia had a tracker in her shoe, the GPS on her phone switched on and exactly zero time to practise her acting skills. She fast walked to Canary Wharf tube station and did a couple of jumping jacks to get herself out of breath before calling Mr Smith. It was testament to the city she loved that nobody so much as broke stride, the pedestrians simply flowing around her as she aerobicized as if it was perfectly normal.

'I need help,' she said as soon as Mr Smith answered. 'It's me. Someone just... Fleet...' Lydia found that it was easier than she had expected to cry. The pent-up feelings about Ash, the fear she had been carrying since Fleet had been shot and then the adrenaline rush of the gunshot in the lift. She had come far too close to losing the man she loved.

'Where are you?'

'Canary Wharf,' Lydia managed. 'I'm going into the station. I need to get away from here fast. I can't see anybody following, but...' She broke off, looking behind her in a panicked way. There was little chance that Mr Smith's resources stretched to commandeering street CCTV in real-time, but it was easier to commit herself entirely to the performance.

'What happened?' Mr Smith asked. 'Are you hurt?'

'No, I'm okay. I think I might have hurt him, though.' She swallowed as a wave of pure fury engulfed her. Mr Smith had set her up, had been threatening her for weeks, trying to intimidate her into needing him. Trying to make her believe that she was too weak to lead the Crows, that she was in danger. When that hadn't worked, he had taken aim at the one she loved. Her voice was shaking with emotion when she spoke and she just hoped that Mr Smith couldn't tell it was anger and not grief. 'He killed Fleet. He just shot him. And I wasn't in control. He was choking on the ground and I ran.'

'Fleet was choking?'

'No, the hitman. He had a gun. I'm guessing it was your assassin.' No need to let Mr Smith know that she had met Felix before and recognised him. She also hoped that he would assume Felix had dialled his number but had been unable to speak. 'I don't know what to do.'

'Get the DLR to Tower Gateway. I'll meet you on the bridge.'

'Just you,' Lydia said. 'If I see anybody else...'

'Of course,' Mr Smith said, his voice soothing.

Lydia cut the connection and followed Mr Smith's instructions, acting terrified and jumpy all the way. It wasn't difficult, as the moment she sat on the scratchy seat of the train and saw her face reflected in the window opposite a truth hit. She had just killed a man. A bad man, for sure, and it had been panicked self-defence, but still. She had thrown out her power with no control and no real grasp of the situation. She began to shake and wrapped her arms around herself. This wasn't the time to break down for real. Still. There were many faces reflected in the train's windows, blurry and indistinct and, for a moment, Felix's dead face was among them.

Emerging from the station, the squat fortification of the Tower of London on her right and a fresh breeze whipping rain directly into her face, Lydia made her way to Tower Bridge. She hoped Mr Smith wouldn't be in his car as she definitely didn't want to get into it with him. She walked to the middle of the bridge, dodging tourists and people heading out on dates and nights in the pub and all the normal things that suddenly seemed so desirable. Fleet isn't dead, she reminded herself.

She forced herself to stop moving and lean against the blue-painted balustrade with its intricate iron trefoil design. It was London twilight and thousands of windows glowing with yellow light shone in the gathering night. The Shard stabbed the purple sky, a futuristic obelisk straight out of a science fiction film. Looking at it in the context of the skyline, Lydia could hardly believe she had climbed halfway up. At least no one would be mad enough to try to get higher.

On the other side of the river, the Gherkin marked the City. The distinctive dome of St Paul's Cathedral was further away and, just beyond it, the central criminal courts. Lydia wondered whether Alejandro was sad to leave the place. Or whether it was weight lifted from his shoulders.

She felt a rush of motion sickness and heard crashing waves just seconds before Mr Smith said: 'Lydia. Thank God.'

She turned to the man she had made a deal with and who, once upon a time, had honoured his word and healed Henry Crow. She had always known that he had wanted to use her, but she had never suspected that he would go so far. And now she was a killer. She tasted bile in the back of her throat and swallowed. 'Was it your rogue assassin?'

'Possibly,' Mr Smith said, he moved as if he wanted

to touch her but then seemed to check himself. 'Did they say anything? Tell me what happened.'

'But why would they target me? What could I have done to get on their radar? I've got nothing to do with international smuggling or toppling governments. Nothing that high level.'

He tilted his head and Lydia could almost see him thinking. He was trying to work out how much to say, how best to keep her afraid and scrambling. Lydia decided to push on with her act, pretending that she believed Felix was an international assassin. 'You. You put them onto me. Why?'

'It's nothing personal,' Mr Smith visibly relaxed. 'We just wanted to ensure they came back to London.'

Back to London. Lydia didn't miss his phrasing. He had relaxed too much and done exactly as Lydia had hoped. Revealed something new. 'So, when you said you didn't know anything about this assassin you were lying. You know exactly who they are.' The final piece fell into place and Lydia resisted the urge to smack herself in the forehead. Instead she stepped back, feeling stupid for not seeing it before. 'They were working for you.'

Mr Smith looked down. 'The service contracted them, yes. But then we lost contact. They've been behaving erratically and we need to bring them in as a matter of some urgency. I didn't want to involve you, but I'm not the only one making decisions. Matters were taken out of my hands.'

'Fleet is dead,' Lydia said.

'And I'm sorry,' Mr Smith reached for Lydia and, if she hadn't known he had ordered it, she might have been

281

taken in. She had to hand it to the secret service, that spook training was top notch. 'But you're in a precarious situation, now. You have to be smart.'

There was no way Felix was the top-level international assassin at the centre of Operation Bergamot, which meant that Mr Smith was acting alone. Lydia felt sure that this was his own personal crusade, building assets for his own, Family-focused department. 'The meeting was for Charlie,' Lydia said, watching Mr Smith's face very carefully. 'I thought it was Alejandro.'

Mr Smith didn't blink. 'Alejandro is far away from London, now. Safe location. New identity. The works. It's the sort of thing we could do for you.'

Lydia nodded as if she was seriously considering his offer.

'Or you could join my department. Help me with my research. It's valuable work. And I can keep you safe. You need people around you, Lydia. You're not safe on your own.'

Lydia made her body sag in defeat. 'Okay,' she said quietly. 'I need to put my affairs in order and then I'll come with you.'

'You shouldn't be alone,' Mr Smith began, but Lydia interrupted him. 'I'll meet you at the old safe house in an hour.'

IT WAS ALMOST eleven o'clock when Lydia's phone buzzed with a text. She ignored it and the three which followed. She was in the cafe, finishing some much-needed lasagne when she saw a familiar car pull up outside.

Mr Smith got out of the Mercedes. He was irritated but clearly trying to pretend that he wasn't.

'You didn't show. Is there a problem?'

'Have you heard about Felix?' Lydia asked and enjoyed Mr Smith's quick frown. He was so good at controlling his expression that every time he failed felt like a triumph. 'I killed him.'

'I don't know what you think you know...'

'I know you booked a sub-standard contractor to make me feel afraid.'

Mr Smith didn't miss a beat. 'For the greater good. You are in real danger and I just wanted you to understand that.'

'How kind,' Lydia said. 'I believe I will take my chances. No more deals.'

'Let's talk about this. I can see you're upset, now, but when you have time to think things through...'

'You've lost,' Lydia said flatly. 'Any chance you ever had to work with me or study me or use me has gone. It's over.'

Mr Smith straightened very slightly.

Lydia could feel the waves of his unusual signature rolling from him as his temper rose. He might be able to control his expression, but he couldn't control that. There, Lydia knew she was ahead of him. 'You made me into a killer,' she said. 'I crossed a line today and I will never forgive you for your part in that. But there is something else you should know,' she held his gaze and pushed more than a little Crow into her words, 'I became a killer today.'

There was a short silence as Mr Smith seemed to contemplate her words. Then he shifted slightly, rallying. 'You're making a huge mistake. I can be a really good friend to you.'

'I have enough friends,' Lydia said. She turned and indicated The Fork. The cafe lights were blazing and warm light spilled onto the pavement. The figures inside were clearly visible through the windows. Mr Smith's gaze shifted and Lydia enjoyed the change in his expression as he took in Fleet, who was standing next to Maria Silver. Henry Crow was seated at Lydia's favourite table with Aiden and they were laughing about something.

'So be it.' Mr Smith turned away. 'You're making a mistake, but I can see your mind is made up.'

Lydia crossed her arms and watched him leave. He paused, one hand on the handle of his car door and spoke without turning around. 'Check your pocket.'

Lydia waited until the car had moved away down the street, the tail lights disappearing as it turned the corner. Then she waited a little longer, just in case Mr Smith changed his mind and came back around for round two.

When the street remained empty and quiet, she reached into the pocket of her hoodie. There was something papery, folded into a neat square. A ten-shilling note.

CHAPTER TWENTY-SEVEN

Two days later and Lydia was watching Jason spray a tower of whipped cream onto a mug of hot chocolate. He added marshmallows and then grated a sprinkling of chocolate with the tiny grater Lydia had bought him for the purpose. 'Tell me what you think.'

It would be perfection, like every single mugful he had made this week, but Lydia obediently took a sip. 'Gorgeous,' she said, licking cream from her upper lip. 'I think you've got the ratio just right.'

Jason beamed.

Lydia took another sip. It really was good.

'You know what you need with that?' Jason began opening the cupboards.

'Whisky?'

He shot her a fond look. 'Something to dip. Like a biscuit. We don't have any.'

Lydia could sense this escalating. Before he could start talking about baking, Lydia warned him that Fleet was due home any moment.

'Was he all right to go back to work?' Jason asked. 'Isn't his shoulder still healing?'

'I wasn't sure,' Lydia said. 'But he said he didn't need to be fully fit to sit in meetings.'

'Are you going to tell him about the note?'

Lydia put the mug down, her appetite suddenly gone. 'Yeah. Soon. I will.' She had told Jason about Mr Smith leaving a ten-shilling note in her pocket, but hadn't wanted to worry Fleet. She knew it was falling back into old, bad habits, but the instinct to handle things on her own was strong.

It was probably just a mind game, anyway. Mr Smith had tried to frighten Lydia into joining him and it hadn't worked. The note was just a face-saving exercise. Probably. At least they had the identity of the sniper. The police had raided Felix's flat and found a cornucopia of equipment, including a rifle and long-range scope. Ballistics were checking to see if it had fired the bullet which had hit Fleet, but Lydia was pretty sure it would match. Felix's phone had shown a text from Mr Smith on the day that Fleet was shot, which seemed enough. Lydia had told the investigating team that the number was connected to a member of the secret service, but it was a burner, of course, and she didn't expect to see Mr Smith in handcuffs anytime soon.

FLEET ARRIVED NOT LONG AFTER, his jacket damp from the rain. London in the spring was a damp affair. He kissed her full on the lips, pulling her close in a decidedly rambunctious manner.

'You're happy,' Lydia said.

'Interesting day.' Fleet went to the fridge and pulled out two beers. He looked at the half-finished mug of hot chocolate. 'You want one of these?'

'Yes, please.' They clinked bottles.

'So,' Fleet leaned against the kitchen counter. 'I had a very interesting meeting today.'

'That's not a phrase you use often.'

'It was an unofficial meeting, really. My boss invited me for a coffee out of the building, so I knew it was off the record. She said that Operation Bergamot was being wound up, that it was a budgetary decision for the Met.'

'So the wider operation will continue with all the other agencies?'

Fleet turned his hands palm up. 'Probably. But the rumour is that a key member of the operation here in London was carrying out unapproved actions and the inter-departmental heads want to distance themselves from the London portion.'

'Mr Smith?' Lydia said. 'Sounds like he's in trouble.'

'Good,' Fleet said, raising his bottle,

The last thing Lydia wanted to do was ruin Fleet's mood, but she knew it would get harder to share the longer she waited. She was learning.

'What's that?' Fleet frowned as she pulled the note from her pocket.

'A parting gift from Mr Smith,' Lydia said. 'There was one like it in Mark Kendal's wallet and Aiden told me it was Charlie's old way of letting people know they were in trouble with him.'

'In trouble?' Fleet arched an eyebrow.

'Imminent physical danger,' Lydia clarified. 'Marked.'

'You think he's letting you know he killed Mark Kendal? Why would he do that?'

'I think it's more that he wants me to stay scared. He's told me that his department has access to a high-level assassin. I guess he wants me looking over my shoulder and this is his way of saying I'm still in danger.'

Fleet thought for a moment. 'Why did Mr Smith target Mark Kendal, anyway? Was it just to make you look like a bad leader?'

'I assume so,' Lydia said. 'And to make me likely to lean on him. He swooped in quick enough to offer help. Besides, he's the only other person who knows about the ten-shilling notes. Apart from my family, I mean.' Lydia didn't want to dwell on how Mr Smith would have got that particular piece of information from Charlie. She had put Charlie and his situation in a locked room of her mind and she had no intention of going inside.

EARLY THE NEXT DAY, Lydia watched Fleet get dressed for work. He had an enthusiasm that had been missing over the last few weeks. 'Getting shot suits you,' she said. 'You're glowing.'

'Bit extreme as far as self-help advice goes,' Fleet said, smiling like the sun. She got out of bed to kiss him goodbye, pressing up against him until he groaned quietly under his breath. 'I'm going to be late, now. You're a bad influence.'

. . .

HALF AN HOUR LATER, once Fleet had left, Lydia stretched out in the bed and tried to hold onto the relaxed calm that head-banging morning sex had bestowed. Her phone buzzed with a text and she rolled over to retrieve it from the floor. It was a message from an unknown number.

St Thomas' Hospital. Roof. Come now.

A moment later, another message came through.

Don't make me visit Emma.

LYDIA STARED at the black letters until they became fuzzy, the words dancing in and out of focus as she fought the urge to throw up, to run, to scream. For a suspended moment in time, every muscle in her body flexed. The tension was like a sacred covenant - if she didn't relax a single fibre, then Emma would not be in danger. Nothing would happen to her, nothing would happen to her children. She would have erased the text message through an act of denial. And then the moment passed and Lydia knew she must move.

LYDIA WAS up and out of the flat without conscious thought. When she found herself in a taxi and on her way to Westminster Bridge she was just relieved to see that she was dressed. The journey seemed interminable. She texted the unknown number to say that she was on her way. Then again to ask the assassin to wait.

It had to be Mr Smith's rogue assassin. He had to have commissioned a hit on Lydia. The ten-shilling note hadn't been an empty threat or a continuation of their dance. Mr Smith had taken his defeat hard and decided to end the game. Lydia couldn't think of any alternative explanation and she was in no state to reason it out.

Getting onto the roof of the hospital was nowhere near as difficult as Lydia had imagined. She had always thought that walking to her own death would feel harder or take longer. As it was, she felt nothing but a calm sense of inevitability. She would not let anybody else get hurt on her account. The idea that her life, her position, her choices, would lead to Emma or her children being harmed in any way was unthinkable. There was no choice to be made. This was what it meant to be the head of the Crow Family. Everything stopped with her.

Coming out of the stairwell and onto the roof, Lydia was slapped in the face by a stiff breeze. At least she wasn't clinging to The Shard, she told herself, while scanning the collection of stone buildings and low walls. She moved around one locked structure with a yellow 'danger of death' notice on the door and the space opened out. Over by the low wall which signalled the edge of the building, there was a slight figure. For a moment, Lydia thought that it was the Pearl King. And then they turned and she realised her mistake.

It was Maddie.

THE END

THANK YOU FOR READING!

I hope you enjoyed reading about Lydia Crow and her family as much as I enjoyed writing about them!

I am busy working on the sixth book in the Crow Investigations series. If you would like to be notified when it's published (as well as take part in giveaways and receive exclusive free content), you can sign up for my FREE readers' club online:

geni.us/ThankYou

If you could spare the time, I would really appreciate a review on the retailer of your choice.

Reviews make a huge difference to the visibility of the book, which make it more likely that I will reach more readers and be able to keep on writing. Thank you!

LOVE URBAN FANTASY?

Discover Sarah Painter's standalone
Edinburgh-set urban fantasy
THE LOST GIRLS

A 'dark and twisty' supernatural thriller.
Around the world girls are being hunted...
Rose must solve the puzzle of her impossible life –
before it's too late.

ACKNOWLEDGMENTS

I am beyond thrilled by the response to this series, and am deeply grateful to my wonderful readers for taking to Lydia Crow and her London with such enthusiasm. Thank you! I will keep doing my very best with the characters and the world.

2020 hasn't been the easiest year in which to write, but I am very lucky to have a wonderful support team. Thank you to my fantastic children, Holly and James, and to family and friends for your love and encouragement. As ever, thank you to my brilliant author pals; Clodagh Murphy, Hannah Ellis, Keris Stainton, Nadine Kirtzinger, and Sally Calder.

Thank you to my editor, cover designer, early readers, and ARC team. You are all wonderful. In particular, thanks to Beth Farrar, Karen Heenan, Judy Grivas, Paula Searle, Ann Martin, Jenni Gudgeon, Stuart Bache, Kerry Barrett, and David Wood.

Finally, my deepest love and gratitude to my husband. I truly couldn't do this without you.

ABOUT THE AUTHOR

Before writing books, Sarah Painter worked as a freelance magazine journalist, blogger and editor, combining this 'career' with amateur child-wrangling (AKA motherhood).

Sarah lives in rural Scotland with her children and husband. She drinks too much tea, loves the work of Joss Whedon, and is the proud owner of a writing shed.

Head to the website below to sign-up to the Sarah Painter readers' club. It's absolutely free and you'll get book release news, giveaways and exclusive FREE stuff!

geni.us/ThankYou